Gordon R. Dick[...] [...] since 1950. Over [...] of his short stories and novelettes have been published and widely anthologized. He has written over thirty sf novels including *The Outposter*, *Naked to the Stars*, *Mission to Universe*, *Ancient, My Enemy* and *Time Storm*. He won the Hugo Award in 1965 for *Soldier, Ask Not*, the Nebula Award in 1966 for *Call Him Lord*, the E. E. Smith Memorial Award for Imaginative Fiction in 1975, and the August Derleth Award of the British Fantasy Society in 1977.

Mr Dickson is a member of the Science Fiction Research Organisation, the Author's Guild and Mystery Writers of America. Much in demand as a speaker on radio, TV and at sf conventions in the United States, he lives in Minnesota.

Masters of Everon

GORDON R. DICKSON

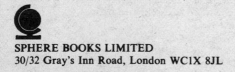

SPHERE BOOKS LIMITED
30/32 Gray's Inn Road, London WC1X 8JL

First published in Great Britain by Sphere Books Ltd 1981
Copyright © Gordon R. Dickson 1979
Reprinted 1984

Printed and bound in Great Britain by
Cox & Wyman Ltd, Reading

Masters of Everon

1

MIKEY CALLED.

It was not a loud sound, but it was loud enough. As if triggered by the light of the sign on the wall of the spaceship's debarkation lounge that announced they were now breathing Everon's planetary air, the immature maolot's massive, leonine head lifted from Jef Robini's lap. The unopened eyes stared blindly and from the half-parted jaws came a deep bass hum of excitement. A sad bitterness rose like the foretaste of sickness in Jef's throat and chest.

"Shh . . ." he said softly, closing his hand around the powerful, open jaws. "Easy . . ."

But the damage was done.

In the lounge, rotating freely now on its gimbals in preparation for landing, the fresh air was now heavy with a new silence. Forty-two passengers, most of them first-wave Everon colonists returning from vacation to Earth, and the rest Earth people with business on Everon, had abruptly broken off their conversations. Shielded by the partitions hastily erected around this bank of seats to enclose Mikey and himself, Jef could not see their faces; but he did not need to.

"Did you hear that?" The hoarse voice of a man rose in the stillness.

A pause, while the other voices still waited.

"I said—did you hear that just now?"

Another pause.

"The board of directors on this spaceline'll hear from me," went on the voice. "As if we don't have enough of

I

those vermin growing and breeding here naturally, they have to let someone re-import one from Earth; and carry it in here, with the rest of us, in the passenger area . . . "

The voice grumbled down into unintelligibility. Most of the homecoming passengers were hung over from the last-night party aboard the evening before; and some of them were still drunk. These were not the people Jef had been expecting to find out on one of the new worlds. Not these people with their overuse of Earth colognes, their obsession with Earth fashions, their apparent dislike of talking about anything connected with their newly-settled worlds—and, above all, their deep hatred of the Everon-native wildlife such as Mikey.

Men and women, they had drawn aside from Jef all during the voyage, even without having seen Mikey, only knowing that he had been traveling on special permit in Jef's cabin.

Jef stared out over the maolot's head now at the brass plate with the name and symbol of the spaceship line on the partition wall opposite him. The sad bitterness was still in him—an ugly feeling that he knew too well. For generations in his family the Robini temper had been infamous. But Jef's father had struggled to keep his family alive in the Bad Years, when the U.S. had become an impoverished nation, after letting languish and die its lead in the development of space. In a country become bankrupt, starving for lack of the space-based industries that would let it compete economically with the rest of the world, a temper was an unaffordable luxury. Ira Robini had determined that his younger son, at least, would not have to carry that disability.

In form he had made it so, if not in fact. Ordinary anger was buried so deeply in Jef now that only the most extreme provocation could evoke it. In its place was the sensation he was feeling at this moment, and which he had lived with for most of his existence, the grim feeling of sad bitterness that sometimes seemed as if it would tear him apart inwardly. He was lonely—but he was self-controlled.

He had not been expecting to feel it so, on this ship to Everon. After his parent's death, he had thought he was beyond being touched by anything more. Also, being here at last with Mikey, funded at last and free to do the work with Mikey that he had dreamed of doing for years, he had expected to enjoy this trip. The last thing he had anticipated was isolation from his fellow passengers and their obvious hatred.

He sat, stroking Mikey and hearing the now-unintelligible grumbling of the voice behind him. In the highly reflective surface of the partition holding the brass plate, he saw himself darkly reflected. A tall, lean man in his early twenties, big-boned and slightly long-faced, with dark hair and even darker eyes. *Masters of Everon*, announced the engraving on the brass plate. It was the name of the corporation formed by the original colonists of this world to which he was descending, this world that was Mikey's birthplace.

Mikey butted his massive head against Jef's chest, comfortingly. There was a rapport between Jef and the Everon native, even in his arrested immaturity the size of a large St. Bernard dog, which seemed close to telepathy at times.

"It's all right, Mikey. All right . . ." he murmured to the maolot.

He made an effort to shut his mind to the other passengers. Reaching into his jacket pocket, he took out the single sheet of paper he had found after his father's death among the few letters his older half-brother William had written home. The paper showed a crude map drawn in black ink, showing a route from Everon City on the coast, back through the grass country and into the mountains. The dotted line marking the route ended at a point marked *Valley of Thrones*; and there were three words written and encircled beside that name.

"Found Mikey here."

It had been Jef's hope that taking the Earth-raised maolot back to the place of its birth would turn up the reason why Mikey had never opened his eyes, nor developed to full physical maturity. At the very least it had seemed not unreasonable that, once back on his home world, Mikey would show some response to justify Jef's Ph.D. thesis—that in the maolots lay a clue to the greater understanding of Everon itself, and perhaps to the greater understanding of other colonized worlds. It was that hope and that thesis that had put Jef on the search for the research funds that had now brought them both here. Which was why he must not let the attitudes of his fellow passengers get to him. Things could not be allowed to go wrong after all this, no matter what he and the maolot were called on to endure. He put the map away.

The man who had spoken before was raising his voice again. Jef tried to ignore it. An empty feeling in him had come to join hands with the sad bitterness. These people, and others like them, would be the fellow humans he would be depending on for existence and help once he was down on Everon's surface. How was he going to enlist their help if they were determined to react like this?

The voice would not be ignored. It was rising to the audible level again; and the sad bitterness suddenly took control of Jef. He put one hand on the seat beside him, ready to lift himself to his feet and go back to have it out with the speaker. But on the bare heels of that thought, with the startling response the maolot had always shown to Jef's emotions, Mikey's head came up again. Catlike and supple, his heavy body tensed. The great lion-head turned back toward the invisible speaker; the upper lip curled back from the scimitar-shaped teeth, already capable of shearing off a human arm; and the unopened eyes stared straight in the direction of the voice. Stared, as if the maolot could see not only the metal partition and the human bodies that would be beyond it, but

4

through them to the speaker himself.

"No, no," whispered Jef, jarred back to self-control. "It's all right . . . all right, Mikey. Lie down!"

"If it was up to me—" The voice rose again above the lighter chatter of the other passengers. "If it was only up to me—"

"Ah, and if only it was," another voice unexpectedly interrupted: a light brisk baritone with an odd lilt to it that sounded almost Irish, or perhaps Welsh, and had almost a faint sneer hidden in its tone. "If it were up to you, sir, the universe would be run a deal more sensibly, no doubt. But now then, it isn't—is it? And the beast'd hardly be here instead of the baggage section unless there was some good reason for it and an equally good permit. Aren't I right about that now, my dear sir?"

The voice had been approaching Jef as it spoke. Now a tall, wiry, black-haired man with a wide, thin-lipped mouth under a thin, black mustache and green eyes, appeared suddenly around the corner of the partition behind Jef's seat section. The mustache and the eyes, taken together, gave the man's whole face a sardonic, devilish look. He was no one Jef had seen before during the two weeks of their trip out from Earth; but then Jef had stayed close to Mikey in their own compartment most of the time. Now, reaching them, the other smiled and dropped into the facing double-seat opposite without waiting for an invitation.

Jef looked at him warily. Neither life nor his father had taught a belief in unexpected friends. Part of him even resented the intrusion of the other. There was no good reason this individual should come to their rescue; and right now Jef was in no mood to talk to any of his fellow humans. But the other was obviously trying to be helpful; and for poor people nowadays on Earth, and particularly for poor people from North America, good manners were so much a necessity for survival that they came close to being a compulsion.

"You are, sir," Jef said formally. "I do have a permit

and the maolot needs to be with me all the time."

"Indeed. How else?" said the black-haired man. His voice carried. Both voice and attitude were a little too ironic and sharp-edged to be completely pleasant; but for some odd reason Jef did not find these things putting him off as much as he had at the other's first appearance. The man was no one Jef recognized, but Jef could not put off a feeling of familiarity. It was almost as if the other was someone he had known for some time beyond memory. A strange feeling. With the death of his mother and father, he had come to feel himself completely alone among the trillions of people who now made up the human race. He found himself warming toward the stranger in spite of himself.

"Martin Curragh's the name," the other was saying. "And you, sir?"

"Jef Aram Robini," said Jef. "This is Mikey."

He leaned forward in his seat to shake hands. The movement disturbed Mikey, who lifted his head briefly to point it toward Martin Curragh, then inexplicably dropped it back down on Jef's knee without showing any curiosity at all in the newcomer.

"Thanks," said Jef.

Martin lifted his black brows questioningly.

"I mean," Jef said, "thanks for not trying to pet him. People seem to be either one extreme or another—scared to death of him, or they want to handle him."

"And that's not advised?"

"No," said Jef. "He's an Everon life form, not an Earth one. His instincts and reactions aren't an Earth animal's. If a stranger touches him—and he can always tell a stranger's touch from mine—he gets frightened."

"A dangerous beast, then." But this Martin Curragh did not sound like he really believed his own words. "Perhaps the gentleman just speaking was right."

"Not when I'm with him," said Jef shortly.

"And is that, too, a fact?" Martin Curragh's voice

again seemed to sneer a little, but once more Jef found his strange liking for the man overriding his ordinary reactions.

"That's right," he said. "I raised him from a cub. I've taken the place of his mother. Maolots stay blind until they're adult—as you may know—blind and dependent on the dam that bore them. He trusts me, and he does what I say."

"So, what're the two of you doing coming to Everon, then? Emigrating? Don't tell me you came all the way just to take the beast home to his own kind?"

"As a matter of fact, yes—" Uncharacteristically, Jef found himself with a sudden strong urge to explain himself to this first friendly fellow traveler he had encountered. Words had been locked up inside him for so long now, with no one to listen. "You see, he's been on Earth for experimental observation since just after his birth. Now he's eight years old. His eyes ought to be open and he ought to be three times as big as he is—"

"Three times? Come now, Mr. Robini!"

"Yes, sir. Three times this size. But for some reason he hasn't matured. The assumption—my assumption—is that there was something lacking to him on Earth; so I've managed to bring him back here to see if, on his home world, he'll mature after all."

"Your assumption, you say?" The question was almost sharp.

Jef was suddenly wary, conscious of perhaps having flooded this stranger too suddenly with more information than it was prudent to give. But there was no easy way to stop talking now.

"Mikey grew up with me," he said. "My family were docents with the Xenological Research station in Philadelphia. When I went after a doctorate in Alien Intelligences, I took him for the subject of my thesis; and the thesis helped get me the grant to bring him back here for further observation."

7

"So," said Martin Curragh, "you're an off-Earth zoologist, are you?"

The touch of wariness redoubled.

"Not exactly," he said. "Not yet. The only reason I got the grant was that no one could try this work with Mikey except me. There's no lack of people with qualifications to push me aside, if it hadn't been for the fact that I was the only human he'd respond to—after my father and mother died."

Martin looked at him during a small moment of silence.

"They're dead, then, are they?" he asked.

"Two years ago. An undersea traffic tunnel collapsed." Even after this length of time Jef did not like to talk about it. "At any rate, that's why I'm here."

"All because you were lucky enough to be named a docent to this interesting beast eight years ago."

"It wasn't exactly luck," said Jef.

"Oh?" Martin's eyebrows raised. "What do you call it then?"

"String-pulling, I suppose," said Jef. "My older brother was a Colony Representative for the Ecological Corps here on Everon. I suppose you know what such people do?"

"What do they do?"

"They operate something like glorified agricultural advisers to new colonies in their First Mortgage most of the time," said Jef a little bitterly. "In this case Will was up in the mountains here on Everon and he found a new-born maolot cub, not far from where his mother had been killed in a rockslide. He managed to keep the cub alive and ended up sending him back to Earth for observation as he grew up. So it was probably his recommendation that turned the trick in getting us named as docents— though my father was a fully qualified and thoroughly experienced zoologist and he was working for the Xenological Research Service. Only—well, you know

8

how much influence a North American would have in the intercultural services."

"Not the greatest, certainly," said Martin.

For a second the impulse passed through Jef to ask Martin if he was himself a North American. But his accent made it unlikely and the question teetered on the edge of invading the other's privacy.

"So," said Jef, "as I say, Mikey and I grew up together. Apparently—I say *apparently* because no one had ever succeeded in keeping one alive in captivity before—they attach to a single person only. He'd do anything my father or mother asked him, but the only one he really responded to was me. That's why there was no point in sending him back here with anyone else, and why I got the research grant."

"And this brother of yours—the one who found him—" said Martin, "the beast wouldn't respond to him, either? Not a matter of imprinting, then."

"No. Baby ducks, and some Earth creatures like them, may imprint and follow around the first moving object they encounter, but Mikey belongs to Everon. Not to speak of the fact that he's a lot more intelligent than any duck; or for that matter, in my opinion, more than anything else Earth-born except a human. But, in any case, William never saw him after those first few days."

"He never came visiting home to Earth?"

"He died somewhere in the upcountry here on Everon," said Jef a little shortly. He was now having strong second thoughts about spreading all this intimate history out before a complete stranger. "That was a few weeks after he sent Mikey to us."

"Did he, now?" There was no noticeable note of sympathy in Martin's voice. "I suppose you'll be trying to find his grave, and all that."

In fact that was one of the things that Jef had planned to do, if it was still possible to locate that grave after nearly eight years. A recently colonized world was not

9

the easiest place to track down matters that had probably only been casually recorded to begin with.

"Perhaps." Jef had not meant the conversation to get into these personal areas. At all costs he must put a period to it. "In any case that's a private matter."

"Oh, indeed?"

It seemed to Jef that what he now heard was an open sneer in Martin's voice.

"That's right, Mr. Curragh," he said. "I've a right to privacy, I think?"

"Oh, you have that." Martin rose to his feet in one smooth movement. "You needn't fear I'll pry into your secret business. You may be a very John Smith now, and no one suspecting it. Good day, Mr. Robini."

He turned and walked off.

Jef sat where he was, torn between resentment at Martin's attitude and a feeling that he had perhaps rebuffed the man too strongly. But though Martin would have no way of knowing it, he had struck a painful nerve with his gibe about Jef being a "John Smith," that name which was the cover identity for those top-ranking members of the interworld Ecological Corps, the Planetary Inspectors. The Inspectors held awesome powers to recommend economic sanctions by the family of inhabited planets against any world not managing its ecology properly; and the "John Smith" cover name was designed to protect these men and women in their personal lives, from political and other pressures. No one but the Corps knew the real identity of any John Smith.

Jef had dreamed once of being an E. Corps Inspector, himself. That had been before Will, the older brother he could barely remember had applied for the position and been rejected by the Corps. That had been sixteen years ago; but Jef could remember the heavy blow of disappointment on the family household when word of Will's rejection arrived. Jef's father had endured that defeat, too, without a word. But, young as he had been then, Jef had felt the pain lying deeply within the elder Robini, silent but inextinguishable.

In spite of the rejection, Will had made his own way to the new worlds and finally caught on with the E. Corps in a subordinate position. He had gone on to give more than half a decade in faithful duty, ending here on Everon, his last post. And how had the Corps rewarded that service . . .?

Jef wrenched his mind from the memory. He thought again of Martin with a harsh contempt. What could someone like him know of what went into the making of a John Smith—

The voice of a ship's officer from a ceiling speaker sounded over Jef's head and he came back to himself with a start. All this time the spaceship had been dropping steadily down toward the surface of Everon and the space there without his realizing it.

A few seconds later there was the slightest of jars as the ship touched down. Suddenly, beyond the partitions around Jef and Mikey, people were standing up, collecting their portable belongings and beginning to move toward the still-closed airlock of the debarkation lounge. As the first of the passengers from behind the rear partition enclosing Jef and Mikey began to pass, Mikey lifted his head sharply.

"Easy . . ." said Jef, putting his arm around the heavy shoulders of the maolot. "We'll just wait. Wait, Mikey! Let the rest of them off first."

2

THE LOUNGE HAD EMPTIED. Jef snapped a leash to a collar around Mikey's neck and led the maolot out. They went down a short corridor to their left and out through the opened airlock at its end, to step down on to the landing stairs leading toward the cement pad below.

The brilliance of Everon's large sun, Comofors, dazzled Jef's eyes as he stepped out of the relative shadow of the ship's lighting. The light did not glare, but it was so strong Jef could not focus. Everything seemed touched with glints of gold. The air itself appeared alive with shimmers of it. Jef was aware of Mikey beside him, lifting his head sharply, sniffing deeply at the native atmosphere he had not breathed since William had carried him, then no larger than a month-old St. Bernard pup, aboard just such a spaceship as this, on his voyage to Earth eight years ago. A violent current of excitement seemed to wash out from the maolot and stain Jef himself.

He found himself, also, spreading his nostrils to the Everon air, inhaling deeply; for it was strange, with soft odors resembling those of cinnamon and crushed clover —unlike anything he had ever smelled on Earth. Automatically he began to descend the narrow landing stair, with Mikey's head bumping into him from behind at every step.

All at once he was caught up in an awareness he could only remember feeling a few times before in his life. Without warning, what was Everon—and what Everon was to him—had sprung upon him like a tiger from cover. His vision was dazzled, but at the same time he saw everything with sharp-edged clarity. He was intensely conscious of the three-dimensional reality into which he now descended. He could feel, so sensitively that the touch of it was almost painful, the hard roundness of the metal handrail against his palm and fingers. He saw as if in a carving the faces of the people on the field below, the woman in a dark blue Customs uniform standing at the foot of the ladder, the landing attendants in their white coveralls, the silver-gleaming metal posts of a fenced enclosure holding a handful of the passengers, and the large mass of other passengers, boarding a grey and green airbus a little farther off. Beyond the fenced enclosure, some two hundred meters distant, was the yellow-brown building that was the spaceport terminal —lounges and foreign officers' headquarters under one roof. It, and the silver metal of the fence enclosure, were the only two touches of color in the landscape that did not seem gilded and transmuted by the golden light from Comofors, standing now at a little past midday in the sky.

It was one of those rare and aching moments in life. Sensations poured in on Jef, overloading him as he went blindly down the landing stair. There was too much to absorb all at once, and he was absorbing it all involuntarily. This was part of what he had come here to find. It was differentness; it was freedom after the boredom and the crushing restrictions, the drabness, overcrowding and loneliness of Earth. Here, without conscious effort, he had become suddenly a part of everything around him. He breathed with the grass beyond the white concrete landing pad, he warmed with the soil of the low, forested hills on the horizon. The breeze brought him a thousand separate messages at once, and the whole world of Everon, this world he had never in his life seen before, called to him with a voice stronger than the voice of his own familiar world of home.

"Passport?" said the Customs official at the bottom of the landing stair. He had reached ground. Looking at her from centimeters of distance, now he saw a tall, middle-aged woman with faded auburn hair and tired brown eyes.

"Here," said Jef, handing it over, along with the special Ecological Service permit for the cabin transportation of Mikey. "We're red-flagged."

"I see," she said, glancing at the red-tape sticker at the top of the passport. "Research. All right. Left, there. Move along, please. . . ."

Jef turned left, entering the small cluster of people standing waiting inside one steel-fenced area. Through the golden sunlight he stared at the wide windows on the upper level of the terminal, where the foreign officers' headquarters would be. It would have been up there that William would have had his office for most of the year before his death that he had been stationed here.

Mikey rubbed his head against Jef's hip. Remembering the official's directions, Jef moved off toward the enclosure where the six other people—undoubtedly, like himself, red-flagged for special handling by the Everon Customs authorities—were waiting.

As he brought Mikey up to them, Jef recognized only one of the six. Martin Curragh was deep in conversation with a small, heavy-set, grey-haired man. The others, Jef guessed, had all been from the individual cabins up front in the first-class passenger section. Unexpectedly, Martin interrupted his conversation to give Jef an odd, penetrating look, a look almost of warning. Jef blinked, but the black-haired man turned immediately back to his conversation without further gesture.

To their left the airbus was filling up with the mass of general passengers, but the red-flagged six in the enclosure as yet had no transportation visible. However, several of them were keeping a watch toward the south, over the tops of the variformed oaks that enclosed the spaceport, in the direction of Spaceport City as Jef remembered it from his brother's maps. A minute or so later a small, ducted-fan aircraft emerged above the oaks in that direction and came swiftly to hover a dozen feet above their enclosure before settling straight down to a landing. From the aircraft—some sort of police courier ship, to judge from the markings on it—stepped a very big man, tall as well as heavy, in a khaki-and-blue uniform with gold stars on the shirt pocket and carrying a clipboard in one hand.

He did not come to the waiting people, but took two steps only out from under the shadow of the ducted fans in the wings of his aircraft and halted. He looked at his clipboard.

"Robini, Jef Aram," he called, without looking up. "Also a maolot."

The rest of the red-flagged passengers turned to stare at Jef and Mikey. Jef led Mikey forward until they stopped in front of the man. As they did so, Jef realized that unconsciously he had been stretching himself up as tall as he could, and this effort was making him as tense and stiff as a guy wire under load. In spite of Jef's own height, this individual had six centimeters of height on him, and outweighed him by at least forty kilos.

The other said nothing, but held out his hand. A stubborn coal of anger began to kindle inside Jef; and instead of responding he merely looked at the hand.

"Passport," said the big man sharply.

"Sir," said Jef, slowly taking the passport and Mikey's permit from the inside pocket of his jacket, "may I ask who I'm speaking to?"

"Avery Armage. Everon Planetary Constable." Armage pulled the papers from Jef's grip. "I'll take those."

"Constable?" Jef stared. The title meant that this man was the top police official of Everon. "Can I ask why we're being met by the Planetary Constable?"

Armage chuckled. For a second he looked cheerful and friendly, his face squeezed into small bunches like knots of muscle. But the sound of his humor was throaty and lacked warmth.

"You can ask . . ." he said. He was busily scanning Jef's papers. "What's this about bringing in your maolot permanently? We've got enough trouble with the ones we've already got killing off our wisent herds, now. All right—the animal's impounded, by my order."

"Hold it a minute!" said Jef, as the other started to turn away. "I've got a Research Service permit. It says—"

"I know what it says," Armage turned back to him, smiling; and Jef abruptly understood that what the Constable might find amusing was not necessarily what most people would consider so. "But the situation's changed since you applied for your grant over two years ago. Everon paid off its First Mortgage to Earth early last year. The Corps hasn't owned us for a year and a half. All they have is supervisory rights. The minute you and your maolot touched ground here, both of you became subject to local law, Everon law; which law reads that any maolot caught within settled or ranching areas is to be impounded or destroyed."

"Destroyed!" Jef stared at Armage for a moment that was too stark for speech. "You can't destroy him! Look at the *reason for travel* on my passport. This is an experimental animal concerned in a grant from the Xenological Research Service. I've been sent out with him from Earth specifically to study his reactions to being reintroduced to his native habitat after being laboratory-raised on Earth. The results of this study can affect the way native life forms are handled on a dozen different worlds, worlds already colonized as well as worlds that haven't been settled yet. You can't just destroy an animal like that—"

"Well, now, that's too bad—what you tell me," said

Armage softly. His dark eyes caught points of light, as a cat's eyes might, from the yellow sun overhead. "But the law's the law. I'm sorry about it, of course, but—"

"Come now, don't be sorry, Constable," broke in the voice of Martin Curragh; and the black-haired man was suddenly there, standing together with Jef and Armage, his thin-lipped mouth quirking in a friendly curve at the huge police official. "Instead, why don't you just wait for a moment to hear the whole of the matter, before you do something you might later regret. Surely Everon's not so rich and powerful yet that it can ignore the wishes of the Xenological Research Service, which has as its concern the good of all humanity—as we all know, don't we?"

Armage's face drew into hard lumps again, but this time not humorously.

"And who are you?" he said to Martin.

"Who am I? I've a dozen or two different names, if it comes to that," said Martin cheerfully. "But I won't trouble you with them."

He handed Armage a thick sheaf of papers topped by a red-flagged passport.

"You can call me John Smith," he said, "seeing that's the name folks like myself are best known by. The fact is, I'm a Planetary Inspector, sent out to pay you a small visit. It seems Ecolog Corps headquarters were thinking it was time one of us Smiths had a look here to see all was in order. I heard you saying how you'd paid off your Mortgage, but there's supraplanetary law yet to be thought of. I'm sure there're no violations here, and all that; but you understand I'll have to look about a bit, anyway, just to satisfy the order that sent me out."

Armage stood holding the papers Martin had handed him. The Constable had not moved or changed expression. He looked to Jef like a three-dimensional image in a cube of transparency.

"And as far as Mr. Robini's concerned," Martin said, "of course his work is no concern of mine. My only concern is how Everon fits in with the family of worlds in which we all are children, as the saying goes. But for your private advice, I might mention that I had quite a talk with Mr. Robini aboard the ship, and found myself impressed indeed with this research of his. It may well be that not only Everon, but worlds yet unsettled may have cause to bless the name of Mr. Robini and his beast for the work they'll be doing here to benefit all humanity. But of course, my dear Constable, as you point out, it's up to you entirely and your local laws how you deal with him, the maolot, and the whole matter."

Armage had been staring unmovingly into the smiling countenance of Martin all the time Martin was talking. The face of the big man still had not moved a muscle. Now, however, he smiled as if he was seeing not only Martin, but Jef, for the first time.

"It's a great pleasure to have you both visiting us, gentlemen," he said. Almost absently, without looking at Jef, he handed Jef's papers back. "Everon can use as much good attention as she can get. You'll be guests of mine, of course, while you're here in Everon City. I insist."

"And of course I accept," said Martin, "and without being able to speak for Mr. Robini, I would venture the thought that he would find being your guest pleasant as well. Now, I do hate to be rushing you, Constable, but Mr. Robini and I both have schedules that leave little spare time. Perhaps we could take off for Everon City with no further delay? You could possibly have us flown in by your craft, here; and it could come back for these five other good, red-flagged folks right after dropping us off at your place?"

As if in a dream, Jef found himself leading Mikey and following Martin on board the aircraft. He remarked, without having the freedom of mind to dwell on it at the moment, that Armage seemed to have taken his acceptance of the Constable's hospitality for granted, following

Martin's smooth rush of words. He coaxed Mikey into a seat beside him. Up front in the craft Armage was giving orders to the pilot.

There was no more talk of impounding and destroying Mikey. In fact, as far as any casual observer might have been able to deduce, the Constable seemed entirely to have forgotten the existence of the young maolot.

3

SEEN FROM THE AIR, Armage's home—by the standards of housing on a world occupied by humans for less than twenty standard years—could safely be called a mansion. Several acres of ground-hugging native vine made a green lawn that surrounded it completely, sweeping past a large, hourglass-shaped swimming pool and scattered, thick-trunked variform oaks, to a windbreak of smaller variform spruce and fir, planted to the side of the building that faced the misty ridges that were mountains, far to the north.

The house itself was a white, two-story building, apparently constructed of color-impregnated metal panels obtained from some dismantled space cargo vessel, rather than of the cheaper native stone, wood, or local concrete. The architecture of it was vaguely colonial. It even had a semblance of a porch across its front and four tall, entirely unnecessary pillars.

During the flight out, Jef had occupied the rear row of seats alone with Mikey, who was continuing to show a good deal of interest in his surroundings, clambering excitedly back and forth across Jef to push the heavy muzzle of his blind head against the cabin windows of the aircraft, first on this side, then on the other. After their near-miraculous deliverance from the law of Everon, Jef had thought it wisest not to let the maolot intrude on the Constable. Consequently, he had kept to the back of the craft with Mikey and left the Constable to sit up front with Martin behind the pilot.

As a decision, it had no doubt been a good one. But it

had the drawback of putting Jef in no position to ask Martin why he had, a second time, come to their rescue. It was not unreasonable that a John Smith should be concerned with justice and fairness to that extent—it was just unusual, and perhaps a little too good to believe.

Moreover, if there was a question naturally to be raised about that, there was as much of a question to be made about the behavior of Armage in meeting the red-flagged passengers personally, the moment they had stepped off the spaceship. Again, there was nothing obviously unreasonable about such behavior; it was just not what might normally be expected.

A Planetary Constable was a highly-placed elected official in the government of a world like Everon. He was much more than a local chief of police, even a chief of police of the largest city on a world—which Everon City was. The natural expectation would be to find one of his staff meeting red-flagged passengers off an incoming spaceliner and then, if necessary, conducting them to meet the Constable at his office.

If Armage had been expecting a John Smith to show up, that might have been a good reason for his appearance at the landing pad in person. But it was difficult to believe that he had—otherwise he would hardly have been so openly indifferent to Jef's papers and a grant backed by the Xenological Research Service. Like all the international Services of powerful Earth, Research was not something to be taken lightly by a newly-settled planet that was still very much dependent for its existence on help from the mother world.

No, Jef was willing to swear that Armage had been as surprised when Martin turned out to be a planetary inspector as Jef himself had been.

Why, then, had Armage met the ship? What had drawn him to greet the passengers personally? And what, if anything, had his being there to do with his arbitrary and devastating decision about Mikey, before

Martin had stepped in to object?

This warm, golden-lit planet had turned out to be darkly shadowed by more uncertainties than Jef had imagined. He had planned to stop overnight in an Everon City hotel, just long enough to arrange for his heavy gear to be shipped to meet him upcountry; and then tomorrow morning he would take off on foot with Mikey for the mountains, to accustom the maolot to being back in his native environment as gradually as possible. Instead, here he and Mikey had been shoved into the spotlight of a VIP situation, a situation he would have been uncomfortable in back on Earth.

At the same time he had to admit to a small pleasure in being where he was. After being teated like a pariah and worse by the Everon people aboard the spaceship, to be invited to stay at the home of their Planetary Constable gave him a certain amount of satisfaction. More than that, perhaps it signaled the beginning of a more friendly relationship between him and the colonists. There had been a definite uneasiness nagging at him that he might find himself in the position of being refused help generally by his fellow humans here on this alien world.

But still, the whole sequence of events was strange. Martin had been the cause of everything that had happened out of the ordinary, first with his speaking up in Jef and Mikey's defense on the ship in the debarkation lounge, and then with his words to the Constable. Why? Why should he have put himself out like that for a complete stranger and a native beast, considered vermin by the humans who lived here? True enough, he was obviously a highly unorthodox type of character, but that raised other questions. How had he come to be a John Smith in the first place? He did have that strange likeability that had so struck Jef. But beyond that one gift, he was at best a raffish, unlikely individual. True—Jef struggled with what he thought might be his own prejudices—Martin had so far done nothing that a John Smith

22

might not be envisioned as doing. But it was undeniable that he did not fit the popular image of an E. Corps Planetary Inspector.

Jef soothed a still-excited Mikey and came slowly but definitely to the decision to corner Martin as soon as possible and pin him down to some answers. It made Jef uneasy not to understand why things were happening. He was a little ashamed of that uneasiness—but it remained. Whenever Jef thought of Will, his mind rebelled at the fact that his brother should have been found unacceptable for a position that a Martin Curragh had achieved. There had been only one flaw in Will's apparent fitness to qualify for the popular image of a John Smith—his Robini temper. One small difference only— and Jef had never seen that temper evoked in his older brother by selfish or petty reasons. While Martin was at variance with the John Smith image in half a dozen ways . . .

But the aircraft had now landed. Armage led them across the tight, intertwined green of the lawn, and a tall, bald-headed man in his fifties opened the front door for them before they reached it.

"Tibur," said Armage to the man. "I've brought some guests. This is John Smith, sent to us from the Ecolog Corps. And this is a Research person from Earth, a Mr. Jef Robini. Gentlemen, my housekeeper, Aldo Tibur."

"How do you, sirs," said Tibur. His voice was ragged, as if the vocal cords had been torn or abraded. From the neck up every inch of his head looked shaven. Even his eyebrows consisted of a few pale-blond hairs that were almost invisible. There was a network of hair-fine wrinkles around the corners of his eyes and his mouth that showed sharply in the bright yellow sunlight.

"John Smith will have the guest suite. Find a room for Mr. Robini close by. Don't worry, Tibur," said Armage, bunching his face in a small smile, for Tibur was staring at Mikey. "Mr. Robini has the maolot completely under control. Haven't you, Mr. Robini?"

"That's right," said Jef.

"I'll see you both later. John Smith," Armage turned to Martin, "will you excuse me? There're those other red-flagged passengers for me to check out. I'll join you for dinner this evening. You will be my guests for a dinner tonight, here at my house?"

"Why not, indeed?" said Martin.

"It'll be a great pleasure—I'll phone you, Tibur, about the guest list and the details. You two and Tibur will have the place to yourselves here until then, gentlemen. I live by myself. I'll meet you later."

Armage turned and left. Tibur turned and led the rest of them up an escalator ramp to the second story and showed Martin to a three-room suite taking up one whole end of the second floor.

Martin stepped in without a word, closing the door behind him. Tibur turned and led Jef with Mikey to another bedroom, two doors down the hall from the suite.

"I'll see your luggage is sent out here from the spaceport," Tibur said, and went away.

Jef led Mikey on the leash about a tour of the bedroom, stopping to let the maolot rub against and sniff all the items of furniture. Maolots in the blind stage had unbelievable spatial memories. After one tour of the room Mikey knew its dimensions and the location of all the objects in it. Jef unsnapped the leash and Mikey walked to the center of the space of carpeting by the window and curled up on the patch of sunlight coming through the wide window in that wall of the room, as confidently as if he could see it.

"Stay there, now. Wait for me," Jef said to the maolot and went out of the bedroom, sliding the door closed behind him. He paused to listen for the *tick* of the magnetic lock that was now keyed over to his thumbprint. Then he went to the door of the suite into which Martin had vanished and touched the annunciator button above the latch button.

24

"Jef Robini," he said.

The door slid open almost immediately, to show Martin standing at the far end of the room beyond.

"I won't say I wasn't expecting you," Martin commented. "Come in. Sit down."

Martin touched a button on the tabletop control deck that closed the door behind Jef and came to take a gaudy, red-padded, armless chair opposite the one in which Jef had already seated himself. The living room of the suite was considerably larger than Jef's full bedroom and had been furnished and decorated by someone with no eye for color or style.

"I'd guess," said Martin, looking at him with the shadow of a thin-lipped smile, "you've got something on your mind to discuss."

"You could put it that way," said Jef. He was once more bracing himself against the strange inclination to like Martin; and the struggle made his voice remote and dry. "I take it you never knew I existed until that moment in the debarkation lounge, just before the ship landed?"

"Did I not?" said Martin.

"I don't see how you could have," Jef said. "On the other hand, you clearly gave the Constable the impression we'd had a good deal to do with each other, on the trip out from Earth, at least."

"Don't be so quick to doubt me, now," said Martin. "Why, it seems to me there may even be a reference to you and your Mikey in my papers."

Jef stared hard at him.

"What are you trying to tell me?" he said at last. "My name's not in your papers."

"Isn't it, then?"

"Will you give me a straight answer?" The familiar feeling of a sad bitterness was beginning to gather once more inside Jef. "Is my name there, or isn't it? And don't tell me you don't know. You'd have to know."

"Would I?" Martin's black eyebrows lifted on his forehead. "Busy as I am, paperwork isn't always something I can check on personally. And those clerks back at Corps headquarters will go making mistakes now and then."

"Then you're saying it isn't there, after all?"

"Did I say that?"

Jef gave up on that tack.

"All right," he said. "Maybe you'll tell me then why you're being so helpful to us? Whether you knew who I was or not, you've gone to some trouble for us twice. I appreciate it, but I'd like to know why you did it. We don't know each other and I've no claim on you. Or are you going to play games with me about that, too?"

"Oh, I don't think so," said Martin. He nodded at the wall that the living room of his suite shared with Jef's room. "That's a valuable maolot you've got over there. The only one ever raised away from its native world."

"Oh, you know that, do you?"

"It hardly takes knowing. Research would hardly have given you a grant to bring him here if your situation and that of your beast wasn't unique. Well, you might say I'm unique, too—here and now, on this world at least, I'm the only John Smith there is. It could be that our two uniquenesses would find a profit in working together."

He paused, looking at Jef.

"Go on," said Jef.

"Very well," said Martin. "But how could I work with your maolot unless the two of you were free and clear to be about the business you'd come to do? So naturally I stepped in when the other passengers seemed to be building a threat against him, and did so again when Mr. Armage seemed about to act in a manner somewhat drastic."

"So it's Mikey you want," Jef said. "What do you want him for? What kind of use could you have for him?"

"Why, none that specific to mention, just at the present moment," said Martin. "I'm only keeping an eye to the future, so to speak, on the basis of my past experience with work on worlds such as this. Maybe you don't know that someone like myself has the absolute obligation of checking out newly planted planets from time to time, to see that the humans on them are using the resources properly, and not wasting them. Habitable, Earth-like worlds, within a reasonable distance of old Sol, are not that easy to come by; as everyone should know these days. If I find something wrong here, I might be obliged to recommend quarantine; and then Everon'd be cut off from all interstellar travel for fifty or a hundred years."

"I know all that," Jef said. "But I don't see how Mikey can help you make your inspections, which I take it is what you'll be doing."

"Well now," said Martin, stretching his legs out and gazing thoughtfully at the white-painted ceiling above them. "Inspecting is indeed a good part of a John Smith's work, true enough. But that's only when the world in question is essentially conformable to Corps regulations and intent. When it is honestly trying to abide by the law; and all there is to be found, perhaps, are a few, unconscious violations of good ecological practice. But it's another story altogether when there are deliberate law-breakers there, when there might be a conspiracy to misuse the world for personal gain. That sort of situation in which the slash-and-burn mentality has gotten out of hand, you might say; and there are some who figure to take with a ruthless hand what they can and carry their profits from it off to some other new world."

Jef stared hard at Martin. It was impossible to be sure if the other man was being serious or not. But the long speech he just heard had been delivered without a smile. If it had not been so hard to believe in Martin as a John Smith, perhaps it would have been easier to take what he had just said at its face value.

27

"You think there are ecological criminals on Everon?" he said.

"Who knows?" Martin shrugged. "But can I take it for granted there are none?"

Jef felt his interior bitterness like a heavy pressure inside him.

"What kind of an answer is that?" he said. "I asked you a straight question. If you don't think there's something ecologically criminal going on here, what do you want with Mikey?"

"Surely a prudent man can be allowed to carry an umbrella on a cloudy day, without being required to predict a thunderstorm?" Martin raised his eyebrows. "It's enough for me that your Mikey might be useful to me, in case of some such eventuality. It ought to be enough for you, shouldn't it, that my speaking when I did saved him from being impounded and destroyed?"

Jef felt guilt.

"Of course," he replied, "I said I was grateful to you for that."

"Then perhaps you'll think a bit on the old adage of not looking a gift horse too closely in the mouth," said Martin. "Now that I've named you as someone in whose welfare I take an interest, the locals are sure to take note of where you go; and if I should need the use of you and your maolot, they could find you for me without delay. That's all. Indeed, perhaps you'll forgive me if I say that in spite of your mild manner, you're as prickly an individual as I've encountered in some years."

There was probably more than a little truth in that, Jef admitted to himself.

"I suppose you're right," he said.

There was a small silence.

"While I'm on the subject of speaking personally," Martin said, "it might be you'd forgive another word or two. No doubt you've your own good reasons for wanting to visit the grave of this brother of yours; but such things on a new planet sometimes give the people there the idea you're searching to stir up some trouble or other. If he was employed by the E. Corps, it might be best just to let the Corps look into the matter for you—"

"I don't think it'd do it very efficiently." said Jef.

Martin's green eyes watched him closely.

"Now what makes you say that?"

"I say that," said Jef, "because I don't think the E. Corps gives a damn about Will—or ever gave a damn about him. There were rumors floating back to us that Will's death wasn't in the line of duty at all, but happened only after he'd deserted—'gone planetary' as they call it on these new worlds. The whole business was very hard on my mother and father in the months right after we got official word of Will's death; and no one at your headquarters ever spoke up to deny the rumors, or called my parents to say they still believed in his loyalty. They did nothing."

"But," said Martin, still watching him steadily, "they did affirm that it was a death in period of duty."

"No. Not even that. All they'd say was that they'd carried him on the books as on duty up to the time of his death. All the details were held back because of that security of theirs—that same security they use to shield people like you from being identified."

"There're reasons for it," said Martin softly.

"Perhaps. But I don't see its application to the matter of my brother's death. They could at least have told us where he's buried." Jef looked back at the other man squarely. "I'm not leaving Everon until I find that out, and also enough about his last few days to answer any talk of his having gone planetary."

"Earth-born persons have been known to do it, one time and another," said Martin.

"Not Will."

The deep emotion in Jef spilled out in the last two words. He heard it in his own voice, a note that sounded savage even to him.

"I see," said Martin again in that soft voice, after a

long moment of silence. "I suppose it's no use then to warn you that that chip you've got on your shoulder against the Corps could get you into deep trouble out here on one of the new worlds, where it's a long way from Earth. —No, I see from the look on your face it wouldn't."

Jef got quickly to his feet.

"Is that some kind of threat from the Corps to keep me under control?" he asked.

"Not at all," said Martin. His voice was level and calm. "It's a warning based on the facts. You've come out here with no doubt in your mind that you'll find exactly what you want to find. But worlds, and people both, don't always turn out the way they're supposed to. You're hell-bent to locate your brother's grave and turn up evidence that will find him blameless. But what if there actually is and was some sort of criminal conspiracy on Everon to plunder the planet?"

"If there was, when he was alive, he'd have found out about it and reported it."

Martin looked steadily into Jef's eyes.

"Unless he was part of it," Martin said.

Jef stared at the other man.

"He wouldn't be," Jef answered. "You didn't know him."

"Do you?" asked Martin. "Your accent is pure Earth. If you'd spent as much as six months of your life on some other world, I could catch the influence of it in your speech. But I don't. That means all your life's been spent on the home world; and almost certainly your brother was gone from Earth for more than the eight years since his death. Possibly as much as half a dozen or more years before that? Since he'd not have gotten the post here without that much seniority as an ecologist in the Corps. You'll have seen him only now and then, when he was home on leave—if he ever did come home on leave. How well did *you* know him? How do you know what wild notion might have taken him under conditions you've never known and could never guess at?"

Jef was silent. It was true. Some furious impulse could have taken Will and caused him to do something that otherwise would have been unthinkable. Unwanted from the back of his mind came a memory of the circumstances under which Will had been rejected by the Ecolog Corps for training as a John Smith. He had always refused to talk in any detail about the events leading to his rejection. But from what little he said, they had gotten the picture of a Will who had passed the preliminary courses with honors and who had been just about to graduate and ship out as a field trainee when something had happened.

All the family knew was that an incident had triggered off that temper of his. He had been discharged " . . . *with prejudice.*" Afterwards he had returned home, but stayed around only two months before shipping out on a labor contract to one of the new worlds still in the process of being terraformed. Once there, he had worked out his contract, found local employment, and what with the shortage of trained people off-Earth, had finally managed to have the "*prejudice*" set aside so that he could gain a job with the E. Corps after all, as an ordinary ecologist. In the seven years following he had worked his way up to the position of Planetary Ecologist.

"I knew him," said Jef finally, to Martin. "He'd have been dead before he'd have been a party to the sort of thing you're suggesting."

"Perhaps," said Martin. "I know nothing of him, of course. But it's a fact that anyone can find himself doing things under strange circumstances, things that other people would never have suspected he or she might be capable of. You'd probably not do badly to keep that in mind."

Jef got to his feet and went to the door. At it, however, the strong habit of courtesy ingrained in him by his

Earth training made him stop and turn.

"Thank you for your help—and your good intentions —anyway," he said, and hesitated. "No offense, but you're not what most people would expect a John Smith to be like."

Martin's face grew leaner and his smile was a little wry.

"There's a great deal more to being a John Smith than most people know," he said. "Well, so much until dinner this evening, then."

"Until dinner," said Jef, and went out.

He was two steps from the door of his own room when he realized that his mind was a stew pot of emotions. If he went back in in this state, Mikey would sense the fact at once and react; and the maolot should not be excited if Jef was to leave him alone for several hours during the dinner that was upcoming. Best that Jef calm himself first before he rejoined Mikey.

He turned away, took the escalator ramp down to the front door, and went out, to pace up and down on the narrow porch that fronted the building. The tall, unnecessary pillars threw bars of shadow across his way as he walked back and forth. He had been deeply stirred without really knowing why—unless it was the ghost of Will, evoked in his conversation with Martin, that had disturbed him.

The afternoon had been sunlit, with warm, still air. Jef sneezed suddenly, rubbed his nose in some perplexity and sneezed again. He looked around himself for a cause, but could see nothing different except a line of dark clouds, led by an anvil shape of strong thunderheads building up on the horizon to the west.

As he watched, however, the dark cloud-line spread rapidly forward. Evidently, the clouds were being driven almost directly in this direction. He stood watching them, his pacing forgotten. A gust of much cooler air, running before the shade that the cloudbank was now spreading over the countryside to the west, seemed to clear his mind of the rolling emotions that had been troubling it. The clouds boiled on, their leading edge forming changing shapes that his imagination could translate into towers and mountain valleys, horse heads and crocodiles. The cloud edge spread to cover the sun and he saw its shadow race suddenly across the lawn of Armage's house and envelop him in a gentle twilight.

A melancholy seemed to ride the pinions of the gathering squall. A not unpleasant melancholy. Jef felt himself caught up in the interaction of the land and the weather, drawn into an action nostalgic and sad but, in its own way, beautiful. The clouds had covered all the sky now, as he watched; and the first gust of rain flew about him. But he did not retreat from it into the house, or back under the meager shelter of the narrow porch roof. Instead, he stood there, feeling a pleasure in the wind, and the touch of the raindrops, even as the wind strengthened.

It came harder out of the west. The rain was a downpour suddenly; and in an instant his shirt was soaked to him like another skin. Thunder cracked in the clouds, and all at once the rain was not rain, but hail, pearled spheres descending, bouncing on the lawn and lying glinting in the dimmed light.

Now he did move back, reluctantly, under the porch roof out of the direct fall of the hail. The wind, sounding about the house, the loud pattering of the hail on the steps and the porch floor, as well as on the roof overhead, blended so that he could almost imagine it making a music—music that seemed to sing of hope and tragedy combined, of beauty and sorrow.

There was a struggle in the song of the storm sounds, but it was a good struggle, a natural struggle, like the struggle of a child and its mother in the birth process. The gusts of wind were strong now and the hail was large. It hammered the ground. The wind tore at the

33

false pillars of the house and the clouds streamed by overhead with rollings of thunder. Gradually, as the minutes went by and he watched, the volume of the storm song diminished, the hail began to give way to simple rain, heavily falling. The overcast lightened and the wind dropped, dropped, until it was hardly noticeable at all; and the main theme of the song was only in the steady drumming of rain on the porch roof.

The rain slowed. The overcast lightened even more . . . and far on the western horizon he began to see a thinning and breaking of the clouds, a clearing with blue sky beginning to show through. The clear sky grew and approached. The rain dwindled and ended, and fifteen minutes later the fleeing overcast uncovered the sun once more, so that golden light shone down all around on lawn and trees, now shining with wetness and still pearled with occasional unmelted hailstones, scattered here and there.

Jef took a deep breath. For a moment he had been one with the storm, had been a part of its forces, a part of this planet. He felt cleansed and freshly at peace with himself and the situation that held him. He turned and went back upstairs to his room.

4

"I'LL BE RIGHT DOWNSTAIRS," Jef said to Mikey a little later. "I shouldn't be gone more than three hours at the most."

He went out, locking the door of his room behind him, and took the ramp down to the ground floor of the house, which was already noisy with the voices of the guests gathered in the main sitting room. Tibur had brought him a printout list of those invited, with pictures opposite the names, and he had made an effort to memorize these, but there was no telling whether his memory might not desert him when it came to meeting the actual people. He had never been very social; and the prospect of making small talk with thirty or forty strangers who had no real reason to be interested in him, was not attractive. This dinner, after all, was obviously being given to honor and curry favor with a John Smith. If there had been any polite way to do so, Jef would have stayed in his room with Mikey.

At the foot of the ramp he put the list in the pocket of his jacket and went into the sitting room, pausing just inside the doorway. No one there seemed to have noticed his entrance. They were involved in conversational clusters about the room. His sensitivity, heightened by solitary habits and the empathic bond he had developed with Mikey over the years, gave him a feeling of things hidden, of the ugliness of some imminent explosion waiting below the surface chatter going on in the room. Tibur was behind a table set up as a bar in one corner, and for lack of something better to do immediately, Jef went over to it.

"And what would you like to drink, Mr. Robini?" Tibur asked.

"Anything. What do you have in the way of beer?" Jef asked.

"You might like to try our Everon City ale."

"Fine," said Jef. "Thanks."

He accepted a tall glass of a bitter malt beverage with a thick head of foam. Sipping it, he turned to look the room over again.

What was most noticeable about the people assembled there was that they could hardly have been told from a similar group at cocktails back on Earth. The interesting reason for this was that here, light years from Earth, most of these colonists were wearing the latest in Earth styles and fashions. On a world this recently planted, this could happen only in two ways. One would have been if all the individuals in the room had been back to Earth in the last year or so, and had a chance to update their wardrobes while they were there. Another would have been the existence of a black market, or at least a grey one, in late-fashion clothes that were being imported instead of the customary equipment and other supplies. Earth did not care what it shipped out to new worlds like this; but Jef would have expected that somewhere outside this room there were colonists who cared more for improving their planet than for the latest fashions.

Beyond the fact that those here were, as a group, dressed in style—and not inexpensively so—their common denominator seemed to be an age level running from the late twenties to the late forties. Men and women both—and their number seemed about equally divided as to sex—they had a sort of capable, almost brutal, look. Perhaps, thought Jef, watching from the drink table, this was only natural, seeing the jobs they held. The guest list he had been given had read like a catalogue of the people

36

controlling Everon. There might be individuals important on this world who were not here this evening. Certainly there were none here who were not important.

Clearly, however, the one who outranked them all was Martin. Unlike Jef, who would have preferred to go unnoticed all evening, Martin seemed to be enjoying the attention he was getting. Some of it barely stopped short of fawning, yet Martin appeared to be taking it all at face value. They're making a fool of him, thought Jef, and his inner sad bitterness stirred at the observation. He also noticed, as he assumed Martin had not, how the whole gathering was quietly being orchestrated by the Constable, who moved soft-footedly and continually among the guests, putting in a comment here, a laugh there.

Martin was at the center of a little knot of six or eight people. He shared a sofa with a woman Jef's guest list had identified as Yvis Suchi, an organic chemist and one of the original officers of the Masters of Everon corporation. She was a tall individual in her thirties, wearing a sort of fuchsia pants-suit, thin and quick of gesture, with a wide mouth, narrow lips and a particularly carrying voice, even when she seemed to be trying to use it confidentially. One of her hands held a drink, the other kept hold of a leash connected to a brilliant-studded collar around a lemurlike creature just under a meter in height, one of the native Everon fauna. It was an omnivore—Jef could not remember its scientific name, although most of the larger species on the planet had been catalogued on the original survey.

The colonists, according to Jef's studies, called such a creature a *jimi*. It was easily tamed and housebroken; its small paws with opposed thumbs could manipulate anything a human hand the same size could manage; and the jimis were quick to learn fairly complicated physical routines. However, they were docile to the point of dullness and outside of the manipulative abilities seemed to have not much more intelligence than a dog of Earth.

There was another jimi present. Across the room another woman, named Calabria deWinter and wearing a wide-collared blue suit, stood holding a leash that kept her pet close beside her. DeWinter was also tall, but fifteen or twenty kilos overweight, grey-haired and with a round, unlined face that would have fitted a much younger body. Beside her, her jimi looked small and fragile—it also looked different from Suchi's jimi in a way that Jef could not identify until it suddenly struck him that deWinter's jimi was female—Suchi's was male. Most of the warm-blooded species on Everon were bisexual and mammalian—an unusual and fortunate parallel to Earth life.

However, once he had become aware of the femaleness of deWinter's pet, Jef was a little sorry that he had noticed the fact of sex. The small pair of breasts under the soft grey fur had not been readily apparent, low down on the front of the jimi's body. Now that he was aware of them, they seemed to make the creature more like a small, trapped human; and the whole business of keeping it on a leash became vaguely repulsive.

"Mr. Robini! Mr. Robini, come and join us!" It was Martin calling cheerfully from the couch. Yanked out of his anonymity, Jef walked over and someone produced a straight chair for him.

"You all know Mr. Robini . . . you don't?" Martin proceeded to introduce him to Yvis Suchi and the others standing or seated around. "We're talking about vari-forms of our Earth meat animals, Mr. Robini. Mr. Clare Starkke here is a wisent rancher—"

He nodded at a man in a brown half-robe, seated in an armchair, who at first glance looked as if he might be almost as tall as the Constable. His face was deeply tanned, heavy-boned and beginning to show wrinkles, although his hair was still full and dark brown.

"Honored, sir," said Jef to Starkke.

"Honored to meet you, sir," responded Starkke in a

somewhat brassy voice. "We're talking about all the troubles we have here, fighting this world so that we and our beefs can survive."

"Oh," said Jef.

He assumed that what Starkke had just said was a standard complaint of colonists. Variforms of Earth animals or plants were never introduced to a newly settled world without an exhausting preliminary round of tests and studies by the Ecological Corps. The variforms that were finally introduced had always been genetically tailored to the biological patterns on the world for which they were intended, and to that world alone. In nearly fifty-seven years since the techniques of variforming had been perfected, there had never been a case of a permitted species threatening the native ecology to which it was assigned. Of course, the variforms still represented an intrusion in the native ecology and their complete integration with it could take some generations of them.

Starkke's wisent would be genetically derived from the European bison, which went under that name. It struck Jef as interesting that it had been from the European, not the American, bison that the Everon variform had been genetically engineered; because the wisent had been a forest dweller, unlike the plains-dwelling buffalo; and on Everon it was the high grasslands below the forest areas to which the wisent herds were restricted. The forest areas, he had read, were restricted to game ranching of other variforms, chief among them being a variform eland.

Jef suddenly became conscious that they were all waiting for him to say something. He felt awkward sitting perched on his chair with his glass in hand. He looked around for some place where he could put it down, saw no surface nearby and bent over to set the glass on the floor by his chair.

"No doubt—" he began.

Yvis Suchi's jimi picked up his glass and apologetically, gently, handed it back to him.

"Leave him alone!" said Suchi sharply to the Everon animal. "We're not at home!"

She looked at Jef.

"I don't like things left on my floor," she said.

"I see," said Jef.

"You're the one with the maolot, aren't you?"

Her tone was not friendly; and the temperature of the atmosphere of the group around him seemed to lower ten degrees.

"Indeed he is!" said Martin energetically and cheerfully. "With the most remarkable subject of a highly important research undertaken back on Earth for the benefit of you good people. Mr. Robini's to be commended for the years he's put into it already, and the task he's undertaken to come out here and pursue it further."

The temperature rose perceptibly.

"You people back on Earth don't know what it's like, sir!" Starkke said to Jef. "Packs of these maolots. They kill just for the sake of killing. I've seen the sun come up and two hundred beefs, eh, lying dead. Or a pack of them'll stampede a whole herd and run them until they drop and die!"

The big rancher's voice was thick with anger, intensifying a tendency Jef had been hearing without really noticing it, ever since his landing—a sort of small, rhythmic halting in the local speech. He had never paid much attention to the stated fact that Basic One, the common commercial and technological language of Earth and the newly planted worlds nowadays, was said to be changing rapidly on many of those new worlds. Now it registered on him that all of those around him, except Martin, had some variation of that same rhythmic halt in their speech—ranging from hardly noticeable in the case of Armage to highly apparent in the case of this rancher.

"The nature of the beasts, no doubt," put in Martin pacifically.

"Their nature?" Starkke turned on him. "The nature of everything that runs, flies or swims on this planet! It's a fight for survival every day, here."

"Now then, it's a pretty, comfortable-seeming planet," said Martin. "It can't be all that bad."

Murmurs of disagreement came from all around him.

"Sir, it is that bad!" said Starkke. "Bad? It's worse! We fight this world for everything we get from it. You clear land and before you turn around there's new growth of grass over everything. Your animals eat it and it turns out to poison them. You plow—and you've bare-ly put your plow away before there's a plague of insects that fly in, light, and burrow into the soil. Before you're ready to plant, the field is sprouting with all sorts of tough, useless growth; and it turns out the tracheae of the insects in the swarm were filled with seeds from somewhere else, and your ground is now a tangle of roots your plow won't cut through. Dam a river and before the dam is done, there's a cloudburst, a flood, and every-thing you've built gets washed away. You saw that hailstorm we had here just this afternoon?"

"Yes," said Martin.

"That hailstorm, sir, came along just in time to flatten a few hundred acres of spring grain that would have been ready for cutting in a week. If it'd done it on purpose, it couldn't have timed the destruction better. None of you Earth-siders have any idea what it's like being a planter on a new world like this!"

"But there're great rewards, are there not?" said Martin. "For example, when your cleared land ends up as downtown blocks in a city such as this, with cor-respondingly increased value to your credit account?"

"Some of us pile up credit, yes—" began Starkke.

"Everyone in this room—or am I wrong?" Martin said.

41

"Of course. No. You're not wrong," said Starkke. "The point is—the point is, though, sir—"

"*Sit!*" said Yvis Suchi sharply, twitching her jimi back on to his haunches. The Everon creature had half-risen to peer at the female jimi across the room. "All right, then, take my glass and get it filled again!"

She unsnapped the leash. The jimi took her glass in both front paws, lifted itself up on its hind legs and walked crouchingly across the room to the table where Tibur presided. There it circled around to Tibur's side of the table and sniffed at all the open bottles. Selecting a couple of them it proceeded to mix a drink and bring it back to Suchi. The group around Martin had stopped talking to watch.

"Very good!" said Suchi, reconnecting the leash as the jimi brought the drink back to her. She turned to the other human. "Actually, it's not that good a drink. But you've got to praise them after they've done something, or they'll simply sit there and shake the next time you give them an order."

"There was some thought of using them in factory-type work, assembling parts," a male member of the group said to Martin. "But it didn't work out."

"No, no. Of course not," Suchi said. "They can't understand the concept of work. It's all play to them . . ."

She continued with a description of the limitations of the jimis in practice; but Jef found his attention distracted. Through the doorway of the room he had just caught sight of someone he had not seen before, a younger man with black hair receding from a high forehead and carrying something like a small attaché case. He stood talking to Armage in the hall outside the lounge for a second, then turned and stepped on the ramp leading to the second story of Armage's home. As his weight came upon it, the ramp surface began to move, carrying the newcomer up, out of sight. Armage turned and went away down the hall in the direction of the dining room's other entrance.

Jef frowned for a second, feeling uneasy for some reason that would not quite identify itself to him. Then suddenly his mind put the second story of the building and the attaché case together. He went swiftly to the ramp; but the new man had already reached the top and disappeared. Jef ran up the ramp after him, not waiting for its automatic machinery to transport him at its leisurely pace. The upper hall was also empty; but Jef turned directly to the door of the room that had been assigned to him, punched its latch button and stepped through as it rolled aside.

Inside was Mikey, his head lifted questioningly from the patch of sunlit carpet where he lay; and less than three meters from him the thin man was opening his attaché case.

"What's going on here?" Jef asked.

The man stopped with the attaché case half open.

"Who—who're you?" he demanded, with the Everon dialectical halt in his voice very evident. He closed the case quickly and went on before Jef could answer. "I'm Doctor Chavel. What're you doing here?"

"This is my room," said Jef. "What are you doing here?"

"I—Constable Armage asked me to look at your maolot—"

"You're a veterinarian?"

"I am. Avery—the Constable wanted to be sure that this beast hadn't brought in any animal infections or diseases that might affect our native stock. You're quite lucky the constable called me like this. Otherwise your maolot would have had to have been impounded and taken down to the local menagerie house for examination when the schedule permitted—a wait of at least three weeks—"

"Mikey doesn't have any diseases," Jef said. "There's a veterinarian's certificate from Earth in my papers. The Constable must have seen that."

"If he did, he didn't mention it to me. Now—" Chavel

had been opening his attaché case as he talked. Abruptly he produced a small, green, pressure syringe. "There's no need to make a fuss about this. I'll just give your beast a prophylactic injection—"

"You're not giving Mikey anything," said Jef. "He doesn't need a prophylactic injection."

"I'd advise you not to stop me." Chavel turned toward Mikey.

"I'd advise you not to try it!" said Jef. "*Mikey!*"

The maolot was suddenly on his feet at the new sound in Jef's voice. His blind head swung to aim its muzzle at Chavel, and a drone began to issue from his throat.

Chavel was pale.

"If—if I must use a tranquilizer gun—"

"Don't take it out of your case," said Jef. "I can get to you long before you could get it out and aimed. So can Mikey."

"This is—outrageous." Chavel backed away toward a nearby table on which a desk phone sat. Still keeping Mikey in view, he reached down and punched it on. "Constable Armage! Avery—"

The screen did not light up. But after a second Armage's voice came from it.

"Well?"

"I—there's someone here that won't let me do my job. The beast's owner, I think . . ."

"I'll be right up."

The phone fell silent.

"Now you'll see," said Chavel thinly to Jef.

Jef's mind spun; but no helpful ideas were thrown up. He was bluffing about letting Mikey attack the veterinarian; that would be a sure way to get the maolot killed, eventually if not immediately. Chavel did not seem to see through him. But the back of Jef's head was cold with the feeling that Armage would.

He was still trying to think of something when the door to the room slid aside and the big Constable stepped in.

44

"What's the matter, Doctor?" he said almost gently, ignoring Jef.

"This gentleman refuses to let me give his maolot a prophylactic shot."

"Oh?" Armage turned at that, and smiled at Jef. "It's for your animal's own good, you know."

"I don't believe it," said Jef.

"Nor indeed," said the voice of Martin, "do I."

The door was opening once more; and this time it was Martin who stepped into the room.

"There you are, Jef," he said. "First you disappear and then our host here does likewise. I began to feel lost with not one familiar face about me. And now I hear that our Mikey must be given some medication for his own good. But you know, I wonder. How much do we really know about maolot metabolism? Mightn't this medication have some unwished for, even fatal side effects?"

"Sir!" said Chavel stiffly. "We're quite familiar with maolots here on Everon—on their native world."

"To be sure. But you see, this isn't an Everon maolot. He's grown up on Earth, and perhaps that makes a difference. Who can tell for sure? But, in any case my dear Doctor—it is *Doctor*, isn't it—you haven't answered my question. I asked if it wasn't possible that such a medication might not turn out to have some unforeseen, even fatal, side effects."

"Ah—" said Chavel, and stopped. He threw a glance at Armage; but Armage merely raised his eyebrows interestedly and said nothing. "Ah, naturally, in choosing a drug we don't anticipate—"

"Yes," said Martin softly, "or no, Doctor?"

"Who knows?" cried Chavel furiously. "We don't even understand all the differences in human beings. How can I give you a guarantee this maolot might not have some individual, far-fetched, bad reaction—"

"Exactly," said Martin. "And, seeing that's so, and the maolot being important, as I've mentioned to the

45

Constable here, perhaps it's best that no such thing be given Mikey. Wouldn't you say so, Constable?"

He looked at Armage.

"I quite agree," said Armage, and smiled a small cold smile at Chavel. "We don't want to take any risks with this valuable beast, Doctor."

"All—right!" Chavel was getting his attaché case closed again, but his fingers fumbled and made a clumsy job of it. When the closure was finally made, he nodded abruptly to them all.

"Good evening . . ."

He was gone before the sound of his voice had died on the ear.

"And now, back down to the dinner?" Martin said to Armage.

"By all means," said the Constable.

Armage led the way out of the room. Behind the big man's back Martin paused to wink at Jef, before he followed.

Jef turned to go too, but Mikey made a small, questioning, humming sound deep in his throat. Turning back, Jef saw the maolot standing in the center of the room, his head seeking blindly from side to side. A shivering motion trembled the massive shoulders.

"It's all right," said Jef. He came back to Mikey and put his hand on the maolot's head. "I'm not going. I'll stay here with you."

Mikey shoved his blunt muzzle gratefully against Jef, almost knocking him over. Jef sat down on a chair and let the maolot drop his head on one knee.

"They can send me up a sandwich—I hope," said Jef.

It turned out that something more than a sandwich could be sent up. Tibur rolled in a wheeled table with the same dinner the rest would be sitting down to below in about half an hour.

Jef ate, and fed Mikey with the wisent meat Tibur had provided for the maolot. Afterwards, however, sitting listening to the faint sound of voices filtering up from the dining room on the floor below, he found himself back mulling an old problem. Once more Martin had come to the rescue, this time with a glib explanation of Jef's reason for being here with the maolot.

It was not that these efforts of Martin's were not welcome. It was just that they had become too frequent to be comfortable and the unanswered question of why he should exercise himself in this way was becoming a clamor in the back of Jef's mind. If the reason was a good or honest one, why had Martin been so shy about giving it, when Jef had asked? A deep-felt suspicion that there was something less than right about Martin had been solidifying in Jef's mind for some time now.

If only there was some way he could find out more about the man. Jef got up and paced the floor of the room, causing Mikey to lift his head and follow the sound of Jef's movements with it.

"I'll be right back," Jef said to the maolot after a few minutes. "I'm just going to look next door."

He stepped out the door of his own room, locking it behind him, and walked to the door of Martin's suite. But, as he had expected, it was also firmly locked. When he put his hand on the door panel and pushed on it, it did not open—but it did move slightly, making a clunking sound.

Jef lifted his hand away, then pushed again. Once more there was the sound. He tried pushing this way several times, and found that not merely the door, but the frame and door moved slightly when he pushed on it. A little further investigation gave the reason. For all of its colonial impressiveness, Armage's house had been put together either hastily or carelessly. The door was a unit taken from some space-going cargo vessel. But it had evidently been set in a frame in the wall of the corridor that had been cut just a little too large.

Jef checked the amount of looseness. The door could

be lifted almost enough to free the latch-bar from its socket in the frame. But not quite. It held just enough to keep him barred from Martin's room. For a second, as he stood staring at the door, he was struck with the incongruity of his sense of outrage that some inanimate object should be frustrating his attempt to make an unlawful entry. Then common sense was put aside. He must get in, somehow.

He could lift the door, using the very tips of his fingers —which were all that could get a purchase on the barely raised ornamental molding that crossed the door panel halfway up. But the minute he lifted it more than a centimeter, the angle of his fingertips became such that his hold slipped. If he could somehow lift, let go and grab for the handhold he had just made available by lifting the bottom edge of frame and door clear of the floor . . .

He tried. It was impossible. Frustration increased. It was not that the door was too heavy to lift. It was the fact that he could not get a good grip on it.

He was about to give up, when inspiration struck. He went back to open the door of his own room and call Mikey out. He lifted the door, explaining to Mikey all the while.

". . . See Mikey? If you can get your claws under the bottom edge of the door when I lift it. Here, let me have your paw. Like this—no, I don't want to play—"

Mikey had flopped down on his side, when Jef had taken one of his paws and gently tried to turn it over.

"All right, then lie there. And when I lift the door, you slide your claws—and your whole paw, if you can, underneath the door and lift. Try it, now, Mikey."

Jef tried lifting the door several times. Mikey lay watching him, obviously puzzled. The maolot was extremely perceptive and very bright; but he had never shown an ability to respond to words directly, the way a dog or some trained Earth animal might. Eventually, he usually achieved a remarkable understanding of what Jef

48

would try to tell him; but he managed this by some method, or in some terms, that Jef had never been able to identify certainly, although emotion and empathy clearly had a great deal to do with what way he did. In this case the maolot seemed aware, after the first moment, that Jef was not playing at all but engaged in some serious attempt. Clearly, however, Mikey was having difficulty understanding exactly what was wanted.

Jef went on talking and trying to lift the door. He was conscious of being studied—but he had gotten used to Mikey's doing that. The studying process was not something anyone else would have been able to recognize, but Jef had learned to read the almost invisible signals from the maolot that announced it. He continued, therefore; and after a few minutes he was rewarded.

Mikey reached out with one paw, as Jef lifted the door for the fifth time, and placed the pads of that paw, not into the crack Jef had produced, but flat against the panel of the door. Friction alone was the bond between his paw and the door-panel, but with the powerful muscles of his foreleg behind it, he managed to hold the door up.

"Good!" said Jef energetically. He reached down, hooked his own fingers into the space between the door's bottom edge and the floor, which Mikey's pressure was keeping open, and lifted. With a small squeak, followed by a click of the latch-bar coming free from its socket, the door was unlocked.

"All right, Mikey, let it down."

Mikey took his paw away and Jef himself let go. The door dropped back down on to the carpeting beneath it, that ran from the hallway into Martin's room. Jef opened the door and a second later was inside himself, followed by Mikey.

Martin was evidently a light traveler. The sitting room of the suite showed nothing of his. The bedroom held a single piece of luggage, a reinforced suitcase with a few pieces of all-purpose clothing and a toiletries bag. Jef was beginning to reclose the luggage, preparatory to leaving the room, when Mikey's head pushed past his elbow and nosed the inside front corner of the suitcase top.

"What is it, Mikey?" Jef's fingers probed the corner but could feel nothing there but the hard plate anchoring the suitcase's reinforcing metal inner frame. Mikey's paw unexpectedly pushed in beside his fingers and a claw hooked on the covering fabric.

"Look out, Mikey. You'll tear—" But the fabric was not tearing so much as peeling back from an invisible line dividing the fabric at the point where the back of the lid met the edge at a ninety-degree angle. Revealed was the dull metal of the plate—with something of a dark red color showing beneath it.

Jef took hold of the edge of dark red and pulled. An identification folder slid out.

"That's his papers, Mikey," said Jef. "But I thought the Constable took them, along with the papers of all the rest of us who were red-flagged. Maybe Armage gave Martin his back?"

Jef pulled the papers out of the folder. They were not the papers of a John Smith of the Ecolog Corps. They showed a picture of Martin, but identified him as Martin Curragh, a mining engineer on loan from an Earth-based corporation, to Seagirt—a newly planted world of a solar system ten light years from this one containing Comofors. Jef stared at the pages in his hands. If Martin was indeed a John Smith, it stood to reason that he would have a number of cover identifications. But while the John Smith papers Jef had seen Martin hand over to Armage had been spuriously new and clean, these identification papers had obviously been unfolded, refolded, and handled a number of times.

Jef stood there, holding the Martin Curragh identification. All identifications were readily checkable within a few weeks, merely by sending a query back to the identifying authority on Earth who had issued them, since all such papers originated on Earth. In fact the time for the query to make the round trip by spaceship was the smaller part of the time necessary to check an identification. The delay, if any, came from the bureaucratic process of comparing it with the records back on Earth.

False identification was therefore a waste of time; it was so easily checkable, and any identification was checked frequently. In the normal course of things any papers, except perhaps those of a John Smith, would be checked. But who could imagine anyone brazen enough to pretend to be a John Smith?

Possibly just such a strange and verbally quick character as Martin.

It was all conjecture on his part, Jef thought, standing there and weighing the Martin Curragh identification in his hand. But in spite of that self-caution, he was aware of a sinking feeling that Martin was indeed Martin Curragh, only, and no John Smith at all.

Unfortunately, his strange liking for the man still persisted. He could have wished to turn up any evidence but this, which showed Martin to be at least an imposter, and almost certainly involved in some deeper illegality. All at once, like the single added piece of a jigsaw puzzle that suddenly reveals the whole pattern of the puzzle, Martin's motives in aiding Mikey and himself fitted all too well with another set of observations and deductions.

Something rotten was clearly operating undercover here on Everon. That much was obvious in the unusual actions of the Constable, in the gathering downstairs where everyone was flaunting the latest Earth fashions, and in the construction as well as the appearance of this house. The whole situation reeked of special interests and the possibility of corruption in the governing areas of this newly planted world. If Martin was himself on the wrong side of the law it made only too good sense that he should be here to cut himself a slice of the unorthodox profits from whatever was going on.

Seen from that angle, his help to Jef and Mikey made an entirely different sort of sense. It could well be that it was not a case of his seeing that they needed him, but of his needing them to help establish his position. Jef's papers were beyond question. Martin's establishing himself as a defender of the someone who was carrying such papers would support the authenticity of the John Smith image in no small way. What better method for Martin to put his authority beyond question, than to act as if it was wide enough to protect others beside himself?

And, indeed, what in fact had Martin done for Mikey and himself? Nothing, really, but use that quick tongue of his to recommend caution and moderation to those who seemed to threaten Jef and the maolot. In no sense, at any time, had he actually invoked the powers that would have been his as a John Smith to aid them directly.

If all these things were added to his exceedingly slippery response to every question Jef had asked him, and above all, to his very unlikeliness as a John Smith—it would take a very stupid or trusting person indeed to go on believing in him. Jef was neither stupid nor particularly trusting.

Carefully he tucked the identification papers back where he had found them and pressed the lining of the suitcase back into place. The hole Mikey's claw had made was small and hardly noticeable. With luck, Jef could count on Martin not noticing it, at least, not for some time. On the other hand, when he did discover it, Jef was prepared to tell the other bluntly why he had investigated, what he had found, and what the certainty of his suspicions were.

He closed the suitcase now and led Mikey out of the bedroom. But at the door of the suite, he found his conscience troubling him. He hesitated. After a second, however, he went on out, setting the latch so it would lock behind him, stepping through the door with Mikey and closing it quietly but firmly behind him. The latch clicked into place.

Still he hesitated. No matter what else Martin was, no matter what his motives of self-gain or self-protection might have been in speaking up, the fact remained he had done both the maolot and Jef a great favor by doing so. And, damn it, Jef could not dislike him, in any case. It nagged at Jef that, clever as his deductions might be, they might also be somewhat lacking in charity to someone who had at least acted as a friend.

After a moment, on impulse, Jef went back into his own room, got a notepad and wrote a brief note to Martin.

> *Dear Martin:*
> *Mikey and I are indebted to you for what you've done for us. We'll be leaving for the upcountry and the mountains early tomorrow. But I wanted you to know that if there's anything in our power to do to help you in your turn, or repay you, let me know.*
> > *Sincerely,*
> > *Jef Aram Rohini*

He took the note out and pushed it under the door to the suite. Coming back to his own room, he felt the peace of a settled mind. If Martin was actually involved in something either illegal or unconscionable—or both—he had been offered what help Jef could give to get him out of it. The note was not specific on the point of the help to be given; but Jef could be plain about what he would or would not do if Martin came to him for help. And if Martin never did—well, the offer had been made. Jef could now, in his conscience, stop worrying about what might happen to the other.

Jef sat down on the bed. What he should do right now was to start to sort out what he would take with him in his backpack tomorrow when he headed upcountry. His heavier supplies and equipment, as well as the excess of the luggage brought from the ship, would have to follow him by supply truck, on one of the monthly vehicle runs to the upcountry supply posts. Jef himself had no wish to wait around for several weeks just in order to ride, rather than walk, part way to his destination; and, more important, he was eager to introduce Mikey to his native environment and begin the study he had come here to do.

Just at the moment, however, the events of a day full of alarms, tensions, and unlikely adventures had gotten to him. He was suddenly aware of being numb with tiredness. He kicked off his boots and stretched out on the bed and, reaching out to the table controls, turned off the room light.

Half an hour's nap, then he would get up and pack . . .

He woke, abruptly, in darkness. He lay still, with the lingering impression that something, some sound, had wakened him; but as he lay there listening, he heard nothing. The door was locked and Mikey would certainly not be lying still himself if anyone had tried to get in.

Jef continued to lie still, half-awake, trying to remember just what time of day or night it was, and what he had been doing when he fell asleep. Apparently he had dropped off instantly on lying down; and his fogged brain was now being slow to respond.

Gradually events began to come back to him, including the note he had pushed under the door for Martin. Remembered now by a slowed mind in a slumber-chilled body, his leaving of the note did not seem such a reasonable move as it had when he had done it. It was true that what he had written did not commit Mikey and himself to anything; but it did set up a moral obligation to someone who might be up to his ears in some criminal activity. At the very least, it left the door wide open for Martin to make demands upon him at some unspecified time in the future, when such demands might be anything from inconvenient to downright dangerous. In short, Jef found himself regretting the note.

He tried to talk himself out of that regret; but it would not go. His mind kept offering unwanted images of Martin on the run from the authorities, asking for shelter; of Martin engaged in some falling-out with other criminal elements, wanting Jef's—and Mikey's—assistance in the struggle. This went on for some minutes in the dark, Jef's imagination presenting pictures of what might happen that were more and more wild—until finally, with a grunt of disgust, he threw off the covers and sat up.

When you make a mistake, he told himself, admit it.

He put his boots back on, got up and unlocked the door to his room. He went out, followed curiously by Mikey, to have a look at the situation. Maybe he could fish the note back from under the door . . .

But as he reached the door of Martin's suite, he stopped. A murmur of voices was coming from within the room.

Too late.

For a few seconds that was all he could think of. Then his ears identified the voices. There were two. One was Martin's and the other, the deeper, softer voice of Armage.

Unconsciously Jef moved closer to the door, bringing his ear almost against the upper part of its panel. He thought he had heard Martin's voice saying something that sounded like " . . . Robini . . ."

He could not be sure. Even with his ear closer to the door now, and straining to hear, he could not make out anything that the Constable was saying; and only now and then did the sharper tones of Martin become intelligible.

" . . . not at all, my dear Avery. Not at all . . ."

" . . . otherwise, I'd not give much for the chance . . ."

" . . . upcountry, of course . . ."

". . . because it's my choice not to, that's why . . ."

The voices broke off suddenly. For a split second more Jef strained to hear, then it burst on him that perhaps something had aroused the suspicions of the two men inside and one or both were even now coming to open the door and look out.

Swiftly, he stepped away, backing into his own room, pulling Mikey with him and closing his door as quietly as possible. Standing inside his closed door, he listened intently for several minutes more. But if the door to the suite was opened, it was done so quietly he could not hear it.

In any case, he told himself, there was nothing more to be gained by his continuing to eavesdrop. Whatever was going on between Martin and Armage—and it was suspicious that Martin had been using the other's first name, when he had always been so careful to address Jef formally—it would have to wait for events to bring it to light, if they ever did. In any case, things were out of Jef's hands now. There was nothing to be said or done until Martin came to him. Then he could lay the whole matter out squarely between them and demand some answers.

Tell the truth and shame the devil.

Almost fiercely, Jef got busy with his packing for the cross-country hike that would begin for him tomorrow.

5

"BRING HIM ALONG! That's right . . . inside, now," said the Constable. He stood with his shoulder against the open door of the rotorcraft, making his big body one side of a corridor which channeled Mikey through into the craft's interior.

It was the next morning. Jef, outfitted with a mapcase, directions, and the rest of the equipment he had brought along for just this use, was embarking with Mikey for a lift upcountry in search of Beau leCourboisier. It was a bright, warm day and everything was fine; except that Mikey did not want to board. He was signaling Jef by every means available to him that they should not board the rotorcraft, but take off across country northward, on foot. The fact was he had never really calmed down since the encounter with Chavel. He was showing now the same sort of excitement he had exhibited on the flight to the Constable's home from the spaceport.

"*In,* Mikey!" Jef finally managed to push the maolot through the entrance and hurried to squeeze in behind him. Seated and holding Mikey wedged against the farther side of the craft with his knees, Jef turned to say a last word to Armage and Martin.

"I appreciate all this," he told the Constable. "You'll keep an alert here for anyone with information on the whereabouts of my brother's grave—?"

"Absolutely," said the Constable. "Good luck, now. You understand the pilot's not allowed to take you beyond the edge of grazing territory? It's one of our ordinances aimed to saving fuel and engine-wear. Any travel beyond the plains country has to be on foot or animal, except official or emergency travel."

"It's all right," said Jef. "I knew about that. That's why I brought this backpacking equipment. I'll do fine. Goodbye, then. Martin—"

Martin, who was standing half a dozen steps off, took one small step closer to the craft.

"Yes?" he said.

"I wanted to thank you, too—"

"Never mind. Think nothing of it—nothing at all." Martin's speech was rapid, as if his mind was elsewhere and he resented the time being wasted in social exchange. He had been this way all morning, a complete change of mood from his attitude when Jef had last seen him, the night before. Martin seemed now to have lost interest in Jef and Mikey—almost to the point of regretting that he had ever had anything to do with them. He had not mentioned the note from Jef.

Jef took his determination in both hands.

"I put a message under your door last night—" he began quietly to Martin, as Armage turned away out of earshot.

"Oh, yes. Thank you. Very polite of you," said Martin, briskly. "However, it's hardly likely that I'd have need of your assistance, since our paths lie in different directions. But thank you, by all means—and I believe it's time you were following your beast aboard, there."

"But you did say it was possible Mikey and I might be useful to you, and that was the reason you wanted to keep track of where we were," said Jef a little stiffly. "If you still think that would be useful—"

"Not at all, not at all—the way things look, now that I'm actually here and have a better view of them. Simply disregard what I said, Mr. Robini. And now—"

"Good-bye, then," said Jef, determined not to be hustled aboard this way. He turned deliberately and entered the craft.

"Good-bye, good-bye," said Martin.

The Constable slammed the rotorcraft door closed.

"Strap in, sir," said the driver of the craft, over his shoulder. "Ready to lift."

Jef strapped in both Mikey and himself. The rotorcraft lifted into the air with a lurch and the ground fell away below them as they headed northward, away from the artificially landscaped lawn and neatly planted trees of the Constable's home.

But with the upward bound of the craft into the air, Jef felt a curiously corresponding bound in his own spirits. Suddenly he was conscious of a vast feeling of relief. For the first time it dawned on him that he was now relieved of all obligations—to Martin or to anyone else.

In an unexpected sense, just now, Martin had set him free. If the man had accepted—even conventionally accepted—the idea of a debt of action due on Jef's part, Jef would still have been tied to his affairs and whatever connection they had with the affairs of the Everon colonial government, in the person of Armage and others like him. As it was, apparently both Martin and the Constable were happy to see the last of him; and, more than a little to his own astonishment, he was almost overwhelmingly happy to see the last of them.

For the first time he recognized some of the hidden depths of feeling with which he had come out here. He had been expecting to encounter an alien world with all its differences and dangers—but also he had been expecting the assistance and aid of the people who had come here before him in meeting those differences and dangers.

Unconsciously he had been thinking that everyone who emigrated to a new world like this would be like William. Where he had never expected friendship or help from any among the teeming billions of people on the Earth, on which he had grown up, he had expected those things, automatically, out here. That had been why, he now realized, he had been hit so hard by the hostility of the other passengers on the spaceship, and that of the Constable, on landing.

Now, in the face of his expectations, everything had been reversed. The humans having anything to do with Everon had treated him with coldness and suspicion. But the planet he had been braced to encounter had seemed to reach out golden-green, warm and strangely friendly arms to welcome and enfold him.

He laughed a little to himself. He was being fanciful.

Nonetheless, it was a fact that he had seldom felt as free as he did at this moment, and never in his memory could he remember feeling happier. He was headed out at last to do the research he had always wanted to do, with Mikey, who had always been closer to him than anyone but his immediate family; and there were, as far as he could see now that he had left Everon City behind, no clouds on the horizon of his immediate future to trouble this prospect.

It was a strange feeling but a good one. He fastened his gaze on the landscape below. Ten minutes later there was no sign of city or planted fields under them at all; and they were headed out over a sea of yellow-green grass that seemed to stretch unbroken and unblemished to the uplands and the misty mountains.

They traveled for nearly an hour above the apparently endless grass and occasional herds of wisent, seemingly hidden shoulder-deep in it. Jef found himself surprised to see how small this variform of the European bison must be. As best he could judge from the air, they could not be much bigger than sheep. Then a dark line appeared on the further horizon and grew into a green band of forest, stretching on to a further horizon. The rotorcraft approached to within a hundred meters of the forest edge and slowed gradually to a hover. Instead of landing, the craft held its position ten meters off the ground and the entrance door opened itself on the air. A section of floor moved outward through the opening and became a platform supported by cables slanting down on either side of the entrance.

"Ready to descend," said the driver. "Don't worry, that platform can carry cargo ten times the weight of you and the maolot and it has, lots of times."

"I wasn't exactly worried," retorted Jef. "Just surprised. Why don't you land?"

"Ordinance," said the pilot. "Don't ask me why. It's the law, is all."

Jef got up from his seat and led Mikey out on to the platform. He had been afraid that Mikey would choose this time to be excited as he had been on boarding the craft, but the maolot was now perfectly calm and docile. Jef found himself looking at the horizon, rather than straight down. Ten meters was no great height, but the platform was only about a meter and a half by three meters in area, and it had no side rails. He felt the metal surface tremble under him as the cables extended, and the ground came slowly up to meet them until they touched, flattening the grass beneath.

Once down Jef stepped off, staring about himself. This grass was as tall as his own head. Evidently he had been badly wrong about the size of the variform wisents They must be nearly as big as buffalo back on Earth. However, there was no point in worrying about that now. Luckily, he could see the edge of the forest through the heads of the stems.

"All right?" called down the driver. Jef looked up.

"All right," Jef waved. "Take it up. Thanks."

"Luck!" The platform began to be drawn back to the rotorcraft again. It mounted all the way, was taken back in, and the door of the craft shut. The pilot waved through the glass of the windscreen and the craft, gaining altitude, turned and headed south once more.

"All right, Mikey, here we go," said Jef, turning to the maolot. Mikey butted him cheerfully with his head. For a second Jef merely looked down at the animal.

"I don't get it," he said. "You were all wound up back at the Constable's, now you're peaceful as a lamb. What's got into you—or I should say, what's got out of you?"

Mikey only butted him again. Jef gave up and led the way toward the forest edge.

As they came within the shade of the nearest trees— some were variform conifers, but mainly willy-trees, specimens of a cottonwoodlike plant that was native to these regions of Everon—the tall stems of the grass shrank until they were hardly centimeters in height, revealing the bright-green interlacing, ground-hugging part of the plant that gave it its local name of moss-grass. Back under the farther parts of the forest this green seemed to extend forever like an endless carpet. It was a brighter green than most of the more somber colors of the forest, but almost everything growing on Everon was green, including the trunks and branches of native plants such as the willy-tree. The only patches of non-green were occasional pastel patches of flowerlike vegetation and dustings of brown from the dried and fallen-apart, fleshy extensions of the native trees, which took the place of leaves in the Everon vegetation.

Jef stopped to check the mapcase the Constable had given him. It was a device about the size and shape of a pocket-sized book. A computer-loaded compass on the upper part of its surface, however, pointed always in the direction of the destination it was set for; and just below the compass a section of map showed through the window, with a red line marking the direction and distance Jef had traveled since leaving the aircraft.

The compass needle was now pointing straight ahead, and the red line was running nicely parallel to the black line indicating their desired route. Jef put the map back into one of his woodsjacket pockets with satisfaction. According to the map and to what the Constable had said, it would be a short two-day hike to Trading Post Fifty on the Voral River. He could look forward to finding a good camping spot tonight by the ford on the only other actual river between him and Post Fifty. Then at Post Fifty he would either find this Beau leCourboisier or someone who could tell him how to locate the man.

His search seemed to be turning out to be more straightforward than he had thought—thanks to the Constable; or rather, thanks to Martin Curragh, who had been responsible for the Constable's cooperation. For the first time in some months Jef's spirits began to rise as he strode along.

The simple fact that the exercise was warming him, making him more alert and optimistic, could have been reason enough for his increase in cheerfulness. But it was also a fact that the country through which he was traveling was strangely pleasant and exciting. Jef looked about him as he walked, trying to pin down what it was that was so particularly stimulating to his feelings.

There seemed to be no one specific cause. Overall, there was almost a fabled quality to the place he was in. Everything was as green as the Land of Oz, which gave the forest an unreal, magical appearance. But it was not just the green color alone, thought Jef, that produced the magical effect. It was the way the oversize yellow sun sent its light in amongst this verdant world, so that the greenness itself seemed touched with gold leaf and even the air was golden-green and particularly alive. Adding to all this was the occasional, musical sound of a clock-bird, a small native creature like a flying lizard with a cry like a small, silver chime, repeated at precise intervals four to seven times in succession. The sound, Jef knew, was actually a challenge to anyone passing through a particular clock-bird's territory; but the sweet, clear tone of it on the still air contributed to the magical-country impression.

Still, even with all of this, it was strange to the point of absurdity that he would be feeling such an outward-bursting impulse of happiness and anticipation. It could only be that remarkable liking of his for this world running away with him, again—a jerk at his right hand, the one holding the leash of Mikey, brought his attention back to the maolot. Mikey was not merely leading the way. For some time now he had been straining to pull loose from Jef, which was amazing. Jef took a quick step forward and caught the maolot's head, turning it to see if Mikey had suddenly lost his infantile blindness and acquired the sense of sight that would come with male adulthood. But Mikey's eyelids were as firmly closed over his eyes as ever. The maolot pulled his head impatiently out of Jef's hands and jerked forward against the leash again, as if he could not wait to get to some long sought destination that was just over the next rise in the ground.

The remarkable thing about this behavior was that Mikey had always been fearful of unknown territory. Until he had fully explored a place, he had always hung back, his head against Jef's leg, to pick up clues of directions and pace. But now the maolot plainly wanted to lead. Of course this was not unknown territory, in one sense. Instinct might be directing him. As an experiment, Jef pulled himself up close on the leash and unsnapped it from Mikey's collar.

Mikey took off the second he was released, literally running. He loped forward, passing unerringly between two trees, and half-circled another, before he halted and turned his head back to look over his shoulder as if he could see as well as Jef, if not better.

"I'm coming!" Jef called to him. "Just don't get lost."

Mikey broke into a lope again, disappearing among the trees. For a moment Jef felt uneasiness. If Mikey did manage to lose himself . . . But, within seconds, the maolot reappeared, loping back unerringly almost to Jef, then turning and heading out once more like a frisky dog, unable to hold himself still, but unwilling to leave his owner too far behind.

In all the years he had known him, Jef had never seen the maolot so happy and excited. He seemed to be bursting with happiness and anticip—

Jef checked himself in mid-stride. He stood still. Three seconds later Mikey reappeared, galloping at top speed to skid to a halt before Jef and nuzzle his hand concernedly.

"It's all right," said Jef absently. "All right. I'm just thinking."

In fact, he was thinking very hard. It had been some years now since he had accepted as a fact the strong impression that at times he could sense what the maolot was feeling—and vice versa. Certainly he had come home from happenings that had upset or angered him and found Mikey apparently duplicating his emotions.

But this faint indication of communication had never been backed up by any concrete evidence Jef could pin down. It was just a general impression he had gotten at times, something there was no way of proving; just as the Xenological Research Section had been unable to prove anything by studying Mikey for the eight years Jef had owned him.

But here was Mikey, evidently intoxicated at being back on the home world he must only dimly remember. And here was Jef, also feeling intoxicated for no strongly apparent reason . . .

Jef examined his inner sensations. They were still of a bounding excitement and joy . . . and there was no real reason for him to feel that violently happy. No reason at all, unless somehow he was picking up Mikey's emotions and duplicating them in himself.

Jef began to hike forward again, but his feet moved automatically. He was still wrapped up in his thinking. If he really had some kind of an empathic link with Mikey that was going to become stronger now that they were here on Everon, that fact alone was worth investigation.

The question then became—if there was such a link, how could he prove it was there? How to test it?

Nothing came to mind to answer those questions. Jef strode along, going around and around the problem in his head, until his mind began to wander from the subject through sheer weariness at going over the same puzzle too long. Gradually he put his questions aside and became more aware of the forested upland he was passing through—giving himself over to the excitement and stimulation he assumed he was getting from Mikey, long since gone back to his running ahead and back again. Under the influence of the shared emotions, he found himself acutely aware of the wooded country through which he was passing; and he began to pick out both the ways in which it resembled a comparable Earthly forest, and the ways in which it was different. His mind shifted the basis of its observation, unconsciously beginning to classify as intruders on the scene all the familiar shapes of trees that were variforms of Earth's black oak, Scotch pine, Norway spruce and balsam fir; and the strange shapes of the native vegetation, which he had never seen before except in pictorial representation, began to feel like comfortable familiars.

He discovered several parasol trees as he went along. They were a species of vegetation very like a low, spreading-limbed tree of Earth. Their difference lay in the fact that the Everon parasol tree did not have true leaves, but the same fleshy branch and twig extensions as the taller, slimmer willy-tree—and for that matter, all native Everon vegetation. Only, in the case of the parasol tree, these extensions were a brilliant green, and clustered thickly on the last half-meter or so of new branch growth, so that the parasol tree looked as if it was holding a thick umbrella-shape over whoever passed beneath it.

Less frequently seen—but he passed one before lunch time—was a milepost: a short, thick-trunked specimen of Everon vegetation, which in the present dormant season of late summer in the northern hemisphere of Everon seldom seemed to be more than three meters tall. However, during the active, winter season, the top of the thick trunk would send up slender saplinglike branches with feathery tips to catch and feed on the pollens and microscopic spores released by the other Everon plants at that season. In a few short weeks the milepost would accumulate a year's supply of sustenance; then its saplinglike extensions would wither and die until next winter, while less than a centimeter was added to the height of the thick, central body.

This, the willy-tree, the parasol tree, and some dozens of other lesser flora and fauna which Jef identified, had been part of a working ecosystem for Everon millennia before men thought of colonizing the world. Then when the decision was taken by the human race to move in, it had been the Ecolog Corps that had taken on the delicate and complex job of reseeding and restocking the planet with just those genetically adapted variforms of Earth fauna and flora that could integrate with the native forms to form a new, but viable, ecosystem. The fact that such a combination could be achieved at all was a miracle, to which the intermixture of Earthly and Everon forms now testified—from the simple variform earthworms through the complex and powerful maolots, themselves.

But simply to put the two together would not be enough. It would require several hundred years of careful control of the colonists and careful watching of the blended ecology, to discover all the secrets of the planet's living forms, both native and imported. Even then, it would need at least several hundred years more to guard against something dangerous coming out of the blended system. Too many questions were still unanswered.

For example, what was the benefit that the native system derived from the mileposts, which seemed, as far as study could tell, to operate as part of the Everon ecosystem, but brought nothing to it beyond the material of their stump after death? Why should the maolots remain blind until adulthood; and did the empathic contact he was ready to swear he was experiencing now with Mikey imply a similar communication between the immature members of that species and the adults with whom they associated? Did the adults also communicate in this fashion—

He broke off in mid-thought, just in time to catch himself from falling over Mikey, who had planted himself crosswise to his path, firmly in the way.

"Mikey! What are you doing?"

He turned to go around the maolot, and Mikey moved to continue to present a barrier.

"Stop that, Mikey!"

Jef made another try to go around the maolot until it dawned on him that Mikey might have some other reason than mere playfulness for what he was doing. Jef ceased trying to go around him, stood still and looked about.

He had come almost to the banks of a very small and shallow stream—not more than ten meters across and showing itself through the clear water to be only centimeters deep. He was in the center of a narrow winding glade, through which the stream ran, with forest behind him and forest in front, beyond the small open stretch of vine-covered ground that bordered the far side of the tiny stream. There seemed no reason not to wade the stream and go on; but clearly Mikey did not want him to do so.

"Why?" he asked the maolot. "What is it, Mikey?"

Mikey pressed against him. He was radiating—if that was the right word—something very like a strong warning. Not the sort of warning that goes with a violent sense of imminent danger; but the sort that goes with a stern caution to engage only in right conduct.

"All right," said Jef. "I'm just standing here, Mikey. Now what?"

Mikey pressed reassuringly but still warningly against him.

68

"All right, I'll wait. For a bit, anyway," said Jef.

He stood, waiting . . . and became suddenly aware that no clock-birds were sounding. In fact, there was no noise from the forest about him at all. Even the breeze seemed to have decided to hold its breath.

Without warning a galusha trotted out from the forest on the far side of the stream. This was one of the smaller predators of Everon, in appearance something like a heavy-shouldered fox with a green-black pelt; but much larger than a fox—about the size of a small wolf. It trotted down to the far edge of the stream and looked across at Jef and Mikey. Behind it two more galushas— adult but slightly smaller—emerged from the wood and stood, looking but not approaching the edge of the water.

The galusha by the streamside bobbed its head suddenly, with a motion in which Jef recognized a similarity to one of Mikey's, when the maolot was inviting him to play. Then the smaller predator turned and galloped back to its two fellows, who broke out of their immobility and raced upstream in the open area, dodged as the first galusha caught up with them, and then raced downstream again.

For several minutes as Jef watched, the galushas in perfect silence played up and down the opposite bank of the stream. Then, breaking off their actions for no apparent reason, they turned and disappeared into the forest beyond; the largest galusha running fast and the two smaller ones racing after him.

Jef was left standing with Mikey, staring across the water at an empty streamside. He woke to the fact that the clock-birds were sounding again. Mikey moved away from his legs, out of his path.

"It's all right to go on now, is that it?" Jef asked him.

Mikey bobbed his head as the galusha had done. Turning, he ran across the stream and paused on the far side, looking back over his shoulder and waiting.

Bemused, Jef followed. The water, as he had expected,

came barely above his ankles; and the bed of the stream was pebbly and firm. He emerged and went on into the forest beyond, with Mikey racing ahead of him once more, as the maolot had done all day.

"What was all that about, Mikey?" Jef asked him as he caught up with the Everon native momentarily, under the trees.

Mikey nuzzled him affectionately. To Jef's empathically sensitized emotions there seemed to be an air of indulgent laughter about the other. Mikey chased off ahead, again.

Jef followed thoughtfully. He checked his compass, but he was right on course. Another puzzle had been added to the long list that Everon had already visited on him since his landing from the spaceship. Some clue to what had happened undoubtedly lay in the behavior of the galushas. Jef wished that he had his reference tapes on Everon life forms, but these of course were with the equipment that was to follow him later. He tried to remember what he knew about the galushas, in hope of turning up some insight—but nothing came. The galushas were merely upland predators who made the staple of their diet out of the oversize insect life forms of Everon. There was no help in that knowledge to an understanding of what had just taken place.

All the same, as he went along, now it seemed to Jef that he was conscious, in a way he had not been before, of being watched. There was not the slightest visible or auditory sign to justify this feeling, but it persisted. He could almost feel himself being watched as he went, of being at the center of a ring of eyes that viewed him from all angles and traveled with him as he moved, so that he was continually under observation.

He could not shake this feeling. Still . . . he looked at Mikey gamboling on ahead and then dashing back occasionally to touch base briefly with Jef before taking off again. Mikey was showing no awareness of such a watch upon them, or in fact any awareness of any difference in things since they had started. If something was going on, Mikey certainly ought to be able to sense it.

Or should he?

Could it be that Mikey's being raised on Earth had deprived him of some Everon-normal sensitivity . . . Jef made an effort to shake the whole question out of his mind. He was getting away from the area of reasonable speculation and into such areas that he might as well be dealing in fantasies.

Still, these and similar questions continued to throng his mind as he and Mikey made their way through the gold-tinged greenness of the Everon forest. But by the end of the day he still had answers to none of them. He had, in fact, even stopped watching Mikey's dashes and runs by the time they came to the ford of the Voral River and set up camp on the near bank. It was already growing dark, and while the map showed the ford was nowhere more than a meter deep, and with a level, gravel bottom, the idea of crossing the considerable width of that dark stream once the sun had gone down did not appeal to Jef.

So, by the time the light had completely gone and before one of Everon's two small moons had risen, he had his shelter tent up and his fire built. He fed Mikey and himself with the concentrated rations he was carrying. There was not enough bulk in such for Mikey, but it would do for the two days they were taking to walk to the first supply post. Once there he could buy some eland meat, if nothing else—and if Mikey did not rediscover a hunting ability in the meantime.

With Mikey curled up across the fire from him, Jef sat, staring into the flames. His sleeping bag was laid out and waiting, but it was barely past sunset and he did not feel ready for sleep yet, in spite of the long day's walk. The curious sensation of being observed was still with him, but now it was as if the observer or observers had drawn back, respecting his small circle of privacy marked out by the firelight. Strangely the feeling had not, from the start, been one of being watched by anything inimical. It was more as if a circle of shy but curious woodland animals had become fascinated by him.

He was free to ignore the feeling; and, effectively, he had. Something else—a feeling of sadness and something like loneliness—was affecting him now. He had been thinking for some time about the puzzle of the mileposts, and the fact that they seemed to contribute nothing to the ecosystem; and from that his mind had veered off to consider the colonists, here and on other newly-planted worlds, and his fellow humans back on Earth.

In one sense he had been like an alien among the others of his own race all his life. He had spent his time as much as possible in the outdoors of the wild parks, and at the zoos, mingling with his fellow humans only as necessary to live, to get himself an education and to find a job. He had always felt, instinctively, that a life should be lived to some purpose; and, lost among the endless hordes of people on Earth, he could not believe that he would ever find any purpose to his own existence as long as he swam as one of their endless multitude, one minnow among countless other duplicate minnows.

He would not have minded being one of those uncountable billions if he could have found his own people something to like and admire. But, in the mass, they had never evoked those emotions in him. As individuals, they could be kind and sensitive and responsive; but the moment they banded together in anything from a community to a nation, they began to react according to the lowest common denominators. The impulse to kindness became the impulse to selfishness, sensitivity was lost under callousness, and responsiveness gave way to a frantic urge to compete, to survive at the expense of anything and anyone else. In his own lifetime the two giants of governmental bureaucracy—which employed sixty percent of the work force—and organized crime, which dominated, if not employed, twenty percent—had been locked in an endless power struggle on the battlefield created by the existence of the great mass of unemployed, living on citizen's benefits.

Only in the small fringe area of the international services, and in the research areas, could altruism and hope for a higher sort of humanity exist. And even here—as it had in the case of Will's death—the selfish concerns of governmental authority could step in and interfere.

Twenty-three years of life on Earth should, he told himself now, have taught him that the human race, transplanted to the other worlds, would be no better. But still he had come to Everon expecting just that. He should not be disappointed in the characters he had discovered in Martin, Armage, and the others he had met at the Constable's. Illogically, though, he was.

Moodily, now, he poked the fire with a branch; and a stream of red-gold sparks shot up into the dark like the rocket-trail of some tiny, invisible spaceship. Humanity, in the final judgment, was even worse than the milepost. Not only did it not give, it had no intention of doing anything but taking. Here on Everon, and back on Earth, where a whole world had been carved and altered to support a human race multiplied like a plague virus, his racial fellows offered nothing and planned to take everything.

Still, it need not be that way. In the midst of all that his race had done, down the red-dyed history of mankind, a spark of warmth and gentleness, like that Jef had found in the members of his own family, had continued to exist—chronicled in story and picture and music, taught in quiet corners, clung to in little corners of the mind. The other side of the coin from human selfishness had always been there, too. Only—it never seemed to gain the upper hand, never conquered—

Unexpectedly Mikey, who had been lying still all this time, leaped to his feet. With one swing of his heavy head, he knocked Jef flat on his back and stepped forward to stand over him, while for the first time since they had left Earth, from the maolot's throat came the deep, rumbling drone that was a true equivalent of a warning snarl.

"Mikey!" said Jef, and tried to get up. Mikey put one heavy forepaw on him and held him down, still staring blindly off into darkness, still rumbling his drone of warning.

Then, eerily, from the darkness came the sound of a high-pitched, human voice, shouting.

"All right!" it called. "Peace—nobody hurts nobody —I'm coming in. All right?"

Mikey took his paw off Jef and stood back. The droning in his throat ceased. Jef scrambled to his feet, staring at the maolot, and then off into the utter darkness of the forest into which Mikey was still facing.

There were a few seconds of waiting, and then a faint rustle from the obscurity was followed by the sudden appearance into the firelight of a slim figure a head shorter than Jef, dressed in leather jacket and green-brown check pants of thick-woven local cloth, with something slung on its back so that a gunstocklike end showed above the left shoulder. There was a quiver of what looked like short arrows at the belt. Jef blinked. It was some twelve-year-old. No—it was a young woman with close-cut brown hair and a lean, tanned face.

"Peace," she said again, stopping on the far side of the fire. "All friends—nobody hurts nobody like I said. But you're real lucky you've found how to make a watchdog out of a maolot. Before I saw that, I'd half a mind to put a bolt into you first and ask questions after."

"Put . . ." Jef shook his head. The words made no sense. "Why?"

"Why you're on my place—and no message sent you were coming through!" the girl said.

Jef blinked again. Her place? She looked to be somewhere between a dozen and sixteen years old.

"Strangers," she was saying now, "get shot on sight in these woods nowadays, when they show up without warning. Everybody knows that. Why don't you?"

74

6

JEF STARED AT HER.

It was a good question.

"Nobody told me," he said. The words sounded foolish in the quiet night above the crackling fire. There was that difference in her speech that he had noticed with the Constable and others, the faint pause in a sentence every so often. "Your place?"

"That's right," she said. "I'm Jarji Jo Hillegas, and this is my ranch—from Silver Meadow to Way Down Creek. I've got over six hundred head of eland running these woods. All the ranches around here are Hillegas ranches. My oldest sister's got the next one south, and my next-to-youngest brother's got his just north of mine. My dad's space backs us all up, eastways."

"Oh," said Jef. "You're an upland game rancher. But—" he hesitated, "You're young for that, aren't you?"

"I'm twenty-two—Standard."

"Oh." Jef continued to stare at her, uncertain as to whether she had simply taken him for an outsider who would believe anything, or not. In no way, he told himself, could she be only one Standard year younger than he was. Not the way she looked.

"And who the hell are you?" she was asking.

"Jef Aram Robini," said Jef automatically. "I'm—I'm here on a research project. I'm headed for the trading post—Post Fifty—right now. But I'm taking Mikey here—"

He gestured at the maolot.

75

"—up to the mountains. He's been raised under observational conditions on Earth; and now I'm trying to find out how he'll adapt, back on his own world."

"The mountains? Why didn't you ride up with one of the supply-truck trains?"

"I wanted to get Mikey back into his natural environment as soon as possible. He's actually eight years old—"

"No, he isn't."

"As a matter of fact he is."

"I don't know who told you that, Robini, but anybody who knows maolots can tell you he's not more than four years, Local. If he was eight years old—"

"As it happens," Jef found an actual pleasure in interrupting her for a change, "he is. That's one of the reasons I brought him all the way back here. On Earth he didn't mature as he should have. If you'll let me explain . . ."

She listened while he talked, but without shedding the air of general skepticism that seemed to wrap her like an invisible poncho.

"Now, I didn't know I was trespassing on your territory, or that I was supposed to check with you first," he wound up. "But in any case, I'd have wanted to come this way. I've been hoping to find out about my older brother's death. He died here on Everon eight years ago—"

"Died? How?" An edge of hardness had come into her voice and Mikey droned abruptly on a note of warning. "What do you mean—'died'?"

Jef felt the sad bitterness gathering in him. For too many years he had suffered the misunderstandings of other people where William's death was concerned. Mikey droned suddenly on a note of warning.

"I mean *died*!" He came down hard on the word. "There was a man named Beau leCourboisier who was there when it happened. I'm hoping he can tell me more about it than the E. Corps could. My brother was a Colony Representative for the E. Corps here on Everon—"

"He was, was he?" The hard edge in Jarji Jo Hillegas's voice sharpened. "Beau know you're looking for him?"

"No. But since he was a friend of Will's—"

"Oh . . . friend." The edge went out of Jarji's voice. The warning note singing in the back of Mikey's throat faded away. "Still, if you were coming through here, you should have radioed ahead."

"Nobody said anything about that, I told you," said Jef. "Do you shoot anyone at all who happens to come through here, if you don't know they're coming?"

"Now and then," said Jarji dryly. "But if your brother was a friend of Beau's I guess I might hold off—in your case."

"Thanks," said Jef grimly. "Weren't you the one who yelled 'peace' just now? I'm not going just to stand here if you try to use that thing you've got. Neither is Mikey."

"Oh, I think I might handle the two of you, if I had to —the maolot first, of course," she said. "It wasn't any doubt in my mind about being able to do that, that stopped me when I first saw you. It was trying to figure out why anybody from the city or the wisent ranches would come up here with a maolot as a pet. They make pig-food out of maolots on sight down in wisent territory."

Abruptly she came right to the edge of the fire so that only its flames were between her and Jef. With a single smooth motion she swung her weapon off her back and sat down cross-legged, laying the device out before her on the ground, beyond easy reach. Seated so, on the green moss-grass, painted by the red-yellow colors of the firelight, she seemed so much a part of this nighttime forest scene that she looked more like some creature of Everon herself, rather than a human, twenty-two-year-old, game rancher with a killing machine on the ground before her.

"I said peace, and I meant peace," she said. "Sit down. Let's talk."

Slowly, and more clumsily, Jef sat on his side of the

77

fire. Mikey crouched beside him, one heavy shoulder against Jef's leg. Reaching out with one arm, Jarji picked up a dry branch of variform pine from the pile Jef had accumulated, and tossed it on the blaze.

"A little more light, here," she said.

The flames caught at once on the dry needles and flared up, pushing back the darkness of the surrounding forest. The scent of the burning wood rose into Jef's nostrils; and suddenly he was seized by the same faculty of acute observation he had experienced as he stepped off the spaceship. The smell of the fire, the dance of its flames licking against the night, the leaping illumination playing with the colors of Jarji's rough clothes and lining her face with moving shadows ... all these and the polished wood of the weapon and the movement of the night air made him feel as if he had fallen into a trance where everything about him was twice as real as reality —and twice as wonderful. This alone, he thought suddenly, was worth his coming to Everon to experience. This, alone—

He wrenched himself out of the moment of transport with an effort, and straightened his back, staring across the fire at Jarji. She sat still, the weapon lying a meter ahead of her, and less than that from the edge of the campfire. Jef's eyes focused on it. The dark wood of its polished stock and frame was of some kind he did not recognize. A backward-curving length of metal was set crosswise near the front of the frame; an arc of metal, like a short bow, with a wire for a bowstring.

The wire crossed the frame at a point where a metal groove ran down the length of the stock. There, guides caught it, and the guides seemed to be fixed to a pulley arrangement running back along the side of the stock to a drum holding eight metallic cartridges perhaps three centimeters in diameter, so that one cartridge at a time engaged one end of the pulley system through a slot in the cartridge's curved side.

"Never seen one of those before?" asked Jarji. "Called a crossbow."

"I . . . guessed that," Jef said, remembering illustrations of devices like this in his history books on the wars of the late middle ages in Europe. "But what are those?"

He pointed to the cartridges in the drumlike part of the weapon.

"Spring-pulls," she said.

As Jef watched, she leaned forward, picked up the crossbow and rotated the drum so that the next cartridge in line took the end of the pulley into its slot. She punched the outer end of the cartridge with a quick stab of her thumb, and the cartridge whirred abruptly, like an angry rattlesnake. The pulley wire spun back through the slot in the cartridge and out again; and the guides swiftly pulled the wire bowstring back the full length of the stock.

"Lucky for you I just rewound a full wheel's worth of spring-pulls," said Jarji. "Wouldn't want to spare one, otherwise."

She took one of the short arrows from her belt quiver, laid it in the groove along the top of the crossbow stock, and nocked its feathered end into the wire bowstring. Casually, she lifted the heavy weapon in one hand, pointed it off to one side, and fired.

There was the sharp, musical twang as the wire released, followed in almost the same instant by the sound of a solid impact.

"You see?" said Jarji, laying the crossbow down again. But Jef was still staring off in the direction the arrow had gone.

"What—what did it hit?" Jef managed to say.

"Hit? Oh, I shot the quarrel into a willy-tree trunk," she answered. "Don't mind showing it off to you; but I'm not going to go hunting all through the woods at night for a quarrel, just to demonstrate."

She got to her feet, walked off into the darkness and

returned after a moment sliding the short arrow she had called a quarrel back into her quiver. She sat down again.

"Could you see that tree you shot it into?" demanded Jef unbelievingly.

"Of course not," said Jarji. "But I knew it was there. This is all my place, these woods. Didn't I tell you?"

She laid the crossbow down before her feet once more. Jef pulled his gaze away from it with an effort.

"Why do you use a thing like that?" he asked.

"Well, now—" Her voice was abruptly bitter and mocking. "You know none of us law-abiding upland woods ranchers would go using a real energy weapon."

Jef blinked across the fire at her. Jarji stared back, hard-eyed, for a moment. Then the tight line of her jaw relaxed.

"I guess you really don't know anything, do you?" she said. "There's a law against carrying regular weapons, any place but down in the city. Never mind . . . you were going to tell me about this brother of yours."

Jef pulled himself together. As briefly as he could, he told her essentially what he had told Martin about Will's death, disappearance and the difficulty his family had encountered getting details about it from the E. Corps.

When he was finished, Jarji sat without saying anything for a long moment, frowning and poking at the fire with a piece of pine branch from which the twigs and needles had been singed away. Finally she threw the stick aside, as if she had come to some decision, and raised her eyes to Jef across the fire.

"I guess I've got to say you're right, Jef," she said. The unexpected, familiar sound of his own first name jolted him after the formality of Martin and the Planetary Constable, down at Spaceport City. "I'd guess the chance is best your brother is buried upcountry here somewhere. Might be, though, you're looking in the wrong place for him."

"Wrong place?" Jef stared at her.

"I mean—he might be buried down around the city, or on one of the wisent ranches," she said. "You see, I figure if Beau or one of us game people knew something about his dying, they'd have sent word to you and your family a long time since. That's maybe why you better be braced for Beau not being able to help you."

"But Beau's the only one I know to talk to, here on Everon," said Jef.

"Oh, sure. I don't mean you shouldn't try to talk to Beau. Just that you shouldn't go expecting too much from him right away. And that's another thing—" said Jarji. "You're going to have to find him first."

"Find him? But I thought he was at Post Fifty," said Jef.

"Had a ranch there, four years ago," she answered. "Wisent ranchers courted him out of it."

"Courted him?" said Jef. "I don't understand."

"Guess you don't," she said. She picked up again the stick she had been using to poke the fire and dug the stiff, charred end of it into the ground before him as she talked, watching the little tufts of earth she turned up, instead of Jef. "What do you know about wisent and eland ranching, here on Everon?"

"I know there were two large meat animals variformed to coexist in the Everon ecology, and that their embryos were imported to be raised here," Jef said. "The Ecolog Corps decided two species would be enough. The buffalo —I mean, wisents—"

"Call them buffalo, if you want," Hillegas said, frowning at the earth she was digging up with her stick, "we here call them wisents—but that's just Europe-type buffalo to someone like you from Earth."

"I meant to say wisents," said Jef. "I know they were brought in to graze the prairie and open country and the variform eland were brought in for wild-game ranching in forest areas like this. I don't remember how many

81

were first brought in to seed Everon with the two species. But they were put here as part of your First Mortgage, weren't they?"

"Doesn't matter how many," Jarji said. "To start out, there was a balance of them—just enough wisent for the open land, just enough eland for the woods. Making allowance for natural increase, of course, as the human population increased and we moved beyond the boundaries for settlement that the E. Corps set up for us under the First Mortgage, wisent ranchers began crowding us wild-game raisers out."

Jef frowned, trying to understand, but finding that she made no sense at all.

"How could wisent ranchers crowd you out?" he said. "I mean, they're out in the open country and you eland ranchers are in the woods—even if the E. Corps would let them do anything, they just wouldn't, in any case."

"E. Corps gave over direct control when we paid off Mortgage One," growled Jarji. "That's the rule. We didn't even have to take a Second Planetary Mortgage. We could have got on without people to teach us how to expand factories and plan highways and land spaceships —not saying anything against your brother; but we could've got on without a Second Mortgage and people like him. Other new worlds have done it."

"But the most practical thing—" began Jef, quoting almost word for word from one of the books he had studied, "is for a new world to take up the first three available mortgages offered under the Corps and Earth assistance plans. Every world needs the First Mortgage anyway, to pay for the original E. Corps survey, the seeding of needed variforms of Earth flora and fauna, and the direct E. Corps control personnel who have to be in charge until the First Mortgage is paid off and the new inhabitants have learned to handle their new world. But almost every world can benefit from a Second Mortgage too, which pays for teaching personnel and the professional help to

82

expand the basic colony set up on the new world under the First Mortgage. What the First Mortgage sets up is primarily an agricultural-trading society; while the Second Mortgage helps this to expand into a semi-industrialized—"

The stick in Jarji's grip broke with a snap.

"What is this?" she snarled. "The sort of stuff they feed you back on Earth?"

Startled and somewhat embarrassed, Jef admitted it was.

"Well, forget it!" snapped Jarji. "That's all. Forget it. It doesn't go here in the wild. You understand me?"

"No," said Jef honestly.

"Well, you listen," said Jarji, dropping what was left of the stick and looking straight at him. "Every world's different, that's what. Every world's a brand new problem—to the E. Corps *and* to the colonists like us. What you were just quoting makes it sound like there's just one blueprint for all new worlds, like this, and things always go one-two-three. Well, they don't! Second Mortgage means not only E. Corps giving up direct control of a world—it means there's a lot of value that comes in, in the way of equipment and materials bought with Second Mortgage money to expand the colony. Means there's chances for some people to get rich. Means some people get the chance to be more important than others!"

The word "rich" rang oddly on Jef's ears. He remembered the elaborate home of Armage.

"I still don't understand," said Jef.

"There's a law here on Everon—E. Corp's approved it," said Jarji. "If wisent don't do well on a certain range, then any wild rancher running eland in forest touching that area can go to court and sue for the right to plant the area to forest and increase his woods-range. Same way, if eland population drops in a forest area, any adjoining wisent rancher can sue to clear the area for wisent grazing."

She stared almost fiercely at Jef.

"Wisent ranchers been suing and winning the right to clear forest area ever since the E. Corps moved out of here," she went on. "You asked me why you probably wouldn't find Beau leCourboisier at Post Fifty, when you get there. I'm telling you why. His woods range got challenged for a wisent grazing area. It was condemned and cleared by a downcountry rancher a little over a year ago."

"But . . ." Jef puzzled over this information, "you said no one could take over forest unless the eland population was down. You mean Beau leCourboisier lost a lot of his eland—"

Jarji laughed shortly.

"Lost!" she echoed. "Lost, all right. You mean poisoned! Well, not all. Some drove off, some poisoned, some just plain disappeared—just as if five or six downcountry aircraft had come along, the night before the head count was made for the court—five or six cargo aircraft full of wisent ranchers armed with laser hand-weapons to kill and carry out every eland they spotted on their infrared scopes."

She laughed again, on a harsh note.

"It's because of things like that, that you radio ahead when you're coming through a person's woods nowadays."

"But," said Jef, "there's no aircraft allowed to fly this far up. The Planetary Constable told me so."

Jarji said nothing. She merely leaned deliberately and spat into the fire. Her spittle exploded with a sharp crack as it hit a red-hot ember.

"Then," said Jef after a few moments when it became clear that she was not going to say any more without prompting, "you say the wisent ranchers have been moving in on your forest territory under the excuse of some law. But I didn't know that; and even if it's true, there's nothing I could do about that. You want to notify the E. Corps—"

"You really don't put two and two together too well, do you?" said Jarji. "Remember I was saying you might be looking in the wrong place for your brother? If he was a real good friend of Beau's, it could be the people who made your brother disappear were the same people who stood to gain by driving Beau out."

There was a long moment of silence. Then Jef heard his own voice speaking, as if it was somebody else's voice, some distance off.

"You don't mean that," he heard it saying. "What you're hinting at is the possibility of my brother being deliberately murdered. If that was the case, why would the E. Corps not tell us about it . . ."

"Not talking about any such thing!" said Jarji. "Just mentioning how things are here. You take it from there, if you want. Figure it out for yourself."

Far off in the night, a sound interrupted them. It was a low, moaning sound that rose gradually up the scale, and in volume, until it became a full-throated, if distant, roar. That roar rang about them for a full minute and then died away again slowly, as it had begun. Mikey shoved violently against Jef, almost crawling into his lap, shivering violently.

"Sure," said Jarji, looking at Mikey. "*He* knows."

"What is it?" demanded Jef, his own voice a little shaky. "Was that—"

"What else? A male maolot, full-grown one. Mine, maybe."

"Yours?"

"Mine," said Jarji. "Oh, not like your pet there. I mean the full-grown male whose hunting territory overlaps my eland range. Up here in the woods we aren't like the wisent ranchers. We don't go out deliberately to hunt down the maolots. But that maolot old man out there keeps other male maolots away. He takes the eland he needs to eat and I don't complain. He and I got a truce on. He goes his way and I go mine—and we both kind of see to it the ways don't cross. He'll measure near two

85

meters high at the shoulder as he stands on four legs. You'll see that for yourself if you ever come face to face with him."

Jef shivered in spite of himself.

"Will he . . ." Jef hesitated. "Will a full-grown male like that stay out of any human's way?"

"Unless there's a reason—probably." Jarji looked over the now-low flames of the fire at him thoughtfully. "Nothing bothers anything here, without a reason. You're going to have to learn that, if you figure to stick around."

"I know," said Jef.

She looked at him with surprise, and some approval—for the first time.

"You might manage to get by, after all," she said, "if you don't get killed before you learn your way around. If you don't know something, don't guess at it. Ask somebody, if there's somebody around to ask, or stay clear until you do know."

Jef nodded. The puzzling behavior of Mikey when they had encountered the galushas came back to nag at him.

"I ran into something odd earlier today," he said slowly.

"Oh? What was that?"

He told her. When he had finished describing what had happened, she nodded.

"That was their mating dance," she said. "Now that's just what I was telling you."

"Mating dance—you mean the galushas?"

"That's right. They'll start playing like that—a dozen or more of them at once, and break up into smaller groups, and then, one by one, an extra male, or an extra female'll drop out. It's a way they have of choosing."

"But why did Mikey act the way he did?"

"I *said*!" She came down on the second word with emphasis. "Here on Everon nothing interferes with anything else without a reason. Any species that's mating,

86

they're safe from the predators that'd ordinarily take them. Individuals from two species that'd ordinarily fight on sight, don't fight. Maolots are territorial, but at mating time they cross territory lines and there's never any argument."

"Is there any connection between that and the way this male maolot of yours has a truce with you?"

She shook her head.

"That's something different. You'll have to live here a few years to understand that. That truce's just between him and me."

"Then, if I run into him—"

"No telling, like I said." Jarji frowned at the fire. "Probably he'll leave you alone, because there's no reason to do otherwise. No, wait. Come to think of it though, he won't bother you as long as you have that one there with you."

"Mikey?" Jef looked down and put an arm about the still-shivering body that huddled close to him.

"Sure. A full-grown male won't hurt any female or cub, or even a young male with his eyes still closed, like yours, there," Hillegas said. "Come to think of it, yours ought to know a full-grown one wouldn't touch him. Now, if he was another full male, it might be different. Any two males'll fight, whenever they meet, for territory. But your maolot ought to know no adult would hurt him."

"He's grown up on Earth, the last eight years," said Jef out of a dry throat. "Maybe he's forgotten, or never learned. My brother found him when he was only a few days old, beside his dead mother."

"Could be he doesn't, then," she said thoughtfully.

Jef's eyes went to the crossbow at her feet.

"I—don't suppose," Jef said, "you could lend me that, or one like it?"

Jarji shook her head.

"These are handmade," she said. "This is the only one

87

I've got. Stay by the fire tonight; and travel in the day. You ought to be safe enough, once any male sees you've got that young one with you."

She got abruptly to her feet, picking up the crossbow as she did so.

"You'll make Post Fifty by noon tomorrow," she said. "My territory doesn't run that way more than another five kilometers, but I'll radio ahead for you and you won't be stopped by any other uplanders. Night!"

As unexpectedly as she had arrived, she was gone into the darkness beyond the now-feeble firelight. Jef listened; but there was no sound from the woods to signal the direction in which she had left. Hastily, he built up the fire.

The flames licked high again. Once more, from farther off, came the long, droning roar of a huge, adult male maolot. Mikey nuzzled Jef and curled up once more against his legs. Jef petted him absently.

7

JEF WOKE AT DAWN, to find the fire out and Mikey still pressed against him.

He got stiffly to his feet, made up the fire and cooked breakfast for them both. With the new heat of the fire and his own reawakening, he began to feel more alive. A by-product of the alive feeling, however, was becoming aware of a rawness to his neck, face and the back of his hands. He had had a good tan on Earth, but apparently the golden sun of Everon was something special. He had become sunburned on the exposed parts of his skin during his hike yesterday. He looked through the small first-aid kit that was part of his pack supplies; but found nothing in there for sunburn. A little sheepishly, he ended up going back to the cooking supplies. He had some butter there in a vacuum pressure can; and he coated his areas of sunburn with that. Mikey tried to lick the butter off his hands.

As soon as possible he put out his fire and got moving. He had slept badly, waking from time to time under the sleepy impression that he had heard the roar of the adult maolot close at hand, then dropping back into sleep to dream that the great Everon predator was standing over him. But with breakfast in him, and the warmth that exercise brought to his sleep-chilled and stiffened body, the dreams of the night before began to fade.

It was a beautiful morning. The forest was open here, with tall variform western white pines shading out any undergrowth, and the yellow-brilliant shafts of sunlight came in at angles to brighten the green low carpet of the forest form of the moss-grass. It was almost like taking a stroll through a park back on Earth. The clock-birds chimed cheerfully all around them and occasionally some small scurrying native creature could be glimpsed —although not for long. They were all clearly wasting no time in getting out of the way of these two strangers. Jef wondered if it was he or Mikey—young as the maolot was—that was making them scurry for cover in such fashion.

But there was no way of answering that question. Jef consulted his mapcase from time to time; but the black line marking the route of his actual passage continued to run right beside the red line of his indicated route. Something about the area of the map displayed in the case bothered him, however; and it was not until the fourth or fifth time he consulted it that he put his finger on what was bothering him.

According to the map Post Fifty was deep in forest territory with no open country closer than twenty or twenty-five kilometers. But Jarji had said that Beau leCourboisier's game ranch, which had been close to Post Fifty, was now cleared for open range and wisent grazing. But if so, the map did not show the change.

It was hard to believe that up to twenty kilometers of what had been forest had been cleaned out completely and turned into pasture. Not that there was anything physically impossible about it, even with the sort of tools that were all a new world like Everon would have obtained with its First Mortgage. But it seemed inconceivable that woods territory would deliberately be destroyed on that scale by colonists on as young a world as this. Surely the E. Corps would get around to checking the world, sooner or later; and surely the Corps would never approve that kind of massive interference with the native ecological pattern?

The question hung in Jef's mind without an answer, nagging him until he forced himself not to think about it anymore. Happily, a glance at the mapcase told him he was now less than eight kilometers from Post Fifty. It was already mid-morning of the twenty-five-hour Everon day. He should reach the post as Jarji had said, by noon —or even before noon.

Jef gave up thinking and went back to enjoying his hike. Mikey paced beside him, apparently also relaxed and peaceful, only brushing the side of his head lightly against Jef's hip from time to time as if to reassure himself that Jef was still there.

About four kilometers from Post Fifty, something bluish-green flickered in the farther shadows under the trees ahead and Jef stopped suddenly, Mikey bumping into him. For a second Jef squinted in the direction in which the movement had been visible, without seeing any further sign of what might have caused it.

Then his vision adjusted; and he realized that he had been looking directly at what had moved without identifying it, because the colors of its sticklike body blended so well with the green of the trees and the moss-grass underfoot.

It was a so-called leaf-stalker, one of the native Everon life forms. The leaf-stalker, he remembered from his studies, was an entirely harmless, insectlike creature which lived on the tiny life infesting the moss-grass itself and the trunks of the trees. The only remarkable thing about it was its size. It stood about sixty centimeters high on its brilliantly blue-green, sticklike legs—larger than any insect on Earth. A pair of false wings half-lifted from its back, shimmering with a play of all colors of the spectrum. Now, as Jef watched, it moved both stiffly and daintily forward, probing the branches of a small bush with its dark-blue, rod-shaped head.

Ashamed of himself for his moment of alarm, Jef paused to admire the leaf-stalker. It was like some strange, impossible, but lovely creature out of a fantasy, with its soft coloring and odd movements. Then, as he watched, it suddenly stopped moving; and with the stopping almost disappeared once more into the colors of its background.

At the same time Mikey crowded suddenly out in front of him, so suddenly that Jef stumbled and almost went down. A second later the deep droning roar of a mature male maolot broke the silence. Not from the far distance, this time, but from close at hand.

Catching his balance, Jef froze—as the leaf-stalker had frozen.

The roar broke out again. The sound of it mounted, rising until the whole wood seemed to vibrate to it. It came from ahead of them, from behind them—there was no telling from which direction it came, because it seemed to echo and re-echo from every quarter.

Then, slowly it died away. But, even after the woods had gone back to silence, Jef still stood motionless where he was, stunned by the memory of that sound still in his head. Gradually his head cleared; and he remembered that Post Fifty was now certainly no more than a few kilometers distant. Once in sight of the Post . . .

But, as he was about to start moving again, a thought stopped him. The roar he had just heard had come from only meters away from him; but in what direction? What if the full-grown male was directly between him and the Post; and by going forward he would walk right to it?

He stood, chilled, trying to remember where the roar had seemed to come when it had first begun. But memory was no help—and then he became aware that Mikey's head was turned, facing blindly in one direction; ahead, but a little to the left of their path toward the Post.

He looked the way Mikey's muzzle was pointing, to see a close patch of trees and a clump of darker shadow —and then, as he watched, the maolot adult male walked into full view, less then thirty meters away.

Jef stopped breathing. He had read about the adults; he had heard Jarji describe one last night; and he had lived with Mikey for four years; but the actual sight of one was something for which nothing could have prepared him.

As Jarji had said, the male now facing Jef and Mikey stood almost two meters tall at the shoulder. His head, lifted on a powerful neck, looked toward Jef and Mikey from more than two meters in the air. He was in fact no taller than a good-sized Earthly horse. But the comparison to a horse did not begin to do justice to the impression of enormous physical power and majesty that radiated from him.

His shape was catlike, but his bones—and in particular the heavy head—were massive even in terms of that size. In the books Jef had read about Everon, there had been mention of an adult male maolot picking up a fullgrown wisent—one of those heavy, buffalo shapes—in his mouth and carrying the wisent off the way a cat might carry a mouse. Now, face to face with this wild hunter of the Everon woods, Jef realized that there had perhaps been more understanding than he had thought in Jarji, when she had refused to supply him with a crossbow. Perhaps in her trained hands a crossbow could do some damage to such a beast as Jef now faced. Certainly if Jef had been holding it now, it would have seemed of as much use as a slingshot.

Jef's knees felt weakened. He began to breathe again, but shallowly. He was as helpless before this adult male as a small bird would have been at the paws of a house cat, back on Earth. One cold, long shiver ran through him and for the first time in his life he faced the fact that in a few seconds he could be dead.

Then the miracle happened.

Mikey had been pressing against Jef's legs in ordinary fashion. But when Jef shivered, without warning Mikey stepped away from Jef, toward the adult male. Roughly three body lengths he moved forward, placing himself between Jef and the other maolot; and from his throat

93

came the droning, rising note of warning with which he had challenged the appearance of Jarji the night before.

That one, long moment in which Mikey faced the great, silent form of the other male seemed to Jef to go on forever. But at last Mikey's drone died away and the two maolots confronted each other in silence.

Something happened.

Jef blinked. Neither he nor the two maolots had moved; neither Mikey nor the adult male had made any further sound; but something non-physical had taken place. Something had been accomplished. Without warning, silently as a cloud passing away from the face of the sun, the huge male turned and disappeared. All at once the place where he had stood was empty except for the sunlight and the moss-grass. Off to the right a flicker of blue and green caught Jef's eye as the leaf-stalker began to move and feed again.

Mikey turned about, came back and rubbed against Jef as if nothing had happened.

The touch of the young maolot brought Jef back to full breath and movement. He let the air out of his lungs with a gasp and stared down at Mikey.

"Mikey?" he said. "What happened?"

Mikey butted his head into Jef's stomach as if he had never had a thought in his life beyond play and food. Jef leaned on him for a second, letting the strong, four-footed body support him while the weakness in his knees disappeared.

"All right," he said finally, straightening up. "Let's go, Mikey. But why couldn't you have shown us whatever you just did with that other maolot, in those years back on Earth when the research team was testing you every week?"

Mikey rubbed against him once more. Jef sighed and they moved ahead through the woods.

But now Jef's mind had been pushed back to the whole matter of Mikey's failure to mature and all the other unsolved questions about him and maolots in general. Nowadays, at least in ranching areas, the maolots seemed to live mainly on the wisent and eland that the colonists had imported. But before the coming of this alien source of food, they had apparently lived off a host of native species, including smaller predators like the galushas. The maolots were plainly at the top of the food chain on Everon, but—like the mileposts—their exact role in the ecosystem was unknown.

Most predators on most worlds had a pruning effect on the species that were their natural prey. That is, they normally preyed on the old and sick of those species on which they lived. But the adult maolots, with their speed and their power, seemed able to take any prey they wanted, well or sick, strong or weak, and they did not normally restrict their hunting to those that could best be spared.

In addition, there was a peculiarity about Everon fauna that so far had resisted all explanation. At certain times prey would literally choose to walk into the jaws of a predator, without the predator needing to make any effort whatsoever. Jef had seen no demonstrations of this so far; but the records of the E. Corps during the early survey period on the planet were adequately supplied with eyewitness incidents testifying to it. Everon, in many ways, was the most puzzling of the worlds humanity had tried to settle so far. So it was not merely a stroke of good fortune after all that a research grant had been forthcoming to allow Jef to bring Mikey back here for observation in his native environment.

Because the interest of the Research Service and the E. Corps itself went far beyond the question of why he had failed to grow into an adult on what to him was an alien world. The real interest even went beyond the value to Everon of what Jef might learn. Despite all the studies that had been made by reputable researchers over the last hundred years, no solid evidence of the so-called ex-

trasensory talents—telepathy, clairvoyance, pol-
tergeistism—had been established. But the maolots,
among themselves, and particularly with their male
young that remained blind until they were almost fully
grown, showed some indication of possibly having a
method of communication involving something other
than the ordinary senses.

The maolots showed no sign of being intelligent in the
human sense—although for animals they were as bright
as some of the more intelligent non-human species of
Earth. That much had been definitely established. But
establishing it did not help in solving the question of
whether they could, indeed, communicate to any great
extent with one another. Why would they need an extrasensory means of communication? Certainly, it would
have seemed simpler for the maolot young simply to have
been born with their eyes open; or to have them open
their eyes shortly after birth, as humans and the young of
most Earth species did.

So said common sense. Imagination, however, suggested something different—something attractive to the
human mind. What if, through maolots, humans might
finally find a way to unlock an extrasensory means of
communication of their own?

On Earth the Research Service had brought Mikey
into contact with a number of humans who had been
reported to demonstrate extrasensory abilities. But the
results of such contacts had always been without result.
None of the humans involved had been able to "receive"
anything from Mikey; and in his turn Mikey had ignored
them completely. In fact, the young maolot had always
been indifferent to most humans unless he felt threatened
by them—the special exceptions being Jef, Jef's father
and mother. Mikey would go frantic if he was isolated
from all three of them for more than about six hours, and
calm down only when at least one of them was reunited
with him.

Nonetheless, Jef himself had always been convinced that something beyond the ordinary was going on in the case of Mikey and himself. Of course, he had always had a special relationship to Mikey; and it was probably true that familiarity with each other had trained them both to read each other's non-verbal signals. Visual signals were no good to Mikey, but his sensitivities in all other physical respects were not merely good, they were superb. However, signal-reading could not explain Mikey's empathy with Jef when Jef was physically separated from the maolot by some distance.

Still, Jef had always been privately inclined to believe that something beyond ordinary explanation was going on between Mikey and himself; and since his landing here on Everon, Mikey's ability to race around in unfamiliar forest without bumping into anything, plus what had just taken place between the young maolot and the adult male, were both startling evidence in support of that belief.

Particularly strong evidence was whatever Jef had seemed to sense happening between the young maolot and the older male. Just as he had never been able to offer solid evidence for Mikey's empathic abilities in the past, so now he had no way of proving what he had felt when the two maolots had confronted each other. But he was damn sure he had felt it. He had "heard" or "witnessed" *something*. He had been there and knew what he had felt. It occurred to him now that there could be a time to stop pretending to have an open mind and to begin to entertain the proposition that you might know something that no one else did.

Deep in thought as he was, Jef hardly noticed that he had left the shelter of the woods until the sun hit him strongly and hotly in the face. He stopped and looked about him.

He had emerged into a clearing filled with several long, low log buildings. Automatically he checked the mapcase, but there was no real need to do so.

This had to be Post Fifty.

He went forward again toward one of the log buildings in front of which the flag of Everon—a single gold star in a blue field—floated in the noon breeze.

8

THE BUILDING HE APPROACHED was a single-story structure, solid with its chinked log walls. Five steps up on the side that faced the flagpole led to a solid door made of three unusually wide, rough, dark-brown planks. A square latch-button of white plastic was set in the door. Jef pressed it and the door opened. He went in, accompanied by Mikey.

His first impression was that he had walked into a warehouse of some sort. The full width of the building before him was filled with what seemed to be Everon-manufactured equipment of all kinds. Parts for water-wheel electric generators and steam electric generators made dark stacks under the log rafters of the peaked roof. Kegs of nails, tall coils of wire, two-handled crosscut saws two meters long, axes, shovels, hammers, tubing, panels, tubs and containers of white plastic, covered the plank floor. Toward the back of the room Jef saw pole racks hung with clothing, most of it in bright colors and bold patterns, made of cloth like that Jarji had been wearing.

The place stank—with an odor that was a combination of the smells of grease and wet fur.

"That's him," said a voice, off to Jef's left.

Jef turned toward the sound.

To his left the stacks of supplies came to an end after about three meters. Beyond this was a good-sized area, open to the plank walls, holding several straight chairs, and with a bar, or counter, along its back wall. The near end of the bar had a sign above it, reading *Pharmacy;* and the wall behind it was built into cupboards, several of them sealed in white plastic as if they might be refrigerated or vacuum-lined to protect their contents. The far end of the bar had a large white container with a faucet in it and shelves behind it filled with rows of white plastic bottles bearing labels Jef was too far away to read.

There were four men sitting around the room holding grey pottery mugs; and another man seated behind the counter on a high stool, as if he was in charge of the place. Jef went toward this fifth man with Mikey beside him and in the face of a dead silence. Since the first words Jef had heard, no one there had spoken.

"I'm Jefrey Aram Robini," he said, when he reached the counter. "And I've got a special E. Corps permit for this maolot. This is Post Fifty, isn't it? Sir, I take it you're the Post Officer, here?"

The man behind the bar smiled without moving off his stool. In contrast to the other men sitting about, he looked almost pale. He was a long-chinned, long-handed man in his fifties, gone heavily to fat, so that what had once been the sharp angle made by his jawbone was now only a crease in a thick dewlap of skin bulging above his collar.

"That's right, Mr. Robini," he said. "Herbert Doty, officer in charge of Post Fifty. We just got a call you and your maolot were on the way here."

"Call?" echoed Jef. "Oh, from Jarji."

"Jarji? Jarji Jo Hillegas?" Herbert Doty's smile shortened. "No, sir. From the Constable down in the city, of course. Where'd you meet that Hillegas girl?"

"I was crossing her game-ranch area," said Jef. "She said I should have radioed ahead I was coming and she told me she'd pass the word along to people farther up."

"Ah," said Doty. He had his smile back again. "Well, she didn't get word to us. You'll find a lot like Jarji in the uplands here, sir. Good people, but no telling when they'll get things done. The only people to count on—"

his glance went past Jef to the other men, "are Post-ranchers. Responsible people like these men."

Jef turned to look at the responsible men and found them closely watching, not merely him, but Mikey.

"It's all right," Jef said to them. "Mikey only does what I tell him."

"Yes," said Doty, and coughed, a thick, throaty cough. "The message about you said that. Otherwise, we'd be bothered, seeing a maolot inside here. We shoot them on sight, you know."

Jef looked back sharply at him.

"You do?" he said. "Jarji said—"

"Oh, Jarji!" Doty waved a hand with long, slender fingers and a plump wrist. "You don't want to go paying any attention to what people like Jarji Jo say. She comes out with all sorts of wild tales."

He slipped down off the stool. For all his appearance of size while he had been sitting up on it, on his feet he turned out to be half a head shorter than Jef, fat-bodied but with skinny legs.

"You've come up here to find Beau leCourboisier," he went on. "Beau'll be here in just a little bit. An hour or two. He wanted to be here when you got here yourself; but he had things still to do at his ranch."

"At his ranch?" echoed Jef.

"Yes, at his ranch—" Doty checked and looked keenly at Jef over the rolls of fat beneath his eyes. "You were going to say something?"

"No," said Jef. In fact, he had been about to mention Jarji's claim that Beau's ranch had been cleared for wisent grazing, four years before.

"You'll be staying overnight, I guess," said Doty, walking away from the end of the bar to a door set in the adjoining wall right beside one of the seated men with the mugs. "If you'll just come this way, Mr. Robini. We'll put your maolot in one of my storerooms, then you and I—"

"Wait a minute," said Jef, stopping. "Mikey stays with me wherever I go. We don't put him in a storeroom if I'm going to be someplace else."

Doty glanced at the other men; and Jef himself turned to stare at them. But their faces were blank; and when he looked back at the Post Officer, Doty's face was also without expression. They were silent, watching him. The atmosphere in the room was heavy. Mikey pressed against Jef's leg.

"I'm sorry," said Jef after a moment, when none of them made any effort to speak. "That's the way it is. Mikey stays with me. If necessary, we'll both wait in a storeroom."

"Well now, Mr. Robini . . ." said Doty slowly, then checked himself. "No, come to think of it, I guess it'll be all right. The maolot can stay with you. We just aren't all that used to them as pets."

"He's not a pet," said Jef. "He's a research subject."

But there was no answer from any of them to that, either. Doty turned and opened the door toward which he had headed. Jef followed him through it, Mikey close beside him, into a narrow corridor lit with electric glow-tubes, where the smell of grease and fur was, if anything, even thicker than it had been before. Doty led the way past several plank doors set in the walls of the corridor, until he came to one on the right that seemed to be locked. A key from his pocket unlocked it and he swung it open.

"There you are, sir," he said, standing aside with something that was almost a flourish. "You'll find a comfortable bed, in case you want to rest, and a washstand in case you want to clean up. You won't have to wait long."

Jef passed him and went in, Mikey at his heels. The room was dark except for one window in its far wall; and for a moment on entering he had to stop and blink to make out his surroundings, even after the rather dim artificial light of the corridor.

As he stood, trying to see, the door closed behind him, cutting off what little additional light from the corridor there was. He turned to open it, but it refused to yield to the white plastic button of the latch.

"Just a minute!" he called through the plank panel to Doty. "The door's stuck!"

There was a low-pitched laugh, almost a gurgle, from beyond the door, then silence.

Jef looked back into the room; and his eyes, now beginning to adjust, picked out a bare box of an enclosure. There was no bed and no washstand—in fact, no furniture at all, except a heap of what seemed to be rags and old clothing in one corner. He spun about and hammered on the door with his fists.

"What is this?" he shouted. "What's the idea of locking me in here?"

Again, he heard the gurgling laugh; and, after that, the sound of boots going away down the plank floor of the corridor outside. Then there was no sound whatsoever.

Mikey pressed close against him, making throaty sounds.

"All right, Mikey," he murmured absently, petting the maolot reassuringly, "it's all right."

But it wasn't. Jef went over to the single window of the room. The window itself was large enough for him, and even for Mikey, to crawl through; and it was no more than a meter and a half from the floor. But a heavy wire mesh had been fastened over it beyond the window pane. With some trouble he finally managed to open the window latch in the right edge of the window's frame; and open the window by swinging it inward upon its hinges on the left side of the frame. But when he took hold of the wire mesh and shook it, he only bruised his fingers. The wire was as thick as fence wire and could not have been more immovable if it had been anchored in concrete rather than wood.

"All right, Mikey. It's all right, I tell you." Jef turned

from the window and went back to soothing the worried maolot. "We'll just wait. They can't keep us here forever."

But, as the day wore on and the shadows of the variform oak branches and leaves above the window lengthened on the small patch of bare ground and moss-grass visible outside, Jef began to lose his confidence about someone eventually coming to let them out. Doty would only need to leave them here without food or water until they died—simply forget about them until it was all over; and who would bother to check up on them? The Constable down in Spaceport City would simply assume that Jef had gone off someplace with Beau leCourboisier. Eventually, of course, the Research Service back on Earth would get worried having no word from him, and send an inquiry to Everon. But by that time, he and Mikey could be buried someplace in the woods and their graves hidden beyond discovery under a new growth of ground vine or moss-grass. . . .

Jef reined in his thoughts with a jerk. Mikey was obviously sensing his present dark mood and getting more and more upset. Besides, the mental picture he was painting was too far-fetched to be true. If the wild-ranchers wanted to get rid of him and Mikey for some reason, it would have been a lot simpler to shoot them with a crossbow such as Jarji had been carrying and then bury them somewhere in the forest, than to go to all this trouble of locking them up and waiting for them to die from lack of water and food.

It was unreasonable to think of any possibility but that somebody would be along eventually to open the door of their prison; and when that door was opened—Jef told himself grimly—he and Mikey would have something to say about things before whoever opened it managed to lock them in again.

They settled down to waiting. Jef investigated the pile of rags in the corner, but they were so dirty that he decided against having anything to do with them. He and Mikey made themselves comfortable on the floor against the wall holding the open window, through which a faint breeze drifted, now and then, to cut the thick atmosphere inside.

Happily, he still had his pack and the rations in it. He shared some food and water with Mikey, although he was wary of using more than a little of the water. There was no telling how long they might have to live off what was in the pack—

A distant whirring sound brought him out of his thoughts with a jerk. The sound grew rapidly louder. He got to his feet and stepped to the open window.

The sound was the sound of a ducted-fan aircraft—the same sort of aircraft that the Constable had told him was forbidden by law from flying this far from Spaceport City. He craned his neck, peering up through the window; but could not see the craft. Then, suddenly, it dropped into view, coming down vertically on to the moss-grass between the building he was in and the next one to it. For a second Jef thought it had landed; but then it lifted again, lightly, and drifted through the air to his right until it was out of sight from his window.

Jef heard the fans of the craft shut down. In the new silence the late afternoon outside went back to its normal noises, the chiming of the distant clock-birds and other creature cries starting up again from the surrounding forest.

Jef himself went back to waiting. Time went past. The afternoon had already begun to fade into twilight outside his window, leaving the unlighted room deep in shadow, when he once more heard the sounds of footsteps in the corridor outside.

Jef got to his feet. The door opened, and Avery Armage walked into the room.

"Constable!" said Jef, moving forward, "you don't know how glad I am—"

"Stay right where you are!" Armage said.

Jef stopped, and Mikey with him. He stared at the laser handgun the Constable held pointed at Mikey.

"That's better," said Armage, closing the door behind him. "You think a lot of that maolot. Just remember, if you start anything I'll shoot him; and probably I'll shoot you, too. Understand?"

Jef opened his mouth, then closed it again. He nodded. He could feel his mind racing.

"Good," said the Constable. "Now, I'm putting this laser back in its holster. Don't fool yourself I can't get it out in plenty of time, before you or your animal can reach me."

Slowly, watching Jef closely all the while, he lowered the weapon and slid it into the holster at his belt. Then he took his hand from it, but he left unbuttoned and open the weather flap that normally snapped down over the butt of it.

"All right, tell me," said the Constable. "Who sent you here? What are you doing on Everon?"

He loomed over Jef like a mountain. There was nothing now in his face of humor, or of the effort to be pleasant that he had shown down at Spaceport City. Jef struggled to control his galloping thoughts and keep his voice calm.

"You saw my papers," he said.

"I saw them," answered the Constable. "I also saw the forged papers your friend had. We've got all the evidence we need to take care of him; and we'll have the man himself in a day or two. So you might as well tell the truth and make it easier on yourself—it's the last chance you'll get."

Jef was still trying to straighten his thoughts. The final words of the Constable sent them spinning again.

"My friend?" he echoed. "What do you mean forged papers? Who's got forged papers?"

"Curragh. Don't play games."

"I'm not playing any games," said Jef. "I just don't know anything about any of this."

The Constable merely stood, staring down at him, the thick lower lip in the big man's face slightly outthrust.

"You're telling me the man you call Curragh *isn't* a Planetary Inspector after all?" Jef asked.

"You know that!" said the Constable. "Anyway, it's not Curragh we're concerned with now, it's his friend. You."

"His friend?" Jef stared at him. "Me? But I only talked to him for a minute or so, just before the spaceship landed."

"And you're just now getting around to telling me so." The Constable's irony was as heavy-handed as the man himself.

"I didn't get much of a chance to tell you anything," Jef retorted. "You'll remember I was stuck in a room in your house with Mikey; and the only times I talked to you were when you looked at my papers, then for a few moments later on when your vet tried to inject Mikey, and on the next day when you put us on the aircraft to start us on our way up here. Come to think of it, how about that law of yours, that you said wouldn't let any aircraft be flown this far away from Spaceport City? You flew up here just now, didn't you?"

"Police and necessary craft are permitted, of course." Armage stared down at him. "Stay with the subject. We know you're Curragh's partner, just as we know he's no John Smith. Now we want the truth about you."

"You've got the truth about me!" Jef stared. "Anyway, what makes you so sure he's a fake? You can't have had time to check his papers with E. Corps on Earth in two days."

"It won't take us long. We're checking with Earth now. We found his real papers hidden in his luggage. In two weeks we'll know all about him. Just as we'll know about you."

"But my papers are legitimate!" exploded Jef—and then had to break off to calm Mikey, who suddenly pushed past Jef and began droning a warning in the direction of the Constable.

"That's right," said the Constable. He had put his hand back on the butt of the laser at his belt, although he had not drawn the weapon again. "If you want the maolot alive, keep him quiet. Quiet and calm."

"I tell you," said Jef, forcing his voice back to a normal level as he straightened up from Mikey to face the Constable once more, "I'm who my papers say I am. Check with the Research Service on Earth, and see!"

"Don't worry, they'll be checked," said the Constable. "But there's no hurry about it. We're spending the funds to send for an emergency check on Curragh; but we can afford to take our time with you. Meanwhile, I'm starting to run out of patience. If you want to save your own neck, stop playing around and tell me the truth. What are you doing on Everon?"

"I keep telling you. I'm here to do what my papers said, study Mikey in the context of his native environment."

The Constable did not say anything more for a moment. He merely stood staring down at Jef.

"You come here," the big man said at last, "with a man who tries to pass himself off as one of the top E. Corps Inspectors. You say you're looking for information about the death, eight years ago, of your brother—who just happens to have had his last contact with Beau leCourboisier. We know Beau leCourboisier. These woods up here are full of hardheads and outlaws; and he's the worst of the lot. Finally, I turn you loose to walk through a couple of areas belonging to wild-ranchers who ordinarily don't let a clock-bird cross their territory without finding out what it's up to; and you stroll through with no trouble at all—"

"You deliberately sent me into those woods, knowing the eland ranchers might shoot me?" Jef demanded.

"They're not quite that trigger-happy. But I thought I might learn something about you—and I did." The Constable stared at him for a second. "Nothing happened but a radio call from that young Hillegas to the wildranchers farther up, saying to let you pass."

He watched Jef for a minute.

"You're too damn cool about all this," he said, "not to know what I'm talking about."

"Cool?" The sad bitterness in Jef had swelled in him until he almost felt it would choke him; but the years of training kept his voice level whether he wanted it that way or not. "I don't know what you think you're trying to do. But my papers are legal. I'm legal; and it's up to you to prove differently if you believe so. What does Curragh say? Does he claim I'm some friend of his?"

"We'll ask him that—just as soon as we lay hands on him. He disappeared the moment you took off, just before I was going to ask him about the papers we'd found with his real name. But we'll catch him. Everon's not that big. And meanwhile—we've got you, and you'll tell us what we want to know."

Something snapped in Jef. His voice stayed level and his face calm, but interiorly he crossed some sort of dividing line.

"I've told you everything there is to tell," he said. "You've got no reason, no right, to question me or hold me. Whether Curragh's a John Smith or not, at the spaceport he reminded you of one thing you might think about now—supra-planetary law. If I'm not out of here in two minutes, you're going to have to answer the charges I'll bring against you in the interplanetary courts!"

"Oh?" said the Constable. He stared at Jef strangely for a moment before going on slowly.

"You push me to it, and I'll find a way to learn what you're holding back—trust me if I don't."

He stepped back suddenly toward the door, the handgun level.

"Maybe," he said, and the note was still in his voice, "you'd better sleep on that thought. By tomorrow morning perhaps you'll have come to your senses—and that'd save us both trouble all around."

He reached behind him without turning and touched the door, which swung open. He backed into the corridor.

"Sleep on it," he said. "Or don't sleep—whichever you want. But you better be ready to answer questions with the right answers by morning."

The door closed with a crash.

Jef was left standing, Mikey pressed against him. But the worried noises had died in Mikey's throat—and suddenly Jef recognized that in spite of the threat in Armage's last words, he was feeling decidedly more solid and in command of the situation than he had before the Constable had walked through the door. Why? Certainly he had not backed down before Armage's questions; but he was still a prisoner in this small room of the trading post, with the top representative of local planetary law apparently convinced that he was illegal in some sense or another. Why should he feel as if he had won any sort of victory . . .

Abruptly Mikey stopped making his throat noises and jerked about to stare blindly toward the window. Jef turned to look, himself.

Against the now darkening sky in the upper part of the window, a dark round shape, as of a head, obscured part of the band of twinkling stars visible there; and the voice of Jarji Hillegas came softly but clearly through the wire mesh that was all that barred the open window from the evening air.

"I knew you were bound to get yourself in trouble," it said, "the moment I first got a look at you. It's a good thing for you I followed up to see for myself."

9

JEF STARED.

"Stand back from the window, now," Jarji's voice ordered. "Stand well out of line with it and me."

A thin finger of shadow came up beside the round shadow of Jarji's head. There was a little wink of light and one of the loops of wire in the lower right corner of the mesh covering the window glowed suddenly white-hot and disappeared in a tiny spurt of red sparks. The loop of wire just above it abruptly glowed with white heat in its turn—

"Wait," said Jef. "What're you doing?"

For a long moment from the first sound of Jarji's voice at the window, he had stood dumb, too jarred by unexpected happenings to react with hope or any other feeling at the appearance of the game-rancher. Then the burning through of the wire mesh had jolted him back to feeling and thinking again.

"Doing?" Jarji said. "I'm cutting this screen from your window. What did you figure I was doing?"

"I shouldn't escape," said Jef. "I'm under arrest . . . I think."

The words came from him unplanned, as if another person within him had uttered them. From beyond the night-dark square of window there was a long second of silence, and then something very like a snort.

"Well, pardon me!" said Jarji. "Pardon me all to hell. I'll just wander on back down to my woods and hope you'll find it in your heart to forgive me for nearly getting you into trouble with the down-country law."

"He's the Planetary Constable—the local police authority," said Jef.

"Sure, he is," said Jarji. "Well, as I say, so long—" Her voice began to move off.

"Wait—" called Jef in a throat-tearing whisper, crowding up against the window. "Wait! I mean, come back. You're right. I do want to get Mikey and myself out of here, law or no law."

There was no response from outside.

"Come back!" cried Jef in a desperately throttled shout.

"All right, all right, keep your mouth shut for a moment!" said Jarji's voice, directly under the window. "Stand back."

Jef stood back. Strands of wire glowed and sparked.

"Now push," said Jarji. "Look out, it's hot."

Jef took off his jacket, wrapped it around his fists and pushed with it on the mesh. The mesh gave and there was a soft thump outside.

"Now, climb through," said Jarji.

"I am," said Jef.

He struggled gingerly through the window, only scratching himself a little. A second later he stood panting on the ground outside.

"Mikey—" he began, turning to the window. But Mikey was already sailing through the window without touching anything, in a beautifully calculated leap.

"Let's go," said Jarji. "Stay right with me, now."

She led off through the darkness. There was no moon presently overhead, but in this latitude of Everon, a cluster of close, bright stars clumped thickly in the western center of the sky gave Jef just enough light to follow her. They passed the lumpy black shape of the ducted-fan aircraft and Jef reached out to touch her on the shoulder.

"Why don't we take that?" he whispered.

"Because they'd find it a half a day after we left it and know that wherever we'd left it was only a half a day's walk from where they could find us," Jarji whispered back. "On foot we'll face them with the distance of a full night's traveling in any direction to wonder about."

They went on, and the deeper darkness of the forest closed about them. But it was not as bad as Jef had expected. His eyes gradually adjusted to the gloom—all the more readily in that he had been locked in an ill-lighted room for several hours previously. Shortly, however, the light about them began to increase.

"Moonrise," said Jarji. Now that they were clear of the post, she spoke aloud in a normal voice. "I suppose you didn't think we even had a moon."

"Of course I know you've got a moon," said Jef. "I read—"

"Actually, we've got two. Two natural satellites, only you can't see the little one in this latitude, except in the summer. You can't even see the bigger one, the one that just rose, until about midnight. The trees hide it unless it's right overhead."

"It's nice to have light," said Jef peaceably.

In fact, it was. As the illumination strengthened about them from the invisible moon, the forest floor brightened until, in contrast to the darkness earlier, it seemed brighter than Jef could remember seeing a night scene under a full moon back on Earth. It was almost as strongly illuminated, Jef thought, as it might be on a heavily overcast day. —Come to think of it, he could not remember ever seeing clouds in the Everon sky, except for the hailstorm. He checked himself on that thought, suddenly remembering he had only been down on the surface of this world for a little over four days. It felt as if he had been here for weeks.

The night air seemed to be intoxicating Mikey—it could hardly be the moonlight, since the young maolot's eyes were, as always, firmly closed. But Mikey was once more running ahead of Jef, as he had been on the hike to Post Fifty. Now he was making little dashes and darts of twenty or thirty meters off into the woods as they moved along the route on which Jarji was leading them. Which reminded Jef . . .

"Where are we going?" he asked the girl.

"As close as possible to where Beau leCourboisier used to have his game ranch," Jarji answered. "Somebody's going to meet you there."

"Somebody is? How do you know?"

"You," said Jarji, "are something to tell the clock-birds about. You really are. How'd you manage to live this long back on Earth?"

"What'd I do?" said Jef, bewildered. "I just asked—"

"Don't," said Jarji.

"Don't ask?"

"That's right."

Jef slowly exhaled. His temper might be deeply buried, but this pocket-sized game rancher seemed to have a knack for excavating very nearly deep enough to unearth it. Not that he was feeling his usual sad bitterness. It was simply that he was . . . almost irritated.

"As a matter of fact," said Jarji, "word got passed. That's all you have to know. I heard it and thought I'd tell you. That's all."

"Well, I appreciate it of course," said Jef. "In fact, thank you for all you've done for me—including getting Mikey and me out of that room we were locked in. But you mean you're going to take me to wherever this person is who's going to meet me? I don't understand. There's no reason for you to put yourself out for me like that."

"Here on Everon, we call it neighborliness," said Jarji.

"Nobody else I've met seems to be all that neighborly," Jef told her. "The Constable. The Officer at Post Fifty—"

Jarji snorted. There was no doubt about it being a snort this time.

"Save your breath," she said. "We've got a ways to go."

That more or less ended conversation for the next few hours.

They tramped on in silence. Jef found his thoughts working their way back to his recent confrontation with Armage. He had not had the opportunity to ponder about it until now, but on this silent night walk, he at last had time to consider why he had wound up that meeting with a definite feeling of having come out of it better than the Constable, in spite of Armage appearing to have all of the advantage.

Why? Jef's own solitary nature and way of life had made him an expert in replaying conversations in his head. If he had been asked, point-blank, what Armage's first words were on entering the room, he would have been as much at a loss as anyone might to suddenly summon them up. But if, as he was doing now, he cast his mind back to the time when he had been in the room and recalled how Armage had entered it, then the whole incident unrolled once more in his mind like a memory tape with build-in sounds and scents.

He ran back over this particular personal memory now, trying to put his finger on the moment at which he had ceased to feel helpless before Armage and had begun to feel he was in control of the situation. But it was not until the conversation was almost over that he located the point at which his change in feelings had taken place— it was the point at which Armage had promised that Jef would tell him what he wanted to know, and Jef had retorted that the Constable had no right to do what he was doing. Remembering that instant, now, Jef recalled threatening the Constable with legal reprisals for his actions and those of the Post Officer. Armage had replied with a threat that he could find a way to make Jef talk, and suggested that Jef sleep on that prospect.

A written transcript might have shown Armage as having come off sounding dangerous enough; but Jef, remembering, was once more left with the firm impression that the Constable's promise had a hollow ring to it; and that, on the other hand, his own threat had struck home in some area where Armage felt vulnerable. There was nothing physical, no definite item of evidence to back this up. It was only a feeling—but it was a very certain feeling.

Armage had bluffed; and he, Jef, had called that bluff.

If Armage had been bluffing, if he was not as in control of the situation as he had tried to seem, then his reason for coming to the room had been only to try to scare information out of Jef. Consider, Jef told himself now, if he had told the Constable whatever it was Armage needed to know, the Constable could have gone out, left the door unlocked, and Jef would have been at liberty to set himself free. Afterwards, Jef could have claimed he had been held prisoner and questioned; but if the Constable and everyone else at Post Fifty denied this, who would listen—particularly when Jef had no proof and obviously there had been no harm done to him?

But if Armage indeed had not been that much in command of the situation, then there must be something he was concerned about—something even, perhaps, of which he was afraid.

Martin Curragh?

And if it was Martin, why was it Martin?

Up until that point Jef's mind had seemed to be making great progress. But facing the mystery of what the Constable might fear, it bogged down completely. Any one of numberless possibilities could be the answer. And there was no way of choosing the most likely. As he, Jarji, and Mikey proceeded through the dim woods, Jef struggled with the problem but got nowhere. After a while the light brightened, as the single moon in the local sky became visible overhead. It made the Everon night about them twice as bright as a full moon would have done back on Earth. Jarji called a halt at last beside a small creek they had been about to wade.

"We're far enough away from the post, now," she said.

"It ought to be safe enough to stop for a bit of food. With this much natural light, we can risk a small campfire even if they've got aircraft already in the skies looking for sign of us—which I don't think they have."

They unslung their packs and Jarji started a small fire under a collapsible pot filled with clear creek water set on the flames to heat. Both Jef and she dug freeze-dried stew portions from their packs and dropped the cork-light chunks into the water to absorb the liquid and the heat together.

"We'll need some more water," said Jarji, gazing into the pot. "Didn't guess you'd be so hungry."

"I put in a double portion—half of it's for Mikey," said Jef. "It's nowhere near as much as he ought to have. He's been eating everything I could give him; and he ran me out. I'd thought I'd restock with food for both of us at Post Fifty, but of course . . . I'll get some more water."

He poured from his canteen into the pot, and then went down to the flowing stream to refill the canteen. When he came back, Jarji was sitting on her heels, stirring the food that was cooking. Her back was to him and her crossbow was laid aside on the grass. Apart from that heavy weapon, Jef thought, she looked like someone out on a picnic. Her appearance and her attitudes were, it seemed, worlds apart. Jef was tempted to ask her about them, so that he could try to make some sense out of her answers. But then, every time he had started out asking her questions so far, they had ended up in something very like an argument.

He decided to say nothing. They ate, put out the fire, packed up and hiked on. It was some hours later and the light of the moon had perceptibly lessened, when the trees thinned abruptly before them and they came to the edge of open country filled with the tall version of the moss-grass standing like a near-two-meter-thick carpet over the treeless earth. They stopped, gazing out at it.

"Look at that—" Jef was beginning; for the sea of grasslike stems stretched as far as the eye could see in the light of the low moon and the night breeze wandering over the surface of that sea made it seem to undulate like an actual ocean. But before he could finish, he was interrupted.

Off to their left there was the sound of a thumping and rustling amongst the tall moss-grass at the very edge of the trees. Jef and Jarji turned sharply to face in that direction, Jarji's right hand snapping the crossbow up into aimed position. The spring-pull whirred as the wire string of the weapon drew back. Without warning Mikey suddenly dashed blindly away from Jef in the direction of the noise, making a variety of sounds of his own.

Without thinking, Jef ran after him.

"Wait—" he heard Jarji call behind him; but Mikey was plainly not going to wait, and Jef could not. He ran on.

Jef caught up with the maolot almost immediately. Mikey had a large shape pinned to the earth, his wide muzzle on its throat; and as Jef came up, the shape gave one last thrashing convulsion and lay still.

"Mikey!" snapped Jef, hauling the maolot back by the fur of his neck. Jef stopped in front of Mikey and bent over the shape.

It was a young eland doe, dead, its head twisted back from its body where Mikey's powerful jaws had plainly broken its neck.

"Mikey—" began Jef and broke off. He had been hoping that a hunting instinct would reawaken in Mikey, not only because the maolot would need it eventually as he returned to his normal life in his normal environment, but because Mikey had now developed food demands that were impossible to meet out of the freeze-dried foods Jef had been packing. At the same time, however, the slender, dead body of the doe was an uncomfortable sight to see. Dropping the carcass, Mikey turned and began butting his head proudly into Jef's chest and shoulder, making the sounds that asked for praise and approval.

Illogically—in view of his emotional reaction to the sight of the killed eland—Jef found himself petting the maolot at the same time as he felt the instinct to withdraw from Mikey's bloody jaws.

"All right, Mikey," he found himself saying, "—all right."

"Looks like that eland was already mostly gone when your beast got to her," Jarji commented dryly at Jef's shoulder. "Look at her belly and mouth. She's been poisoned."

Jef took another look. Jarji was quite right. There was a yellowish foam around the muzzle of the eland, and her stomach was swollen drum-tight. Jef stared at it and pulled Mikey back once more from the carcass.

"No, Mikey!" he said sharply, adding to Jarji, "Was this what you meant when you said something about the wisent ranchers poisoning the elands on Beau leCourboisier's game ranch, because they wanted to clear it for their own herds?"

"That's right," said Jarji. "Well, let's find a place to camp. We're here."

"Here?" echoed Jef. For a second, with his mind on the doe and Mikey, he had forgotten where they were headed.

"At the edge of where Beau leCourboisier used to run his elands." Jarji waved out over the wind-rippled sea of moss-grass. "That was his forest land out there."

She turned her back on the open country.

"Well and well," she said. "Let's find ourselves a place to camp. It'll be daylight in a few hours and you'll find it not so easy to fall asleep with the dawn in your eyes."

She turned back into the forest. Jef followed her; but he had to haul Mikey away from the dead eland by main force.

10

JEF DREAMED that he was out in the midst of the sea of moss-grass he had seen the night before. It was daytime and dark clouds blew up. It began to rain and the rain fell with particular force. One drop hit him on the forehead so hard, the impact of it was like that of something solid. He woke, but the rain kept falling. Something else undeniably solid bounced off his chin.

He sat up in his sleeping bag and found himself looking across the slumbering form of Mikey at a man squatting about five meters away, and tossing small pebbles in Jef's direction. The man was short, ruddy-faced and square-bodied, but dressed in the same sort of woods clothes that Jarji was wearing.

Mikey woke at that minute, jerked his head up and began to drone a warning at the stranger.

"Shh. Easy, Mikey . . ." said Jef, grabbing the maolot. For the newcomer carried a crossbow cocked on his knee and it was aimed in Mikey's direction.

"Easy, that's right," said the stranger. His crossbow shifted to point away from Mikey; and Jef looked to see Jarji also sitting up in her sleeping bag. "Easy all around. Just keep your hands in sight, there, friend."

He glanced back at Jef.

"You're Jefrey Aram Robini. That right?" he asked.

"Yes," said Jef in a husky voice that was still fogged with sleep. He cleared his throat. "Uh—you know Jarji Hillegas? That's Jarji there."

"Heard of her," said the man with the crossbow. "Pleased to meet you, Jarji. Know your mom and dad.

I'm Morrel McDermott. You, Jef Robini, I got a message for you."

"Message?"

"From Beau leCourboisier, man you're looking for. Beau got word you were hunting him. He sent word you ought to come ahead. I'll tell you how to find him."

"How—how did leCourboisier find out I was looking for him?" asked Jef, still trying to get his mind awake and working.

McDermott looked across at Jarji.

"He do much of just going around asking questions right out, like that?" McDermott said to her.

"I guess you knew everything, too, the first time you ever stepped into the woods upcountry," said Jarji. Her voice was sharp.

"Well, pardon me," drawled McDermott.

"Like hell I will!"

"Typical Hillegas," said McDermott, looking over at Jef. "Got the worst tempers on Everon, that family. Only people they don't fight with are each other. All the same, you go around asking questions without stopping to consider, you're liable to end up being shot—"

The whir of a spring-pull interrupted him. He had relaxed a little too much and concentrated a little too much on Jef. Now Jarji sat with her own crossbow cocked and aimed at him.

"All right, now," said McDermott, disgustedly. "I was talking about other people, not me. You figure Beau'd recruit somebody who's a hothead?"

"Just remember you said that, that's all," said Jarji. She flicked a catch on her crossbow and the tension went out of the string. "Peace."

"Peace," said McDermott. He uncocked his own crossbow and laid it aside. Jarji put her weapon beside her on the ground. McDermott turned and stared significantly at Mikey.

"Oh, Mikey'll be all right," said Jef. "I just have to

give him some breakfast—"

"If he wants it," said McDermott. "He's pretty well cleaned up on that dead doe back there."

"Doe—" Jef scrambled hastily out of his sleeping bag. "But that eland was poisoned. Mikey—"

He ran his hands hastily over Mikey's belly and muzzle; but there were no signs of tightness in the maolot's stomach area or wetness around his muzzle. And in fact, if anything, Mikey had not looked so sleek and contented since they had left Earth. Right now he took the touch of Jef's hands as an invitation to play, and snapped harmlessly at them, rolling over on his back.

"Don't seem to have hurt him any," said McDermott. "Maybe that's one reason the wisent ranchers hate maolots the way they do—could be their poison doesn't work on them."

"But why wouldn't it?" asked Jef wonderingly.

McDermott shrugged.

"You're going to tell us how to find Beau, I figure," Jarji put in. She had already climbed out of her sleeping bag and stood facing McDermott.

"Sure. Toss me your mapcase."

Jef dug out his mapcase and tossed it over to the other man. Rising, McDermott caught it easily in one hand.

Squatting again, he punched out coordinates on the keys of the case, fingered the stylus from its clip, and marked in a route on the map section for which he had punched. Then he replaced the stylus and tossed the mapcase back.

"Move by day," he said. "There'll probably be aircraft up from the city, looking for you. But travel along the edge of the woods and hide out in the tall grass if you see any craft in the air. There's enough sunlight reflected from the grasstops to shield your body temperatures from a flyer's heat-scope unless the craft goes right directly over top of you."

He nodded to Jef, reassuringly.

"But if they do land and chase you, run into the woods," he said. He turned to Jarji. "I'll tell Beau it was you not only got word to Robini to come here, but brought him yourself. He'll appreciate. Say hello to your folks for me when you get back."

"I'll tell Beau myself," said Jarji. "I'm going on with Jef."

McDermott's eyebrows went up.

"Now," he said slowly, "there wasn't any thought of that, that I know of. I don't know what Beau'll say. It was figured Robini could come in on his own. Less chance of us being traced through him, that way."

"And more chance his going astray!" said Jarji. "I'll bring him in. You, Beau and all don't like it—lump it!"

McDermott shrugged.

"It'll be between you and Beau," he said. He got once more to his feet and nodded to Jef. "It's about a five-day trek. Luck to you both, that far."

He turned and vanished into the woods. There was no sound of his going.

"All right," said Jarji. "We'd better eat before we take off. Let me see that mapcase."

Jef turned to her.

"Now wait a minute," he said. "Just a second. I told you I appreciated all you'd done for me; but this goes beyond neighborliness. I've got the mapcase. You don't have to go along with me the rest of the way."

"That's my choice," she said.

"Why?" he said. "You don't need to. And it isn't as if you seem to think a lot of me."

"I don't have to give anybody reasons," she said. "And that includes you."

"But," he said, "you really don't think much of me, do you? In fact, you don't even like me."

"I didn't say that." She looked stubborn. "All right, you're from Earth. You don't understand Everon, even as well as the wisent ranchers and the down-city people

123

—and they don't understand it at all. You people from Earth come in here for the Ecolog Corps or on a job for some outfit like that; and you sit in your office down by the spaceport and think you've been on Everon. Far as I'm concerned, you could all stay home. No, I don't particularly like you, Robini!"

"My brother," said Jef, "had an office down by the spaceport. But he knew Everon and loved it just as much as you do. I know, because I've heard him talk about his work here, when he was home on leave. He was as close to this world as anyone on it."

"Might be," she said. "But I didn't know him. If he felt that way, he was the first off-Everon job import I've ever seen who did."

"You know what the matter is with you?" Jef said. He had not intended to say this much, but now he found himself committed. "You're a colonist on a new world, just beginning to make a living under primitive conditions; and you've got an inferiority complex where people from Earth are concerned. So you turn it around and try to pretend that I'm the one who doesn't know anything, and don't feel anything."

"That's pretty," she said. "Where'd you read that?"

"I didn't read it—"

"You," she said, getting to her feet and slinging her crossbow over her back, "better quit right now. I can talk rings around you. I can walk rings around you. I can run rings around you. I can shoot you full of holes. I know these woods and you don't. If I want to go along with you to meet Beau, there's not one damn thing you can do about it."

Jef opened his mouth to retort, and then shut it again. Unfortunately, she was right.

"On the other hand," she said after a pause, "I'll give you something; and that's your maolot. It was seeing him with you that made me take a second thought about you in the first place. You like him and he likes you. So,

I'm giving you the benefit of the doubt because he does. Figure yourself lucky you've got a friend like him to vouch for you, that's all. Now, toss me the mapcase the way I told you and go find us some dry wood for a fire. Like I say, we ought to eat before taking off."

"Are you hungry all the time?" Jef demanded.

"No. And I'm not particularly hungry now," she answered. "But if an aircraft spots us and we have to run and hide and run for a day and night without a chance to stop, we'll at least have had full bellies when we started."

Jef gave up. He went off into the woods to look for fallen tree limbs, or anything else that would burn readily.

His mind was spinning. There was a sort of hard edge of sense to everything she said. Only . . . it bothered him that somehow he always seemed to end up the loser in the argument. It went against reason to assume that he was always wrong, and she always right.

But undeniably she was right now in saying that they should eat while they had the chance . . . the mention of food reminded Jef of Mikey. The maolot had tagged along with him as he had gone out after the wood. He stopped now to examine Mikey again; but Mikey had never looked better nor acted more frisky. Jef ended by going back to look at the eland carcass and was surprised when he found it to see how much Mikey had eaten. Both forequarters and a hindquarter were stripped to the bone. The stomach area was untouched—possibly the reason Mikey himself seemed unharmed.

Jef looked about the little area of torn up moss-grass and brush where the eland had thrashed about in dying. However, there was no sign he could find of any obvious poison. He carefully examined the bushes and the ground. There was nothing out of the ordinary about any of them; and the moss-grass was the typical mixture of the low form of the vegetation with tender stems half as high as those in the open, topped with tiny yellow seeds, like young oats. Jef was suddenly tempted to investigate the stomach contents of the dead animal and see what he could learn. But at that moment a call from Jarji reminded him of the firewood he was supposed to be gathering.

He gathered it, and brought it back. They ate, packed and moved out.

It was still early morning when they started. They traveled just inside the shade of the trees at the edge of the forest area, for the sake of shade. Under the strong, Everon sunlight, the open grass-lands were indeed hot—in spite of the fact that these were the upper latitudes of the planet's northernmost continent and summer was almost over. The route McDermott had marked out for them followed the forest edge in a northwesterly direction away from the greater width of the prairie country leading down to Spaceport City.

They hid from only one aircraft that first day. An outburst of the clock-birds, a tintinabulation greater than any Jef had yet heard from these Everon creatures, was followed by the distant, singing buzz of the approaching craft's ducted fans. He, Jarji and Mikey headed out into the open grassland at a run and dived in among the stalks, crawling some little distance until the feathery tops closed over them.

Looking up through the tops of the moss-grass stems, they saw the craft approach, flying low over the trees, but well inside the edge of the forest, obviously looking for them there. For a moment its fan noise filled their ears and it passed between them and the golden sun, its wings looking black, momentarily, except for a grey circle in each one, where a ducted fan whirled at high speed inside its housing.

Then the craft passed on, its sound faded and was gone. They got to their feet, moved back into the forest edge and once more took up their trek.

During the next few days they had to hide frequently. Jef was astonished that the Constable either could or would put so many vehicles in the air to search for them; but Jarji pointed out that one aircraft could cover a single day's foot-marching distance in a matter of minutes; and that probably what they had seen was the same one, passing and repassing.

Daily, on their way, they ran across more poisoned and dead elands. Always these were at the very edge of the woods where the trees met the grasslands and the young stems of the moss-grass began to take over from the forest vegetation. If the eland were recently dead, Mikey struggled to feed on them; and Jef, after several instances in which Mikey ate and survived with no apparent harm, gave up and let him stuff himself as much as the maolot wanted. After all, Jef thought, all the rations in his packsack together would barely make a snack for Mikey's present appetite.

By the third day Mikey was stopping to gorge himself whenever they came across a dead eland that was still in edible condition. For the first time in Jef's experience, the maolot was beginning to refuse to come when ordered— until he had finished eating as much as he could hold. He crouched on the ground when Jef shouted angrily at him; he made apologetic noises; but he would not go on until his sides were drum-tight with meat.

Jef was frankly baffled. Mikey had always been a large eater; but this was beyond reason, even beyond nature. But Mikey's sudden growth was equally beyond reason. He now stood a good meter and a half high at the shoulder.

It was Jarji who finally brought this matter out into the open conversation, somewhere along in the afternoon on the fourth day.

"Your beast's growing," she said, "at this rate he'll be adult-size in a couple of weeks."

Jef grunted. He could not deny what she said. Mikey's

head had used to butt against his own lower ribs. Now it was almost on a level with Jef's head. In two more weeks at this rate, Mikey would be looking down at him.

"In just a few days?" Jef said. "It isn't possible!"

Since it was not only possible but an obvious fact, Jarji apparently decided to let that remark go by without comment. She strode on, while Jef took time out to fend off Mikey, who, finding himself the center of attention, had stopped in Jef's path and was trying to nuzzle Jef's face. It took some little effort to dissuade him.

"Anyway," said Jef, when he had successfully got them all moving again, "I'm glad he's doing something with that food he's been taking in. I was afraid he'd explode on us, one of these days."

He checked, sobering.

"On the other hand," he said, "I hope he isn't growing too fast."

"How can he grow too fast?" Jarji retorted.

"I was thinking—in case we meet another adult male maolot," Jef said. He told her about the encounter he and Mikey had had with the large male on their way to Post Fifty, after she had left them.

"And you think the big one let you go when he saw Mikey wasn't full-grown yet?" Jarji asked, when Jef was through.

"You told me that yourself—that the adult males wouldn't bother young ones—remember?" Jef replied. "Actually, that was something I already knew—that adult males don't attack any but other adult males. If the one we ran into had been ready to attack, when he saw Mikey he changed his mind. So he let Mikey go, and me with him."

"Never any telling what a maolot'll do," she said. Something in the tone of her voice made him glance at her. She was striding along with a look of abstraction that he had never seen her wear before.

They kept moving without further talk. Jef's thoughts

drifted back to the questions that clustered about Beau leCourboisier. Armage had called him the worst of the up-country outlaws. But Jarji had mentioned something about Beau's eland being driven off and poisoned so that some wisent rancher could get the legal right to clear that part of the forest land for grazing. If that was true, matters had reached a point of open violence between the two groups sometime back. And anyone caught up in that violence . . .

On the other hand, it was a little hard to believe that such things could happen on a world settled so recently that it was still subject to Ecolog Corps inspection. An individual or two might be misguided enough to drive off someone else's herd animals—poisoning? With a small shock Jef remembered that he had been seeing supposedly poisoned eland himself—Mikey had been eating them. But where would plains ranchers get poison in the quantities necessary to be effective against individual animals that each ranged over a number of square miles of territory, and in fact were scattered pretty thinly? Also how could they go about spreading that much poison without getting caught in the act by the game ranchers, sooner or later?

"The next poisoned eland we come across," Jef said to Jarji, "I'm going to have a look at its stomach contents and see if I can find out what it was eating when it was poisoned."

She did not answer. She was marching along with that same thoughtful look on her face. It was as if she had not heard him.

Later on that day Mikey suddenly dashed off from the two humans and did not return. Jef slowed his steps, waiting for the maolot to catch up, but Mikey stayed invisible. Jef stopped and turned around.

"I'm going back to look for Mikey," he said.

"Found himself another meal, that's what," said Jarji. She sat down with her back to the trunk of a willy-tree, leaned her head back and closed her eyes. "Wake me when he's ready to move again. Otherwise, let me be. I feel like a nap."

Looking down at her, Jef was sure it was not so much a nap as some further privacy for thinking that was on her mind. But it made no difference to him why she wanted to be left alone. He turned and began to retrace his steps, looking about him as he went. But though Mikey was only some twenty meters off the route when Jef found him, a good half hour had gone by and Mikey was already done eating.

"Well," said Jef to the maolot, looking with some distaste at what was left on the carcass, "you found me a dissection subject, all right."

It was a clumsy job, performed with only a belt knife and with no stream nearby to wash up in afterward. Jef ended by scrubbing his hands and arms with bunches of young moss-grass to get himself more or less clean afterward. But he was able to identify the stomach contents of the eland—they were the same half-grown stems in which the animal lay, and which he had used to cleanse his hands—the little golden seeds at the stem tips looking lightly tarnished but otherwise as if they could be planted with success in the next moment.

"So here you are," said Jarji's voice dryly, behind him. "What've you been up to?"

Jef finished putting the stems and seeds he had recovered into a plastic bag he was holding that had formerly held some freeze-dried meat.

"I thought I'd get some evidence of what these eland had been eating when they died," he said. "This Beau leCourboisier isn't likely to have someone around his camp who can do a chemical analysis, I suppose, but somewhere I ought to get to a place where these grass stems can be checked for poison—"

The sack was suddenly ripped out of his hand.

"Hey!" he said and took a step toward Jarji to get it

back—then stopped at the feel of a painful pricking just below his breastbone. Looking down he discovered that his chest was touching the point of a knife she was holding between them.

"That's Everon business!" she snapped. Her face was white with anger around her eyes. "Hunt that grave of your brother's if you want, Robini, but stay out of our affairs. Hear me?"

Before he could answer, she stretched out the arm that held the plastic bag, thumbed it open, and strewed the laboriously recovered stems and seeds among the ground cover, where they were immediately lost.

"Don't try that again!" she said. "Now, get your maolot moving. We're going to travel."

"No," he said. She had finally pushed him over the line and he could feel the sad bitterness building inside him, for all his voice kept its usual calmness. "You do what you like, but Mikey and I are going our own way from now on. Mikey, come on!"

He turned and walked off. A second later Mikey's muzzle poked apologetically into his side and back. He went on without a word, Mikey beside him, until he rejoined the route they had been taking earlier, then turned in the direction they had been headed and strode on.

For perhaps a quarter of an hour he was oblivious to his surroundings, completely lost in his own feelings. But gradually he cooled down enough to notice that, after all, they were not alone. Seven or ten meters off to his right, glimpsed occasionally through the intervening bushes and tree limbs, Jarji Hillegas was paralleling his path with silent ease.

He swore; but she had been right in what she had said earlier. There was nothing he could do about her accompanying him if she wanted to. On this frontier world the advantages were all hers.

11

JEF WALKED FOR SOME DISTANCE, staying some fifteen
meters inside the edge of the woods country, before it
began to dawn on him that in stalking off from Jarji he
had overlooked one small item. Even after this occurred
to him, he still kept on walking, taking his course from
the glimpses of grassland he could see occasionally
through the trees, and hoping to come up with some
solution other than the obvious one. Finally, his feelings,
as slow to cool as they were to kindle, got down to a
temperature of reasonableness and he found himself at
last ready to admit that he would be making himself
more ridiculous by keeping on like this than he would be
by admitting he had gone off half-cocked in the first
place. At the same time there was still enough sense in
him of having been mishandled so that he found it difficult to make the first move.

He halted finally in a convenient open space with a
boulder to sit down on, sat down, took off his pack and
began to unseal some food for himself and Mikey. After
a bit Jarji's voice sounded behind him.

"Forgot I had the mapcase, didn't you?" she said.

"Yes," he answered.

She came around in front of him and sat down
crosslegged on the ground, frowning at him.

"You ready to get back on route, then?"

"That's right."

She continued to frown at him.

"It's not your fault," she said. "I don't mean to say it

132

is. It's just that you don't know a thing about what you're mixing in."

He grinned at her, unexpectedly. Now that they were talking again, it was amazing how much easier he found it to be undisturbed by her way of saying things.

"I take it that's your version of an apology?" he asked.

"*Apology?*" She started as if to spring from the ground. "Save your damn life and you want an apology—"

She broke off and settled back down, staring hard at him.

"All right," she said. "I suppose you can't help it. Listen to me, Robini—and try to understand what I'm telling you. This isn't your territory. It's nobody's territory but ours, us who live here and know our way around. Now, something's working for you. I don't know what it is. At first I thought it was all the maolot and you were just riding along on him; but it's something more than that. You and this upcountry are somehow taking to each other more than you ought to be able to do, by rights. But—"

She leaned forward and jabbed a forefinger at him.

"That's got nothing to do with what I'm talking about now. God knows why I should worry my head about you. But there's some hard people on both sides of any question you run into up here; and there's some questions— there's one question in particular—anybody'd be wise to step around. You've got plenty to do with your maolot and finding that grave, if that's what you really want. Just you forget to worry about whether elands get poisoned, or how it happens, or anything at all of that sort. You reach Beau's camp, you ask him about your brother, listen politely to what he has to tell you, then clear out. Don't look back and don't ask any other questions. Do you understand me?"

"No," said Jef.

She drew an exasperated breath.

"What d'you want to do—this research of yours, or get

mixed up in our local wars?"

"Research, of course."

"Then do what I tell you."

There was, thought Jef, a good deal of sense in what she was saying. He did not, in fact, have any desire to get mixed up in local antagonisms. Hadn't he congratulated himself on leaving Armage's place, that he had managed to get away unentangled in whatever was going on with the Constable, Martin and others?

"All right," he said. "You're right."

"Damn right I am!" She continued to stare hard at him for a few seconds longer as if to be sure she had really convinced him. Then her face relaxed. "Well, are you going to sit there stuffing yourself for the rest of the day?"

"Be done in a minute," he said.

He was. He stood up, brushing his hands, and slipped his arms once more through his packstraps. As they moved off again, together, she turned abruptly and shoved the mapcase into his hands.

"Here. Take it! I don't need it, anyway."

"Thanks," he said.

He clipped the case back to his belt.

She led them off at an angle, now, away from the forest edge. The angle was a sharp one. Jef had not thought that he had traveled so far since trying to part from her that he'd gotten that much off the map route. But when he pulled the mapcase from his belt and looked at it, the black line that was their actual line of march had angled off from the red line of their proper route some distance back. So far back, in fact, that it was hard to believe they had not strayed sometime before Mikey had found this last eland.

However, the little dogleg at the end of the moving black line now showed them headed back to rejoin the red one that was already there. They should reach Beau's camp, Jef estimated, in about three hours—not much later than mid-afternoon of the Everon day.

Actually, it took them closer to four hours; and during the last hour and a half they moved through forest that began to show a difference in character from that they had traversed earlier. Little by little, as they mounted to higher altitudes, the Earth variform species of vegetation became rarer and the native species more numerous; until, as they began to get close to their destination, they were finally in an area where there were no Earth-native plants at all to be seen; and among the native species Jef had identified earlier, there were a number of other Everon plants that he could not even name.

While this change had been making itself apparent, the topography of the area had also been changing. Gradually it had become more open and more rocky, with more the look of a northern upland. In fact, though they were plainly walking uphill most of the time—Jef's leg muscles testified to that fact—the change was more than the grade of slope seemed to indicate. It was almost as if they had gotten into mountain country without realizing it. Even the air seemed cooler and thinner.

There was one more difference, which to Jef was somewhat ominous. By mid-afternoon they had begun to hear the occasional distant call of mature maolots. These all sounded a good distance off, and Jarji ignored them. But to Jef's uneasiness, Mikey did not. Instead of pushing up against Jef, now, when a distant call would sound, Mikey was stopping and lifting his blind head in the direction from which it had come, as if at any moment he might call back. In fact, the thought that he might answer worried Jef to the point where he finally spoke to the maolot.

"Now, don't go doing anything foolish," he said, when a call closer than the others broke out and Mikey's head came up. "You're bigger than you used to be, but those out there'll be a lot bigger than you."

"Leave him be," said Jarji. "He's got more sense than you have."

"You forget," said Jef, glancing at her, "I know him a lot better than you do."

"Want to bet?" she retorted.

He ignored the challenge. There was no point, he told himself, in wasting breath on a ridiculous argument.

But as they went on, the calls became more frequent even if they sounded no closer than the one that had touched off the warning from Jef to the maolot. Mikey became more restive with each one. At length he was breaking away from Jef's side to run several steps in the direction from which a call had come; and he did this even when Jef spoke sharply and caught hold of him to try—futilely—to hold him back. The unconscious ease with which he broke loose from Jef's grip sent a small shiver down between Jef's shoulder blades. Even back on Earth before they had come to Everon Mikey had been unusually powerful for his size. But here and now that he was almost full-grown, his strength had become awesome. Worried, Jef spoke sharply to him. Mikey apologized each time he returned to Jef's side, butting his head against Jef's shoulder and almost knocking Jef off his feet, but there was now something absent-minded and almost cursory about this familiar gesture—as if the maolot's mind was elsewhere.

"I tell you," said Jarji at last to Jef, "leave him alone. He's got his own reasons for what he's doing. Not that you could stop him from doing it, in any case."

"I don't like it," Jef said. "How far are we from leCourboisier's now?"

"Minutes, I'd say," said Jarji. "Never been in this area, myself, but I've heard about it. If Beau's where I think he is, we might as likely—"

She was interrupted by the deep-throated call of a mature maolot—this time close at hand. She and Jef stopped instinctively and the crossbow came up in her hands, as the spring-pull whirred and the weapon cocked itself. But Mikey broke loose from Jef's grip and went loping off in the direction from which the call had come. This time he vanished among the willy-trees and did not return.

"*Mikey!*" shouted Jef. "Mikey, get back here!"

He swung about and started to run after the maolot. He had not taken three steps, however, before a small and determined anchor attached itself to his left arm, almost pulling him off balance.

"Give up, you knothead!" snapped Jarji. "Do you think you can catch him on foot? He's half a kilometer gone by now—oh, you will, will you?"

Jef felt himself tripped suddenly and went down on his face. He rolled over on his back and looked up to see Jarji standing at his feet, glaring at him.

"You better act sensible if you get up," she said, "or I'll put you down again in a way'll give you time to cool off before you get up a second time. Didn't you hear me? I said he's gone. Your maolot's gone. I don't know why, any more than you do. But I know you're not getting him back until he wants to come back. Now, can you understand that?"

Jef hooked the toe of one boot behind her left ankle, placed the sole of the other boot against the front of her same lower leg, and flipped her over on her back. He was on his own feet looking down at her by the time she had scrambled into crouching position.

"Yes," he said, and she stopped. "I can understand it. And no, I don't want to fight you, mentally or physically. Maybe you can take me, with no trouble. But there's a few things I know to do, and a few things I can do right, and if you push me to it, I'll do them. But there's no sense I can see in the two of us chewing each other up, so why don't we both just not push?"

She was looking at him rather strangely. He stayed alert, unable to tell whether she was about to launch herself at him, or not. However, she got to her feet, picked up her crossbow, and turned away in the direction they had been traveling. He watched her go for a moment and then stretched his legs to join her. When he caught up with her, she had the same abstracted look on her face he had seen there earlier.

They walked on in silence for another ten minutes, and suddenly the forest opened out before them. They looked slightly downhill into a miniature cliff of bare rocks rising above the tree-height of the vegetation at its far end. Beyond and above the rocks, there was nothing to be seen but the blue of the high afternoon sky and a few torn streamers of cirrus clouds.

Below the rocks, in the clearing on either side of the stream, were four log buildings, each one roughly the size of the trading post Jef had seen. There were no figures moving around between the buildings; but Jarji, without stopping, made straight for them. Jef went along. All the buildings, he saw, had the shake-shingled roofs of the main building at Post Fifty, sharply peaked to shed snow. But here, much more so than at Post Fifty, it was possible for Jef to imagine, in spite of the signs of summer all about him, how, seven months from now these uplands would be under two to three meters of snow and ice; and that the eland would be yarded up in forest clearings, the wisent out on the plains huddled on the northwestern slopes of slight rises in the ground where the wind would have scoured the snow cover from the frozen moss-grass they needed to survive.

He and Jarji were close to the buildings now, and had still to see any signs of inhabitants. But when they were less than ten meters from the nearest door of the long building, it swung open and a tall man came down the five steps of the stair that connected it with the ground.

"Just hold it there," he said, "and we'll find out who you are before you go any farther."

His voice was a soft, but deep, bass; with a strange resonance like a woodwind, as if his chest had a much greater cavity than an ordinary man's. As a voice, it was pleasant rather than intimidating, but his words were backed up by the weapon in his fist. It was no crossbow, but a laser handgun; not a handgun of the military weight and complexity possessed by the gun Jef had seen in Armage's possession, but still something that could cut a human body in half in one second.

"Lift your hands, if you will," he said. "And I'll check you out."

Jef raised his hands; and out of the corner of his eyes saw Jarji doing likewise. The man with the handweapon came toward them.

McDermott had been clean-shaven; but this individual wore a full-grey-white beard. He was a tall whiplash of a man, narrow-waisted and broad-shouldered with slimness that seemed far too young for his beard; and he moved like a man half his apparent age.

He came first to Jef, and ran his free hand lightly over Jef's sides and hips. Then he opened Jef's pack and felt around inside it.

"Clean," he said. "But then I thought you'd be." Unexpectedly, he winked at Jef. Then he moved on to Jarji.

Jef turned to see him holding Jarji's crossbow and searching her but taking more time and good deal more care. He stepped back at last, holding a smaller version of his own laser.

"Cute," he said, hefting it. "Where'd you get it, Hillegas?"

"You think you're the only one knows how to bribe those city apes?" she retorted.

The bearded man nodded, sticking Jarji's laser into his belt.

"I'm Bill Eschak," he said, stepping back and holstering his own handgun. He looked at Jef. "You'll be Jef Aram Robini?"

"Yes, sir," said Jef. "My brother was William Robini. I understand Beau leCourboisier was once a friend of his."

"Don't 'sir' me. I'm no downcountry type," answered Bill. He turned to Jarji. "Which Hillegas are you?"

"Jarji," said Jarji.

"Ah. Number six," he nodded. "Saw you in your cradle, once."

"Is Mr. leCourboisier inside?" Jef asked.

"Beau's away, right now." The soft, humming bass voice of Bill Eschak seemed to linger in Jef's ears. "But we've been expecting you. I'll put you up in the main cabin quarters; and Beau'll talk to the both of you as soon as he comes back, tomorrow."

He turned and led the way back up the steps toward the door from which he had emerged.

"This way," he said.

They followed him up the steps and through the door into a long corridor not unlike the one down which the factor at Post Fifty had led Jef and Mikey to the room in which he had locked them up. The main difference was that this building did not smell—or at least, it did not smell unpleasantly. In this corridor the odor was one of pine wood, leather, and fresh, not stale, cooking scents.

The corridor ended at a larger door; and this let them through into what seemed a wide living room, with a number of wooden chairs and settees, their leather-corded seats covered with cushions made of heavy cloth of various colors.

"Bedrooms through there," said Bill, waving at one of the other doors set around the walls of the room. "Bathroom the same way. We've got power and plumbing here. But you'll find doors that are locked. Just let them be. Until Beau comes home, we've kind of got to keep you boxed in this part of the place. —You hungry? We'll be having dinner in half an hour."

"Good," said Jef automatically. Freeze-dried camping foods were all right; but a steady diet of them for several days was quite enough for a while.

"Come along, then," said Bill.

He led them across the room and through a further door. They crossed another room walled with racks for book spools, like a library, and went out yet one more door into a hall that led them to the largest room they had yet seen, which turned out to be a sort of combination mess hall and recreation room.

The place was indeed not small. Something like fifteen or twenty men and half a dozen women were scattered around it, evidently waiting for dinner, most of them holding clay mugs holding some foamy brown drink that Jef took to be some sort of fermented beverage. The dining-room area at one end consisted of two long tables made of planks set up on trestles with benches pulled up to them. One table was set for a meal, but no food was to be seen. The other was bare, and perhaps a third of the men in the room were seated at the bare table, playing cards or chess.

Bill Eschak took Jef and Jarji around the room, introducing them; but the names came so fast that when the process was over, Jef could not remember more than two or three of those he had met. But by this time food was being brought in to the table set for eating. Bill steered Jef to a seat across from him near the table's far end.

"Steak, eggs and fried potatoes," Bill said. "How does that sound to you?"

"Fine," said Jef. His mouth watered. He took his seat at the table and after a while a man in a white apron came in with already loaded plates, which were passed down the table. Jef accepted the one that came to him and dug into it.

He had not thought it was possible to be so hungry. But, a few moments after he had wolfed down part of the steak, the eggs, and even some of the fried potatoes, he began to slow down. At the same time he became conscious of the men and women nearby him at the table, watching him. Even Jarji had her gaze on him.

"Something wrong, Jef?" asked the deep voice of Bill,

across the table. Looking toward the other man, Jef thought he saw a particular intensity in the pale blue eyes above the beard.

"Wrong?" Jef echoed.

Of course there was something wrong. The steak was steak, all right—but it was undoubtedly variform eland steak; and eland, at that, which had fed all its life on Everon greenery. The eggs may have or may not have been chicken eggs—but if from chickens, these birds also were variforms and had been feeding on Everon produce. Even the potatoes were variform and paid a tribute to having been grown in Everon soil.

Everything, in short, tasted subtly wrong to someone with taste buds trained on Earth. No, thought Jef grimly, that wasn't the way to think about it. These things did not taste wrong, they tasted *different*. At the Constable's —as on the spaceship—the food had not. Clearly, therefore, when the Constable had kept Martin and himself overnight at his home outside Spaceport City, what they and the dinner guests had been fed then must have been from special Earth supplies, brought in by spaceship— no doubt at outrageous prices. The freeze-dried foods he had carried in his pack, of course, were also of Earth origin; since he had imported them himself as part of his passage expense, not knowing if anything like that would be available on Everon.

To sum it all up—what was happening was that for the first time he was encountering the way Everon foods tasted, and the difference of their tastes from those of Earth was more of a shock than he would have imagined. It did not help that there were no good words to express that difference—the best he could do was that it was as if everything he ate tasted strangely woody and a little bitter.

Unconsciously, as he paused to figure this out, Jef had stopped eating altogether. Now, however, something else struck him. The food still tasted strange to him, but now that he had stopped putting it in his mouth he realized he was still hungry; and not just politely hungry—he could have eaten a horse. In fact, he told himself, he could have eaten an Everon horse if there was such a beast.

He laughed and dug into his plate again. The eyes of the others continued to watch him; but since he continued to shovel in the food, they seemed to accept the fact that this was no act. Gradually, they withdrew their attention from him. Jef continued to eat heartily; and a curious result began to make itself noticed. Either the taste of the Everon food was becoming less noticeable, or he was getting used to it.

"I think I'd like some more," Jef told Bill, when his plate was empty.

"I'll get it for you," said Bill.

He took Jef's plate and rose from the table. When he came back with it refilled, a few moments later, the others who had been eating were already finishing up and leaving; and by the time Jef had cleaned his plate for a second time and—with genuine regret by this time—turned down some sort of fruit pie, the table was empty except for Bill, Jarji and himself.

"That was the first time you'd eaten Everon stuff?" Bill asked.

Jef nodded.

"I saw everyone was thinking I wouldn't eat it," he said. "Why all the interest in my finding the taste different?"

"Well," Bill said, "you've got to remember this is our food and we work hard for it. The eland, the eggs and the potatoes don't just appear out of nowhere, and jump on to the plate ready-cooked. When somebody from off-planet turns his nose up at our food, the way lots of them do, it's sort of like he was turning his nose up at us. You ought to see sometime what some people say or do, first time they bite into something that's homegrown here."

"I wouldn't be like that," said Jef. "My brother was a planetary ecologist for the E. Corps here for eight years. He liked all new worlds; and he liked Everon almost as much as Earth. I do, too."

"But you're not figuring on staying," observed Bill.

"I don't know. The Constable's hunting me . . ." The memory of his present situation on Everon came back on Jef all at once, quenching the glow of good feeling that had been kindled by the fullness of his stomach.

"Constable's only one man," said Bill. "Wisent ranchers and city people're only part of everyone on Everon. Don't be so sure you can't do anything you want."

The deep, musical voice of the grey-bearded man was oddly comforting. Jef found himself thinking how different Bill Eschak was from Jarji, with whom conversation was more like an armed encounter. Jef found himself wanting to talk. He had been isolated from communication with other people almost completely since his parents' death, until he found himself opening up to Martin on the spaceliner. Following that first conversation, however, Martin had seemed to lose interest; and Jarji, as noted, had been as prickly as a thornbush from the first moment of their acquaintance. Bill Eschak, here, on the other hand, was like a comfortable grandfather to talk with.

"You know," said Jef to Bill, "I've been trying to understand things here on Everon. You know on the way here, I saw a lot of elands—"

"Oops!" said Jarji; and Jef leaped hastily up from the bench he was sitting on, as Jarji's spilled cup of coffee flooded over the front of his pants.

"Here," said Bill, "I'll get something to mop it up with."

Jef glared at Jarji as Bill came back with looked like a piece of clean, but old, shirt. Jef opened his mouth to tell her off, plainly and openly for once.

"Here, I'll take it," said Jarji briskly. She jerked her

head at Jef. "Stand back out of the way, Robini. And next time don't jog my elbow."

The enormity of this ploy that put all the blame on him, took Jef's breath away. Looking about the room, he was willing to swear that everyone else there was watching him with amusement, completely taken in by what Jarji had just said. What was the use? he thought wearily. The only way to exist with her was not to exist with her—get away from her at the first opportunity and make sure to stay away.

"I think that's got it," said Jarji, handing the cloth back to Bill. "Thanks."

"How about you, Robini?" Bill said. "You got another pair of pants along, or you want to borrow a pair?"

"I've got an extra pair," growled Jef. He gave up the futile effort to wring wetness out of the cloth of his pants legs.

"Come on, then." Bill tossed the wet shirt cloth on to the table top. "I'll show you to the room we'll be putting you up in and you can change."

He led the way out of the dining-recreation room they had eaten in, and back the way they had crossed, down a different hall to a plain door that opened to a room about five meters square. It had a bunk bed, a rough wooden armchair with a colorful blanket draped over its seat and back, and a plain, small wooden table in front of it that looked as if it had recently been used as a writing desk. Beside a thick grey, unlit candle, some charcoal stick pens stood upright in a holder of willy-tree bark and there was a pad of heavy paper lying beside it. Jef's and Jarji's packs were on the bed.

"Get your pack," Bill told Jarji. "We'll be putting you up over in the regular bunkhouse."

"That suits me fine," said Jarji. "This outworlder snores—can you figure that? Step out for now, though, Eschak, we want a couple of minutes to ourselves."

Bill's eyebrows rose above the blue eyes.

"Well, now," he said. "I don't know. Beau—"

"Just latch the door on the way out," said Jarji. "This part's none of Beau's business—or yours."

Bill laughed. It was a strange, almost noiseless chuckle that did not quite fit with the man as Jef had come to think of him.

"I'll give you time to change his pants," Bill said. He went out.

Jef opened his mouth. Jarji slapped a hand quickly over his lips and held it there.

"Now, get out of those pants," she said loudly. She took her hand from his mouth, held her finger to her lips, made shooing motions toward his pack on the bed, and went to listen at the door.

Feeling awkward and embarrassed, Jef struggled out of the clingingly wet brush pants he was wearing, and got into the spare pair from his pack. He was pressing the dry belt tabs together when Jarji came back from the door.

"All right," she whispered, "there's no one listening. We can talk. But keep your voice down."

"I—"

"Whisper, damn it!"

"All right," whispered Jef. "What makes you so sure no one's listening?"

"Just take my word for it. I had my ear to that door panel. If anyone can breath in that corridor and I can't hear him, then he's got lungs no bigger than a crawling mite's. Besides I can smell old Bill Eschak on a dark night five meters away."

"Smell?" he echoed.

"You can't? That's right, you're like those down-country city people. No nose. No ears. Never mind that, though. Listen, you know why they're putting me in the bunkhouse?"

"Uh. No," said Jef.

"Because they don't trust me. With thirty-forty

woodspeople around me, there's not much I can do. That means you're on your own."

"They trust me?" Jef whispered.

"Trust you? They don't trust you, they just know you can't do anything by yourself, so they don't figure to worry about you once they've got me away from you. But pay attention, now. I've done all I can for you. From here out you're on your own; and if you keep on talking about things that don't concern you, these people are going to start thinking you know a lot more than you do. So, if you haven't learned yet to keep that mouth of yours shut, you better do it now, unless you want Bill Eschak cutting your throat for you before tomorrow sunset."

"Come on, now," said Jef. "You can't tell me he's the sort of man to do anything like that!"

"Isn't he? Why d'you think he's Beau's first officer? These people here are all spring-pulls. Old Bill's had his blade into more people than there're teeth in your head. This is a bad group, Robini, and don't you ever forget that. —Now," she broke off suddenly, "you're on your own."

She turned, went swiftly to the door, and pulled it open.

"Come on in, Eschak," she said. "No need to try and sneak up. I'm ready for my own bunk, now."

"Well, that's good," said Bill, appearing in the doorway. He looked past her to Jef. "Word just came Beau'll be in real early in the morning. He'll talk to you at breakfast. Have a good sleep."

Bill stepped back from the doorway and Jarji followed him out. The door closed and Jef heard the sound of their footsteps die away.

He sat down on the bed. Perfect silence surrounded him. Jarji was one of the woods ranchers herself. She ought to know what she was talking about. On the other hand, what she had been telling him about Bill was incredible. People just didn't go around knifing each other, even on the newly settled worlds—barring an occasional psychotic or badly disturbed person. The human race was just too civilized for that, nowadays. Or was it?

He looked at the plank and log walls surrounding him, but they offered no answer. The room was dimming as the sunset died outside its one window. He looked for some way to light the candle, but could find none. Slowly, almost automatically, he got his camping light out of his pack and set it on the table by his bed. He began to undress. He was tired enough to welcome the idea of sleep, at any rate.

He took his clean pants and put them back in his pack, spreading out the coffee-soaked ones on the table to dry. Slowly he climbed in between the rough covers of the bed and put out the camping light. The various scents of the woods of the building around him filled his nostrils and some night-creature sounds filtered to his ears through the window across the room. It was all very pleasant.

Images of Jarji flitted through his mind. She was apparently able to irritate him with a word; but, illogically, at the same time, he continued privately certain that under her prickly exterior she was warm, friendly, and honestly concerned about him—perhaps more so than she wanted to show. On his part, for some time now he had deliberately been trying to avoid dwelling on the thought of her as female and attractive, ever since she had rescued him from Post Fifty. But the effort was beginning to be a little ridiculous, like pretending that the sun was not in the sky during daylit hours. In fact, his reaction to her seemed part—a strange part at that for someone as naturally solitary as himself—of the general good feelings he had been permeated with ever since he had stepped out on to the landing stairs of the spaceship. They were good feelings that affected him almost as strongly as a narcotic. Right now, in spite of Jarji's warning, he could not seem to summon up anything but a comfortable feeling of content with the universe. It was impossible to worry about Bill Eschak and these other people he had come among.

Intellectually, he gave due credit to Jarji's warning that he be on guard against Beau's people, and particularly Bill Eschak. Undoubtedly she knew what she was talking about. Undoubtedly, she was right. But, emotionally, the warning did not seem to have the power to disturb him.

It was probably these general good feelings of his that were lulling him in such a fashion. If that was so, he did not have to look far to find reasons for the way he felt. For one thing, he was heathily tired after tramping through the woods this way for several days. It was true he had been careful to exercise himself into shape before he left Earth. But the differences between practice and reality was still perceptible. He had not woken up stiff on any of these mornings, but he had slept like a log every night. His body was naturally relaxed and that was a good share of it.

In addition, he was here at last, doing what he always wanted to do, in the research with Mikey. In effect he was finally enjoying the fruits of something he had struggled and worked for, for some years. Things were going well; and a lot of the urgency had gone out of matters that otherwise might have had him wound up tight. He was remarkably unconcerned about the Constable, for example, in spite of the fact that technically he was now a fugitive from planetary justice, with the other duty bound to bring him to book. Even the matter of Will's death, and his long-held wish to locate Will's grave, had lost a great deal of their urgency. The hurt and resentment he had always felt where his dead brother had been concerned, had largely faded. He could no longer manage to work himself up over it. Which was strange . . . in fact, everything was a little strange. Give due credit to exercise and success, and there was still a large part of his present contentment unexplained.

It had to be Everon itself, that was the cause. It was a world that seemed as if it had been waiting here for him to fall in love with, all the years of its existence. He wondered sleepily if the colonists felt, or had ever felt, the way he now did about this planet. There was no way to tell. Maybe only some of them felt it. Jarji, perhaps? He should ask her—sometime when she herself was not busy lecturing him or spilling cups of coffee on him.

His thoughts drifted away, back to the pair of pants he had spread out on the table. Half-asleep, he found himself thinking that they should be dry enough to wear by morning. It had hardly been worthwhile, after all, putting the spare pair on.

12

JEF CAME SUDDENLY AND COMPLETELY AWAKE. He lay tense, not knowing what had wakened him, staring into the gloom about him. High in the room, a little distance from the bed, he thought he could see something glowing faintly, the way the eyes of certain Earth animals shine with reflected light in the dark. He blinked, but the illusion persisted, although whatever might be there was so faint that he could not be sure he was actually seeing it. For a second he wondered if he was not merely having some very vivid dream, rather than being awake.

There was only one way to find out. He reached out with one hand to the corner of the table, found his camping lamp, and switched it on.

The room sprang into existence around him in the sudden illumination from the little nuclear-fueled lamp —standing at the foot of his bed was Mikey.

"Mikey!" Jef said. "Where have you been?"

He was out of bed in an instant. At his present size Mikey loomed enormous in the small room, his head upright on his powerful neck so that his eyes would have been at the point where Jef had imagined he had seen something glowing. But it could not have been Mikey's eyes he had thought he was seeing, for these were still, as always, tightly closed.

"How did you get in here?" asked Jef, running his hands over the massive shoulders.

For once Mikey made no move to lower his head and butt his forehead against Jef in the usual fashion. Instead he stood for a second, then turned about to the door, lifted one paw, and with a surprising articulation of two of the pads of his enormous toes, seized and opened the door latch. He pushed the door open a crack and stood, turning back his head over his shoulder to Jef in invitation.

"Where do you want to go, Mikey?" said Jef, perplexed, but remembering to keep his voice down. "Wait —I can't go anywhere until I get some boots and clothes on."

He turned and started to dress. Mikey let go of the latch and put his forepaw back on the floor; the maolot stood waiting patiently while Jef dressed.

"All right," said Jef at last, clipping the camping lamp to his belt. The pants that had been coffee-soaked were not completely dry yet, but their dampness was not enough to worry about. He walked toward the door himself. "Let's go."

Mikey pushed open the door and went into the corridor. Jef followed. There was no one to be seen in the corridors and rooms they passed. Mikey led Jef to the door by which Jef had entered the building, and they went out into the night. Outside it was dark in spite of the fact that there was a moon in the sky. Clearly, the night was almost over. Mikey, however, moved as surely as if it was broad daylight and he had eyes to see with. Whatever sense it was that allowed him to get around on his native world, it was serving him as well now in the outside dark as it had inside the building a few minutes earlier.

Jef followed Mikey among the buildings to the one closest to the cliff. At its door, the maolot once more lifted a forepaw to the latch. This time, however, the latch did not lift and the door did not open. Putting his paw down again, Mikey half turned, put one broad shoulder against the door and pushed. There was a subdued snap, and the door yawned silently inward. Mikey pushed his way through; and, after a second's hesitation, Jef followed.

Inside, this building was as black as the inside of a cave. Mikey and everything else were invisible. Jef unclipped the camping light from his belt and risked turning it on. He found himself standing in what seemed to be some sort of warehouse, piled high with sacks made out of loose-woven, reddish cloth, about one meter by a quarter of a meter in size, and stuffed, apparently, with lumpy objects.

The ends of the bags were sewn shut. Jef felt the contents of one through the cloth and discovered the objects to be about the size and shape of mature carrots, except that each one curved in a semi-circle. Struck by a sudden suspicion, Jef leaned over the bag to sniff at it. A faint, musty, lilaclike odor came into his nostrils; and the suspicion became a certainty. This building was plainly full of the roots of the question plant, a native species growing in the upland areas of Everon. The roots contained aconitine, like the monkshood plant of Earth. The question plant was one of the few forms of vegetation native to Everon that were poisonous to Earth creatures. The plant had rated a picture, as well as a warning paragraph, in one of the books Jef had read about Everon before he had made the trip here. There must be enough of the roots in the sacks surrounding him, Jef thought, to poison a cityful of people.

—Or to poison all the dead eland the woods ranchers were complaining about?

But why would Beau leCourboisier and his group want to poison the eland of their fellow woods ranchers? If it was the wisent they were planning to poison—of course, thought Jef. Beau and the others would be planning to kill off wisent in retaliation for the dead eland. With this much question plant, they could do it—but that was a suicidal tactic. If the two ranching groups started killing off each others' herds, what would the planet survive on after a winter or two of depleted current food stocks?

He was still turning this over in his mind when he noticed Mikey pawing at the base of a pile of sacks against a farther wall.

"Look out, Mikey," he whispered. "They'll all come down."

Mikey paid no attention to the words. He hooked a thick, curved claw of his right forepaw into the lowest sack and pulled. Jef sprang forward to try and stop the stack of filled sacks on top from tumbling—but they did not. Instead, they swung out in one solid unit, revealing themselves as camouflage for a wide door. Jef found himself staring down a short, dark corridor from the very end of which a door that was slightly open sent a slice of white light into the corridor.

Jef stared; and for the first time his ears picked up what Mikey must have already heard with his much more sensitive ears. Something could be heard, coming from beyond the lighted doorway at the corridor's end. It was the soft, steady murmuring of a man's voice, too low-pitched to be understandable at this distance.

"Shh . . ." Jef breathed at Mikey. "Shh . . . not a sound . . ."

He stepped past Mikey and began to tiptoe down the dark corridor. As he came closer to the doorway, the sound of the murmuring grew louder; until, as Jef eased up to the very corner of the doorway to where he would be able to gaze around the doorjamb at whatever was inside, the words he was hearing at last came clear.

". . . to set up and energize incubating units," a voice was saying, "will require at a minimum thirty hours of work by a ten-man working crew, particularly if these men are untrained. The five-hour set-up time for the incubating units you were given by manual implied that the set-up crew would be trained and experienced biotechnicians. To thaw the frozen embryos and begin to

154

process them through the birth stage—you don't want them coming out of their capsules all at once and needing to be taken care of—will take a minimum of another sixty hours. Then, when they start to be born out of capsule, you'd better have at least one person for every twenty eland foals, if these people are untrained at that, too."

The voice broke off, interrupting itself with a comment.

"I can't understand your needing this information all over again," it said. "A full rundown was given your people when our ship went into darkside orbit here three days ago."

"Beau himself took the information with him," answered a voice that jarred Jef—the voice of Martin. "When he left here yesterday, he left without anyone knowing what needs to be done. Now he may not be able to get back tomorrow the way he'd planned."

"He'd better," said the voice. "I'm not going to hang here in orbit around a Second Mortgage planet with sixty thousand variform eland embryos . . ."

Jef eased forward further until he could see around the corner of the door. He looked into a room at which Martin sat in a metal chair before a full wall of equipment of the sort that Jef himself had seen many times as a boy, when he had gone to meet his father as his father was coming off duty, back at some spaceport on Earth.

It was nothing less than the full control-tower equipment necessary to communicate with and guide a full-sized interstellar spaceship out of its parking orbit around a world like this, down to a safe landing on the surface; and what held Jef motionless for a long moment, then, was not just the amazing nature of what he had discovered, but something entirely personal. Seated with his back to Jef in a chair that slid automatically up and down the six-meter length of controls and telltales of the instrument board before him, Martin continued to work and talk with the spaceship, thousands or even hundreds of thousands of kilometers away in space. As he spoke his chair slid right and left; his hands danced skillfully and economically over dials and controls.

". . . Yes, I have you," Martin was saying, his chair pausing before the row of circular screens each with its little pinpoint, or line, of dancing light. "Orbital inclination to planetary plane is point sixty-five hundredths. Fair enough. Better plan on holding until present time minus eighty-three hours approximately—"

"I just told you," the voice from the instrument bank interrupted him, "we're not going to sit up here in parking orbit any longer than another sixty hours, maximum. I'll jettison cargo and write the deal off before I hold any longer. Every hour gives that spaceport control down there that much more chance to notice us, out here. Sixty hours, max. Then I dump the cargo."

"Well, now, and that would be a sweet loss to you, wouldn't it?" The mocking note, with which Jef had become familiar earlier, was in Martin's voice. "I've not been briefed on how this was all set up, being someone Beau brought in as an emergency replacement, as I said. But it doesn't take much of a brain to figure who'll be the big loser if those eland embryos get thrown away in space. Where would a bunch of backwoods game ranchers on a new colonial world like this one get the money for landing control equipment like this, plus the funds to import variform animal embryos on that scale? You'll have put a fair share of your own funds into this deal, Captain—ship and all; in hopes of special landing and other concessions from Everon once these game ranchers get political control, no doubt. Now, give me no more arguments, there's a fine man; and I'll talk you down here, as I say, approximately four days from now."

Martin stopped speaking, and sat waiting. But there was no further argument from the voice that had been speaking to him.

"Well, let's break communications for now, then,"

Martin said finally. "Talk to you again in ten hours or thereabouts. Out."

He reached up and touched a control on the panel. The moving dots and lines of light vanished from the circular screens. Audibly yawning, Martin leaned back in his chair and swung it lazily about so that he faced the doorway. So easily and naturally did he turn, that it was a full second before Jef realized Martin had a laser hand-weapon in one fist and it was pointing directly at Jef. Jef felt a touch of bitterness. Everyone, it seemed, had a weapon but himself.

"All right, Mr. Robini," Martin said. "I'll bother you to come on in; slowly if you don't mind, and without getting excited. Also bring in your maolot, as calmly as may be."

Jef's face and part of his body were plainly visible beyond the edge of the open doorway. But he knew that Mikey was still out of sight behind him; and he was tempted to gamble.

"Mikey's not here," he said.

"Come now," said Martin, and a sharp note had come into his voice, "are you expecting me to take your word for that? Stand aside."

He motioned with the barrel of the laser. Grimly, Jef stepped all the way through the doorway and to one side within it. Martin's gaze went past him, and he reached out with one hand to a switch on the board behind him.

"Well, now," said Martin. "It seems you were telling me the truth, after all."

Startled, Jef glanced over his shoulder. The interior of the outer room was now illuminated—a large power crystal in the ceiling was making the place as noon-bright as the grasslands. There was no Mikey there. He had vanished. Jef was too relieved to wonder how and when. The power crystal and the outer room went suddenly dark.

"I told you so," Jef said, turning back to Martin.

"How'd you get here? And what're you doing here?"

"Questions," said Martin softly. "You should really learn not to ask so many questions, Mr. Robini."

Turning slightly away from Jef, he triggered the laser on the narrow aperture, sweeping its incredibly hot beam back and forth over the control bank before him.

13

METAL AND PLASTIC SMOKED AND MELTED in narrow cuts, looking as if a giant had scrawled with a thick black pencil across the twelve-foot face of the control bank. In seconds the heat of the laser beam reduced to junk what must have been several million credits worth of equipment available only from Earth.

Jef stared at the ruined instruments, too stunned by the enormity of the destruction to react. He had not felt anything for the upland game ranchers until this minute; but seeing something like this destroyed in an instant hit him unexpectedly, almost as hard as if he had been one of Beau's group himself. He opened his mouth to say what he felt—but no words seemed to fit.

Then another thought came to him.

"So," he said, "it's the city people and the wisent owners you're working for, after all, not these game ranchers."

"Well now, Mr. Robini," said Martin calmly, "what makes you so sure that this world of Everon divides itself so neatly into two camps? And, indeed, what makes you so sure that I must be working for either of them, instead of simply following my duties as a John Smith to do what's best for all those who've come to live here, and for the world itself, as well?"

"You aren't still trying to pretend to me you're a John Smith?" Jef said. "The Constable's seen your real papers. So've I."

Martin nodded.

"That night when I was downstairs at dinner, of

course." He looked at Jef; and Jef, suddenly remembering how he had with Mikey's help forced the door of
Martin's room, felt uncomfortable.

"All right," he said. "I'm not proud of digging
through your luggage; but I felt I needed to know more
about you, in self-defense. At any rate, I saw your regular
papers."

"My *regular* papers? Come now," said Martin.
"You're certainly aware—and if you aren't, I've men-
tioned it, I think—of the fact that a John Smith such as
I has many names, many identities as his work requires
it. You should remember that—and so should Constable
Avery Armage."

"I think Armage's already made up his mind about
you," Jef said. "He certainly sounded as if he had when
he talked to me at Post Fifty."

"Ah, he got there before you escaped, then?"

"Yes—how'd you know I escaped?" Jef stared hard at
him. "How did you know they were holding me there?"

"It's my job to know," Martin answered. "In fact, I
was on my way to release you myself, but I gather others
helped you to freedom before I got there. What was it the
good Constable said to you?"

"He wanted to know about you. He seemed to think I
was some kind of partner of yours," said Jef. "But I think
he knew better. He just thought I was so fresh off the ship
he could bluff me into telling him anything I knew."

"And his bluff didn't work?"

"I suggested he'd find himself facing legal action if I
wasn't turned loose."

"But instead of waiting to be turned loose—" Martin
was watching him keenly, "you chose to escape—from a
Planetary Constable."

"I think he's up to his ears in something illegal himself," said Jef bluntly. "Anyway the chance came to get
out and I took it."

"You amaze me, Mr. Robini." Martin's voice was

light. "You've a practical streak in you I hadn't suspected. I'd advise you to use it now, and shake the dust of this encampment from your heels."

"I'm here to see Beau; and I haven't seen him yet."

"You'd be well advised not to see him at all. I'm on my way out myself—"

"I'm not surprised," said Jef, looking at the ruined equipment.

"I'd have a low opinion of you if you were, Mr. Robini. Now, I suggest you give me sixty seconds to get clear and then head into the woods in the first direction that attracts you. Your maolot and other true friends will find you before dawn and by that time you should have put a safe distance between yourself and this camp."

With these last words he stepped into the darkness of the outer room and effectively vanished. Jef strained his eyes to see any sign of the outside door opening to let him out, but against the brightness of the communications room it was not possible. Jef glanced at his watch, in the new silence feeling the rapid pounding of his own heart. He could not leave here. He would not leave here, and give up his only chance of finding out what had actually happened to Will.

He glanced at his watch again. Something over a minute had gone by. He took a step toward the corridor room—and Bill Eschak materialized at the entrance of the corridor. Jef stopped.

Bill came in, staring steadily at him all the way. Then he reached the entrance to the communications room and his gaze went past Jef to the equipment. His face paled above its beard.

He turned and looked full into Jef's face once more; and Jef felt his breath pause in his chest. Now, Bill's eyes bore out the reputation Jarji had given the older man. But he only turned and walked to a small phone handset on one of the side walls. He took it down and pressed its call button several times.

"Beau?" he said after a second. "I found him—in the room at the back of the store building. That's right . . . I was looking outside for him and thought I saw someone moving down this way, so when I got here I checked and the front door was broke open. Beau, the equipment's wrecked. Lasered to ribbons."

"I wasn't the one who did that," Jef said. "A man named Martin Curragh, who's posing as a John Smith, wrecked it. —Listen!"

In fact, even Jef's civilization-dulled ears could hear, distantly through the log walls, the faint mutter of a light plane's internal combustion engine that had sounded suddenly, and was now quickly dying away out of hearing.

Bill's eyes burned above the handset, at Jef.

"You hear the plane, Beau?" Bill said into the phone. "Robini says Curragh did it—and that'll be him getting away now. That'll be one of our birds he took. He'd not have risked having anyone land one of his own in so close here, we could hear him come in. Shall I question Robini? No, I didn't guess Curragh was, either . . . all right, then. All right, if you say so, Beau. We'll wait here."

He replaced the handset. They waited.

A few minutes later there was the sound of boots in the darkened outer room and a man came into the corridor who dwarfed Bill—a man even larger than the Constable.

Like Bill, the newcomer wore a beard; but his was a great red mass, cascading halfway down the wide front of his thick, russet jacket. A knitted maroon stocking cap sat on a mass of hair as red as the beard, so that the overall impression he gave was like that of some great red-furred animal. He threw one quick glance at the destroyed equipment, then stopped and turned to face Jef. For a moment the eyes in his wide face were like chips of green bottle glass. Then, abruptly, they softened, and his beard parted in a smile.

"Hello, Jef," he said in a soft baritone. He held out a huge hand. "How are you? Bill, I'm surprised at you. Will Robini's brother wouldn't do anything like this to us. Will was a friend of mine, Jef. I want you to know that. I wouldn't have come here the way I did, just now, if I'd thought you weren't someone only posing as his brother. But you're a close relative, all right, one look at you tells me that. You couldn't be anyone else with that face."

"Of course," said Jef warily. His nerves had been screwed too tightly for him to relax quickly, even in the face of Beau's apparent friendliness.

"You say it was Martin Curragh did the damage, here?" Beau went on.

"That's right," said Jef. He told the large man the story of his own acquaintance with Martin, winding up with his recent discovery that Martin had deliberately set him up to be deported by the Constable.

When he was done, Beau took off his stocking cap and ran thick fingers through his stack of hair. For a second the gesture made him look weary and much older. Then he put the cap back on and was imposingly vigorous again.

"And you've got no idea where he's going, or who he's working with?" Beau asked.

"No. I mean, I don't know where he'd go. I accused him of working for the wisent ranchers and the city crowd, but he said they just thought he was working for them—you remember, I told you that just now."

"So you did," Beau said. He looked again at the ruined communications board. "We made a mistake in taking on Curragh. Do you know, Jef, it would have been a lot easier if your brother was still alive. He had the experience to handle this equipment and we could have trusted him."

"Will?" Jef felt another sudden shock. What Beau said made no sense. "But you're planning to bring in con-

163

traband eland embryos. That's going to upset the natural ecological balance here. It's against E. Corps regulations. Will worked for the E. Corps."

"He was my friend," rumbled Beau. "He was one of us."

"I know, but—" Jef tried to think of some way of saying it that would make plain what he meant without insulting Beau and the other game ranchers in general. "Will wouldn't do something like that. He always believed in the E. Corps and the E. Corps regulations. No matter how good a friend you were, he wouldn't break regulations—"

"Listen to me!" said Beau grimly. "I said he would have been the man to do it; I didn't say he'd agreed to do it. This was back before we'd even thought of . . . all this. He knew, even back then, the wisent ranchers were behind our eland poisoning. In fact he was in the process of putting in a complaint for us to the E. Corps."

"He was going to put in a complaint?"

"He was," Beau said, "although I'd told him it was already too late for that. All the E. Corps could do if it came in was stop the wisent ranchers from expanding their lands any further by clearing our forests. If there'd been some criminal complaint, or something to do with off-Everon people, it'd have been different. But we were already into Second Mortgage. Even eight years ago, the wisent ranchers were already too far ahead of us."

"What do you mean, too far ahead of you?" asked Jef.

"I mean we'd been too slow catching on—to the fact they were poisoning our eland to get themselves a legal excuse for clearing our forest," Beau said. "They'd cleared too much land already. Everon's already headed toward being a grazing planet for wisent only, and a lopsided economy. The only way to even it up is to import enough eland to turn the scale the other way."

"And make it a lop-sided economy with eland only?" Beau's face hardened.

"I'm trying to explain things to you," he said. "Do you want to listen, or not?"

"I'll listen," said Jef. "But why didn't Will put in a complaint, anyway? I'd think—"

"He disappeared before he could," Beau said. His eyes met Jef's squarely. "That's all I know. All anyone knows. He left here to go back to his office at the spaceport—it was the end of a weekend—but he never showed up at the spaceport."

"And none of you looked for him!" said Jef.

"What are you talking about? Of course we looked for him!" rumbled Beau. "We've got men who know how to track. We tracked him right down into plains country; and then lost his trail where a whole herd of wisent had covered it, going in the same direction for miles."

"Maybe," said Jef. "If you'd just show Mikey and me where—"

"Not now," said Beau. He got to his feet abruptly and lightly. "I owed you that much of an explanation; but now we've got our own problems to look after. The ship with the eland is still in orbit up there and the equipment to land it back here in the woods is beyond fixing."

"We're licked," said Bill Eschak.

Beau shook his head like a red-furred bear.

"Not yet," he said. "We're not going to lose those eland after all this. There's one more set of landing equipment on this planet that can bring that ship down to surface, here at our place, and that's the control equipment at the regular spaceport."

Bill gazed at him.

"Who'll handle it?" the bearded man asked.

"Curragh," said Beau. "All we have to do is take over the spaceport for an hour at the most, to give him time to do it."

"I—" Jef hesitated to intrude on the conversation of the other two, but it seemed necessary. "I don't think Martin'll do it for you."

165

"We'll pay him," said Beau briefly. "If he sold us out to the downcountry, he's buyable. We'll just meet his price."

"Or," said Bill, with one of his near-noiseless laughs, "give him a choice."

Beau looked a little sourly at his lieutenant.

"I think we can name a price this man'll go for," he said. He turned back to Jef. "Where do you think we might find Curragh, now?"

"I don't have any idea," said Jef. He thought. "At a guess, if he was actually working with the city people, he'd head for the Constable."

"That's what I think," said Beau to Bill. "There's no place for him to put down safely in the woods. Too many of our own kind around. There's nothing for him on the open plains; and he won't want to show up in the open in the city, where somebody might recognize him and pass word of it back to us. He'll be meeting Avery Armage some place quietly. Where?"

"Constable's place outside the city," said Bill. "Nice, quiet, plenty of room to put other people up overnight if they want to get a whole bunch together."

"How many planes have we got, ready to go?"

"Well, there's the usual five, Beau. And the courier plane just needs routine overhaul. We could fuel her up and use her if we had to."

"That's fifteen people." Beau thought for a minute. "I think we can raid that place of his with fifteen."

He suddenly seemed to become aware that Jef was still standing there.

"Oh, Jef," he said. "We're going to have to put you up here for a few days until I've got time to talk about Will with you. You can find your own way back to your room, can't you?"

"You never did ask him," said Bill, "how he got here?"

Jef had had time to think about an answer to that question.

"I thought I heard Mikey—that's that young maolot of mine—outside," he said. "Mikey ran off yesterday. I went out to see if I could catch him and got turned around in the dark. I thought this building was the one I'd been in; and then, when I found the door open and saw it wasn't, I saw a light back here and came in to find someone who could tell me how to get back to where I'd started."

"Sure," said Beau a little impatiently. "Bill, why don't you go to the door with Jef and point the right building out to him?"

Bill nodded and started out the door. As Jef was about to follow the older man, a question came to him. He had a good deal of advice against asking questions, but this one seemed harmless.

"Tell me something," he said, as he turned to follow Bill, "is it just Earth variform animals who react to native plants that disagree with Earth stock, or do some of the native animals react, too? I was just thinking Mikey's been eating everything in sight lately; and having grown up on Earth, he may not have the instincts to keep him away from things on Everon that might not be good for him—"

"No, no," said Beau. Bill had come to a complete stop and turned back. "There's nothing to worry about. Nothing at all. Nothing poisons maolots. They can eat anything. The wisent ranchers have tried everything under the sun, and short of shooting a maolot dead center, nothing stops them."

"That's right," said Bill.

Beau's voice had been soothing and entirely convincing in its tone. But Bill's voice suddenly had a new note.

"I wouldn't worry, if I were you," went on Beau warmly. "You know—on second thought, Bill, why don't you walk Jef all the way back to his building? Just to make sure he doesn't go astray again?"

"It'd be a pleasure," said Bill. "Come on, Robini."

He led off. Jef followed. But in this answer, to his ears,

once more, rang the same odd note that he had heard from Bill a moment before. Belatedly, alarm signals began to sound in his mind; and, in the short length of time that it took him to follow the other to the door of the building, fresh suspicion soared into a certainty. He would not have been so sure if he had not seen the look on Bill's face when the other had come in and found him with the ruined equipment. Jarji had not exaggerated. Bill was not only capable of murder—he obviously enjoyed it. And there was a long dark walk between the buildings with Beau's injunction to the older man to see that Jef did not "go astray again." Those three words now rang again in Jef's head with all the authority of a secret command.

Bill was waiting for Jef just outside the door. In the gloom of the barely moonlit night, they started across the grass.

"Too bad about that control equipment," Jef said to break the silence, after half a dozen steps.

"Too bad," echoed Bill. His voice was strange and remote as if he spoke from some distance off, in spite of the fact he was walking at Jef's side. Together they were drawing away from the building they had just left, and the open doorway from which a little light still spilled out. With each step they were getting deeper into dimness.

"Did you know my brother?" Jef asked. "Beau said Will was one of his best friends. I suppose you must have known him, too."

"I knew him."

Bill's voice now seemed to come from even a slightly greater distance. Turning his head, Jef saw that the other man was lagging behind slightly. Jef slowed down, but Bill apparently slowed also, for he did not catch up.

"You weren't one of the ones who tracked him, the way Beau said?" Jef asked.

"No, Robini," said Bill. His voice was almost harsh, now. "I didn't track him. Turn around."

"Turn—?" Jef stopped and looked back.

Bill was a full pace behind him now and standing still. He had one hand inside his shirt past a button that was now unbuttoned.

"That's right," said Bill.

The bearded man was speaking with a peculiar, thick-tongued slowness. Also, his hand was withdrawing from his shirt with the same odd slowness. Jef saw the white of the skin on the back of that hand flash palely in the darkness—and then there was something like a rush of air, a heavy thump, and Bill went sprawling on the ground. In the same second a huge shape loomed up before Jef in the dark, a massive head dipped, clamped teeth on Jef's belt and lifted him easily into the air. He was swung about, and the next moment whatever had seized him was galloping off with him into the night forest as if he had been a small rag doll in the mouth of a playful dog.

14

THE JOLTING HE WAS TAKING was making Jef's senses reel.
He reached up instinctively to cling to the neck to which
the heavy head was attached and touched familiar-feel-
ing skin and muscles. Steel bands under warm-furred
velvet.

"Mikey!" he grunted, hardly knowing how he knew
but suddenly completely certain that it was, indeed,
Mikey and not simply some wild maolot. "Mikey, stop a
moment! Put me down. *Mikey*!"

Mikey, however, did not stop and put Jef down. He
did, however, slow his pace to a much easier one; and Jef
got the feeling, along that particular channel of communication between them, that Mikey was waiting for
him to pull himself around and up on to the maolot's
back. Mikey had grown unbelievably in just these last
few days and now he was almost as large as a mature
male of his kind. Such rapid growth should not be a
physical possibility, but there it was. Clearly, he was not
only large enough for Jef to ride, but had more than
enough strength to carry a rider of Jef's weight. Jef
kicked hard with his left leg, managed eventually to get
a heel hooked over Mikey's broad backbone, and
scrambled up into a position astride that back.

Somewhere in the process, Mikey had released his
teeth from Jef's belt. The change of position could not
have been managed otherwise, but without that firm
hold on him, Jef felt the danger of being jolted off. He lay
flat along the crest of Mikey's back, holding hard with

170

his legs to Mikey's flanks and maintaining a tight grip around the neck of the maolot.

Happily, Mikey's back was broad enough so that he was not uncomfortable to ride and he was traveling now at a loose trot which, combined with the springy way the bones and muscle of his legs took up the jar of their impact against the earth, made staying on top of him less of a problem than it might have been otherwise. After a while Jef began to relax and trust himself not to fall off. For the first time he sat up and looked about to see where Mikey might be taking him.

He had not noticed when they had ceased to have treetops overhead, but they were no longer in the woods. They were out in the grassland. As far as Jef could see under a sky that was beginning to pale with dawn, there was nothing but the shoulder-to-head-high grass in every direction. He stared, finding it hard to believe that they had come this far from the tree-country, this quickly. It was true Beau's headquarters had not been found that far from the edge of the open country; but to get this far out of sight of the forest area this quickly was startling.

Jef stared at the thick carpet of tall vegetation whipping past them on either side and tried to estimate Mikey's speed.

Even half-grown, back on Earth, Mikey had been able to run for hours at thirty or forty kilometers an hour. In fact, he had done just that on weekends when Jef took him out to one of the State Parks, or wild areas, for exercise. Here, at double his Earthly size and with a stride probably twice as long, Mikey must be doing half again that pace, even though he was clearly not straining himself.

"Where are we going, Mikey?" Jef asked into the right ear of the maolot. There was no response. The ear did not even twitch; and the empathy between Jef and Mikey did not return any answer to Jef's question. Jef gave up. He was only a passenger after all. Off Mikey's back and alone out here, he would be helpless and scheduled for certain death. Out here in the grasslands there was no food—for him at least—and no water, barring the infrequent lakes that the variform wisent could smell from miles away, but which in Jef's case could be less than a hundred meters distant beyond obscuring grass stems, and go completely undiscovered.

On his own two feet Jef would be lost and beyond any hope of finding his way back to a wooded area. He could be walking in a circle within three minutes of heading off in what he thought was a certain direction, for among the grass stems all directions looked alike. So there was nothing to do now but ride wherever Mikey was intending to take him. Hopefully, it would not be too long a trip.

It was not—although it was not a short one, either. An hour and a half later, with the sun well up over the horizon and the green of the grass surface touched with rippling glints of gold, Jef saw a dark line ahead of them, which grew and resolved itself into a line of trees. Half an hour after that they loped once more into shade and the grass dwindled to moss height. A few seconds more and all view of the grassland was lost behind them.

"Mikey," said Jef, "I could drink a river dry. How about you?"

Through the voiceless channel of communication came an immediate sensation of agreement. Less than five minutes later they broke out between towering elmlike, native trees of an upland species Jef did not recognize, to stop at the bank of a shallow, fast-running stream tumbling between boulders and over gravel in a bed not ten meters across.

Mikey sat down on his haunches, and Jef slid off. Without any further delay they both drank, Mikey crouching at the edge of the stream, Jef lying full length beside him.

"That's better," said Jef at last, sitting up and wiping moisture from his lips. "Now, if you could just manage to turn up something I could eat."

He sensed concern and regret from Mikey.

"Never mind," Jef said. "I'm not going to starve to death in twenty-four hours. For that matter, I'm not going to starve to death in a couple of days—though I hope I get something to eat before that long. What did you bring me here for, Mikey?"

There was a response of some kind from Mikey, but it conveyed no useful understanding to Jef.

"I'm not reading you very well," Jef said. It occurred to him that there might no longer be any advantage in speaking out loud to Mikey. Perhaps all he would really need to do from now on was think of whatever he wanted to say. Then it struck him that since he had always been in the habit of organizing his thoughts verbally, they would probably be a lot clearer if he spoke them as well as thought them. Having worked this out, he remembered that back on Earth Mikey had also been in the habit of responding as if their communication was by voice alone. So, for that reason, even if for no other, it made sense to go on using sounded words to help out, at least until Jef himself got much better at their wordless, Evcron-style conversations.

The strange thing, it occurred to him now, was the ease with which he had come to take it for granted that he and Mikey could converse non-verbally. Of course, the fact that he had always suspected something like this was going on between them, even back on Earth, played a part in his present easy acceptance of it. But all the same, actual communication of this sort had been a dream for centuries; and here he was the first one to use it as a routine skill. He should be more excited.

On the other hand, came a further thought following like one box on an assembly line belt after another, Mikey himself was apparently taking this wordless communication very much for granted; and a large part of what was being communicated between them had always been emotion rather than information. So if Mikey was not concerned about the ability, it was not surprising Jef was having trouble getting excited, himself.

Now that he had found some water to drink, his general fatigue, coming on top of the excitement of the night and the physical effort of the maolot-back ride, was beginning to make itself felt. For the moment his hunger had moved back into the realm of the unimportant. The morning sun was warming him pleasantly; and now that he had left the edge of the stream, he found himself sitting on a patch of moss-grass that seemed remarkably soft. He yawned.

"I think I'll take a nap, Mikey," he said. "Talk to you a little later. All right?"

He was lying back and stretching out as he said the words. The moss-grass was like a pleasantly sprung mattress. The warmth of the early sun lapped him like a soft blanket. He half-turned on his side and slid off into sleep. A last stray thought, just as he went under, was that it was more than a little providential that he should get this sleepy at a time when he ought to be hungry and irritable; and the faint wisp of a suspicion existed for a second that possibly—he could not think how, but possibly—Mikey had had something to do with it.

Then he was asleep and dreaming of a boat that sailed him over dark blue waters to a place desirable and exciting.

He woke after what felt like a very long slumber—and in fact the sun, far from just having risen, was now in late afternoon position. He lay where he was, comfortably drowsy, letting himself drift back to full consciousness. He had dreamed about many other things after the dream of the boat ride, he seemed to remember. He could not quite seem to fasten on what those other things had been, but the feeling within him was that they had been extremely pleasant, comforting and reassuring, something like the feeling of finding his way back into the home of his childhood and the company of his immediate family back when he had been very young. Pleasant as it had been, though, in some other way he also could not bring to mind right now it had also been very important. Important and full of things he needed to know.

He began to remember; not exactly what his dreams had been about, but generally with what they had been concerned. He had been busy discovering many things, getting straightened out on many matters, some of which were surprising. They possibly would have been so, even though he could not remember specifically what would make them that way—startling, if not repellent, to some other humans. But he had found them to be neither. It seemed that his long acquaintance with Mikey had prepared him to encounter them with a minimum of shock. He had found them different, that was all.

He was now almost fully awake. He rolled over on his other side and saw Mikey, apparently lying unmoved from the same place and position in which Jef had last seen him, his blind head turned as if to watch Jef.

And of course, thought Jef—now made wiser by his dreams—Mikey could see him perfectly well. He did not need his own eyes. He could use any other pair of eyes except human ones, or even a stone or a stick of wood that had been at a site he wished to observe for a certain critical length of time. That time varied from object to object, but essentially it was a matter of the minutes, days or years required for the stick to weather, the stone to settle into the soil it lay upon . . . and so forth. The concept of such seeing was not at all difficult to grasp, just outside the frame of ordinary human thinking.

"Hello, Mikey," Jef said.

Mikey acknowledged the greeting; although, Jef now realized, from the maolot's point of view it was an entirely unnecessary response. After all, they had been together ever since Jef had spoken to him last, including

175

through the dream itself. It struck Jef, not with suddenness but with a strong impact, that he was reading Mikey with much more clarity and understanding than he had before he had dropped off to sleep.

Jef got up, drank from the stream, stirred about and generally got himself back into full operating condition.

"Well," he said to Mikey eventually, "I'm wide awake. What now? I suppose I ought to go back and check on Jarji. You wouldn't think Beau and those others'd hold her responsible for what I did—"

Reassurance flooded from Mikey, together with something else, an image or a scene of some kind, that Jef was not able to resolve. The import was clear, however. Jarji was all right; and the impression Jef got was that she herself was away from Beau's camp and traveling by herself in his direction.

It was frustrating, in a way, he thought. He did not so much receive an impression from Mikey as become suddenly aware that he had already received an impression. It was more as if he heard something said to him in a completely unknown foreign language and following this, experienced his memory of the unfamiliar sounds melting into understandable words of his own native tongue. Not a good analogy to what he was experiencing, he thought to himself now, but the best he could do.

"I should wait here for her, then?" he asked Mikey.

Strongly negative impression from Mikey. He and Jef had things to do—now.

"What things?"

Mikey stood up and came over to him.

"Oh," said Jef. He climbed up on Mikey's back once more, wincing slightly. He had gone into training to prepare himself to hike the surface of Everon, not to ride that same surface on a maolot, bareback. The inner muscles of his thighs were stiff and sore from gripping Mikey's flanks.

But the moment he was on, Mikey was in movement.

15

NOW, AS THEY TRAVELED ON ONCE MORE, the afternoon was waning and almost all of their route lay through forest. As far as Jef could judge, they were following a straight line that roughly paralleled the edge of the grassland, in an area where this edge ran north and south. They were headed north and the country was rough, becoming a landscape of little ridges and hollows. After an hour or so they finally came to a small cliff, very like the small cliff that had stood behind the clearing where Beau leCourboisier had his buildings. Mikey climbed up on the cliff and continued along the line of its top, a little way back from the edge of its vertical face that looked out toward the grassland.

In fact, from up here the grassland could be seen. Only a half kilometer of woods separated the cliff face from the sea of tall, green-gold stems. The ridge ran on at roughly this distance from the forest edge, and they followed it until at last, on one particularly high pinnacle behind a split spire of rock, Mikey finally came to a halt and sat down.

Jef slid off him, grateful to find himself on his feet again. Even with an easy mount, this much distance on maolot-back was making itself noticeable. Mikey lay down, settling himself in position where he could gaze out through the split in the spire of rock. Jef felt himself urged to do the same.

Jef joined him. The rock was not as comfortable as the moss-grass had been at their earlier stopping spot, but he finally found a smooth spot on which to perch cross-legged with his back against an outcropping.

"What are we looking for?" he asked Mikey.

Mikey turned his head toward him and then turned it back to point once more out through the split in the rock. Looking through in the same direction, Jef felt his gaze drawn to a more distant ridge of rock lifting up above the surrounding forest.

He ran his gaze over the edge of that cliff. It was cut and weathered into raggedness and fringed with small trees that were hardly more than meter-high bushes. At first Jef could see nothing but rock and vegetation. Then, little by little, with the pressure of Mikey's mind directing his attention, he began to pick out unmoving shapes, lying still, watching outward and down into the belt of forest lying between them and the edge of the grass.

There was one . . . two . . . three . . . Jef counted fifteen mature maolots lying scattered separately on the cliff-edge over some three hundred meters of distance. There were more, Mikey said, out of sight behind rocks or trees.

"But what are they all doing here?" Jef asked.

His gaze was drawn down into the woods. Once more he had trouble finding anything there but the natural elements of the scene. Then, urged on by whatever direction from Mikey was guiding his attention, he located a single, light, ducted-fan aircraft, pulled in under the cover of one of the large, elmlike trees, at the edge of a clearing just big enough to land in. As he watched, a human figure came out from under the tree, shaded its eyes and looked away into the sunset sky, out over the grassland.

The figure gazed for a second or two, then turned and went back under the tree again.

Something, his feeling from Mikey told him, would be happening soon.

178

"What's going to happen?" Jef asked.

Jef got an impression of other humans on their way here.

"What are they coming here for?" Jef asked.

They were coming, the realization took shape in his mind, to destroy a part of the forest and let the grass take over that area.

Jef felt a cold, growing sense of shock that left his empty-stomached body feeling a little giddy. It was true, then, what Jarji had said. There had indeed been illegal clearing of forest land. This, that Mikey had brought him here to see, had to be illegal or else why would it be taking place in such secrecy? The aircraft hidden from overhead view under the trees, the solitary watcher looking for others that he gathered through Mikey were just now arriving with the beginning of night to do their work, all this pointed toward an action that would not bear the light of day or the open gaze of the law.

He looked again for the human under the tree with the plane; but in the waning light Jef could not be sure any longer that he was making the watcher out of the shadows that surrounded him and his vehicle. Jef looked for the other maolots distributed along the ridge and found them lost also in the gathering obscurity. On the cliff the light was better than in the woods below. But the dimness was enough so that the watching maolots had blended into their surroundings.

I can help you see them, he felt Mikey informing him.

The bond between the two of them intensified. It was as if the maolot was taking Jef's mind on to the back of his own, as he had taken Jef on to the back of his body to carry him away from Beau leCourboisier's headquarters. As it had been with that physical carrying, it was not something he could make happen by himself. His mind offered a ride to Jef's, and Jef, with an effort equal to that with which he had scrambled up behind the shoulders of

Mikey, had to stretch his new capacities for rapport to take advantage of what was now being made possible to him.

It was a small but indescribable struggle that ended with Jef triumphantly riding the current of Mikey's perceptions. Once sure that Jef was solidly with him, Mikey reached out to look at the maolots below, one by one, through the viewpoint of some creature or object near them.

To Jef, the feeling was like riding a roller coaster. He felt himself swoop down into a viewpoint that showed him, from a body-length away, the side view of a majestic, mature maolot female, gazing out impassively between two tall boulders. The image was faintly distorted, as if he looked through the multifaceted eyes of some insect. There was a moment of watching, then another swoop to a new point of view; and now he was looking at one more of the massive watchers, a male lying with paws together and head up, gaze fixed on the distant grassland beneath the sunset area of the sky. This watcher turned his head, as though aware of being observed, until he faced whatever point of view Mikey was using to watch him. But as he did, his eyes closed, so that when Jef became able to look directly at them, they were as blind-appearing as Mikey's.

Jef felt chilled. Clearly, the impression came to him, the large male knew Jef was looking at him; and, equally clearly, he had deliberately closed his eyes to keep Jef from seeing them. There was distancing in that action, a shutting-out. Jef found himself feeling more lonely than he had thought it possible to feel.

Another swoop, and Jef was looking at another large female. Then another male, and another mature female. Mikey moved Jef's point of view along the cliff top, stopping at each of the silent sentinels. Some of these ignored the observation that was being made of them, some turned to look; but all who looked closed their eyes before Jef could see into them.

At last Mikey returned their point of view to his own body behind the divided spire and his mind released Jef's point of view. Jef sat back against the face of rock that supported him, dazed. Once—it seemed like months ago, now—he had thought that it was probably as well Jarji had not been able to supply him with a crossbow; because, inexperienced as he was with such a weapon and powerful as a full-grown maolot must be, he would probably only anger such a creature by trying to defend himself with it. He had been thinking then only of the physical size and power of the adult. Now he faced the fact that if one of these he watched had stepped out then from between the trees of the forest through which he had been traveling, and done no more than look at him with closed eyes, he would still have been as helpless as a small bird charmed by a snake.

Slowly the emotional effect of what he had just seen receded.

Look, Mikey told him. Now they come.

He turned to stare out over the forest and the grassland. The sun was just winking below the horizon, and, as he watched, it went. Now that it was gone he was able to see other little winks of light, several hundred feet above the grasslands and approaching. As these grew closer, he saw they were the last of the last daylight, caught by planes high enough in the air to still be able to do so, and reflected off the shinier underparts of their wings and bodies.

There were four of them. They came in, circled, and went down, one by one, to land in the clearing where the single human and his craft already waited. After gazing at the still-bright sky, the shadow in the clearing below seemed night-dark to Jef. But plainly there was enough light for craft to land safely. As Jef continued to watch, his eyes adjusted to the dimmer scene and he saw them all settle in the clearing. There were figures moving around them on the ground; but it was now literally too dim to make out any details. Without warning, the dazzle of a guide beam for an industrial laser flickered into life at the edge of the clearing, and one of the tall, dark fingers that were the elmlike native trees, began to lean, further and faster as it went, until it came crashing to the ground.

It's begun, Mikey informed Jef; and Jef had a sudden image of the trees and bushes all cut down and the new open ground sown with fertilizer. By dawn the low moss-grass in the cleared area would begin putting up microscopic stems. In a week the grass here would be almost as tall as that full grown in the rest of the grasslands and humans like himself would hardly be able to tell where forest had used to be.

Jef stared as more dazzles of lights appeared and other trees began to fall.

Now the older ones go, Mikey said.

Startled, Jef looked down at the clifftop. It had become too dim, even up here, to see the shapes of the adult maolots; but through Mikey Jef felt that they had indeed gone.

"Where?" Jef asked.

Mikey showed him.

Jef found himself loping through the night forest. The men with the industrial lasers were close, but the adult whose point of view he was now inhabiting mentally paid no attention to them. Ahead was the edge of the grassland. A moment later and he was plunging through the grass with the same gait but much faster than Mikey had traveled in bringing Jef to the cliff.

The grassland was dark. The cloudless sky overhead was a darkness in which only a few first points of stars shone. There was nothing to be seen; but the maolot which was Jef could feel his fellows spread out in a skirmish line five hundred meters wide, sweeping out into the grasslands at a steady pace of better than fifty kilometers an hour.

Come, Mikey told Jef. We need to get started too, so we can meet them afterwards.

"Afterwards—what?" Jef asked, as he remounted Mikey.

Afterwards, said Mikey. Jef would see.

With Jef on his back, Mikey began to move once more along the line of the rocky ridge. It ran for several kilometers before it either lowered to a level with the surrounding land, or the land rose to join it. At first it was dark going, but then a moon rose. Its rising was seen first by the adults out in the sea of grass some moments before Mikey and Jef could see it. Above the waving grasstops it produced as spectacular a picture as had the daybreak Jef had seen. Only this was a picture painted all in silvers and greys and blacks. Seeing it through the mind of Mikey to the mind of the particular maolot with which he was in direct contact, Jef found himself caught up in the identity of the older alien—to the point where his ride on Mikey became the dream and his sensations of coursing through the tall grass on his own four legs, the reality. He snorted the night air deep into his enormous lungs. The moonlight intoxicated him. His feet seemed to barely touch the earth at the end and beginning of each leap, and his limbs felt as if they could keep carrying him so forever. With ten-meter strides he spurned the planet beneath him, sending it spinning with his pads. Ahead were those he sought.

Ahead, Jef became aware, was a darker line against the moonlit grass. It was a darkness that grew until it became recognizable as a mass of animals—a mass of wisents. It was a herd of three thousand of the Earth variform animals, his maolot knew, feeding and jostling each other, with females and young in toward the center of the herd, males toward the outside, their eyes watching, their horns ready, an uneasiness in their dim minds making them alert for possible attack. Not an attack from maolots, but from bulky, oiled-metal things that patrolled around them, keeping them in one tight herd. Riding wisents, the herd animals were used to—though these faster-legged, lighter-weight, close cousins, genetically tailored to be a riding animal for the Everon settlers, were regarded as an enemy tribe by the herd beasts and attacked whenever they could be cornered. Aircraft overhead, they were also used to. But never in their lives had any of them seen one of Everon's few, valuable prototype trucks with their noisy and smelling internal combustion engines, and these filled them with uneasy fears.

The adults were close now. They were no longer bounding forward, but sneaking through the grass below its feathery surface. The adult that Jef's mind rode with was now circling the circling trucks, passing close enough to the men in the bed of one truck, sitting around the industrial laser mounted there on a swivel base like a heavy duty military rifle, so that their talk could be plainly heard. Heard, and by Jef, understood.

". . . how the hell much longer?"

"Four hours, radio says."

"Four hours, and then four hours to make the drive in. Why we got to lie this far out? No sense . . ."

". . . the maolots."

"Hell, we cut one in half, he shows up. Four hour drive! We could lay one hour out and have the trees down and the herd in by midnight."

"Wait'll you made more'n one of these drives. Maolots are smart."

"What good's smart against an industrial laser? Ten script against the first one I see getting away."

"That's no bet. You see one, of course it's not getting away."

"Put or shut . . ."

"Besides, the satellite pictures don't have to show

wisents already on the land. Just helps in court, if they do."

"Sure, tell us, Holbert. How many thousand head do you own? How many new patches you open up before now?"

—Somewhere, on the far side of the herd, the deep, carrying call of an adult male maolot droned in the night.

The wisent grunted and milled. In a couple of seconds the outer ring was solidly composed of bulls, their horns lowered. Their unease over the unknown trucks was drowned now in their certain awareness of the maolots.

Searchlights were on in each of the vehicles. Bright beams were sweeping the grasstop. Voices were calling and speaking by intercom from truck to truck.

"What do you see?"

"Damnall, that's what I see. What do you see?"

"There's only one of them."

"How come you're so smart, Harlie?"

"Get that light over here! I thought I saw something—"

"Use your own light!"

"—Damn, he was moving too fast. . ."

Slowly, gradually the talk lowered in pitch and became less excited. The wisent calmed.

From another quarter a mature male sounded, not a full roar, but a droning, hunting call.

Alarm rose again. The wisents stamped and tried to gather into an even tighter bunch. The trucks put on speed, waving the beams of their searchlights around energetically. Slowly, much more slowly this time, things calmed once more in the silence of the night.

"What the hell, Harlie, one maolot's not going to attack five trucks—"

A drone sounded beyond the side of the herd that faced the recently risen moon. Another answered almost immediately from the other side of the herd.

"There's two of them! I told you, I told you there was more than just one—"

"Shut up! Listen!"

A series of uneasy waves of movement, like waves in the ocean from some underwater disturbance, were rippling through the close-packed wisents. Individual animals in the herd were trying to turn from one threat to face horns-out at another, and finding the herd so tightly pushed together that turning was impossible. Instinct to face danger, head down, warred with instinct to huddle together as tightly as possible.

"—Do something!" a voice from one truck was shouting. "Those maolots keep getting this herd worked up and half of them'll run themselves to death when we finally start moving them into the new patch! Harlie! Ty! Your two trucks break circle! See if you can run those bastards down!"

Two of the circling trucks—one on each side of the herd—turned out from their patrol route and began to swing back and forth in figure eights outside the circle the other trucks were making around the herd. Within the identity of his maolot, crouched now in the grass with heavy jaws open as if laughing while he watched, Jef felt triumph.

"Nothing!" one of the men in the closest truck was reporting by intercom to whoever had ordered the trucks out.

"Keep looking!" The radio voice over the intercom could be heard answering.

"Maybe we scared them off."

"You scared them off all right—like hell you did!"

The man in the nearest truck grumbled something Jef's maolot could not hear well enough for Jef to translate. But the truck kept moving.

A full chorus of maolot voices rang out, one after the other, so fast that the two outside cars gave up their figure eights automatically and simply cruised parallel to the circle the interior trucks were still making.

"That does it!" came the radio voice from the intercom. "Harlie, Ty, back to position. I don't give a damn whether they've got that patch cleared yet or not. I'm not losing money for half of this bunch dead on the way in. We're moving them now; and once we get the wiz there, they're not our responsibility anymore! Back to station, all trucks! Move them out—and keep your eyes open. Those cats may sing, but they're not going to show themselves when someone's awake on a laser. Keep your heads together and we'll get them all in safe—and us home by dawn!"

One truck moved directly into the wisents, and the others drew back. The herd began to move, at first almost grudgingly, but then rapidly speeding up to the trot which was a pace these animals could keep up day and night, if necessary. The trucks herded them, one before and one ahead, one on each side of the moving herd. Outside the protection of the trucks, the maolots also paced the traveling beasts, but without sound and without moving in on them.

Jef, responding completely within the identity of the maolot through whose eyes he was seeing this, felt despair. The herd was traveling now, and there was no way the maolots could get at it, with the trucks between them and the shaggy herbivores. It was true enough that any one of the maolots could have made a quick dash into the dark mass of trotting animals and killed right and left before the gunners on any of the trucks could have laid their sights on him. But such a maolot would never have gotten back out of the herd alive.

Clearly, the adults, fierce and strong as they were, had too much intelligence to throw away even one of their own lives just to do token damage to the herd. Though short of such a sacrifice, Jef did not see now how they would have any real chance of interfering with the drive.

Then he became aware of an effort that his identity-maolot was making. It was a strange sort of effort because it was neither physical, mental, nor emotional. It

187

was something deeper and older than such things and all the maolots following the herd were making it at once.

It was an effort that reached out to encompass, to touch everything. All things moved to it. The earth breathed, a billion microscopic things broke free to wander, the night winds patterned, and overall concentration wove this into a movement and a happening. It was part of blood and bone and soil and seed and air. It was like a great, silent medicine song in which the singer was the music and the music was everything.

The moonlight dimmed slightly. Jef's maolot glanced up and saw a thin veil blurring the light of the single, visible moon. About the trotting herd the grassland was not as clearly to be seen as before. The air was cooler now, with a slightly damp chill.

Something in Jef exulted. It was reaching him through Mikey and through his identity-maolot, but it was originating in him, also. It was a glory—the glory of what was right—the glory of feeling, of knowing and doing. It was as it always had been, always must be, and always would be until the final death. His head swam with feelings so strong it blurred his vision.

The wisent were trotting a little faster now, snorting uneasily. There were the beginnings of fear in them, but also being variforms, they were touched themselves by what was happening, what Jef was feeling. Only the men on the trucks did not feel it. Their voices were low but steady in their talking. Jef's identity-maolot glanced upward again. The moon was almost invisible now—a cloudy blur of light, no more, and the grassland was becoming murky and dark, with little tendrils of mist clinging to the tops of the grass stems.

One of the other maolots sounded.

Another answered.

The searchlights flared out in all directions, but the mist baffled and broke their beams. The wisent coughed and trotted faster. There was a hint of panic in their going.

The maolot calls sounded again.

The herd's trotting broke at last into the beginnings of a run.

The mist thickened. Now the men on a truck at one side of the herd could not make out the truck on the other side of the herd. The truck leading could see none of the trucks behind it. The rearguard truck saw only wisents close before it.

Human voices were making themselves heard, but the sense of their words was lost in the increasing noise the panicking herd was making. Searchlights stabbed out and blunted themselves on the thickening mist, worse than useless beyond a few meters because the light from them spread in the hanging water droplets and blinded the men operating them. The wisent were now in a head-long run and the bass dronings of the maolot voices were sounding in the obscurity right alongside the trucks and among the fleeing herbivores.

Lasers crackled blindly and wildly in the darkness, finding no maolots. Men on the trucks were yelling at each other now, finally infected by the thick aura of fear rising from the terrified wisents.

The maolots sounded all together—and suddenly the attack was on. The maolot that was both himself and Jef came out of the mist like a silent thunderbolt, up and over the rear gate of one of the trucks. The men around the mounted laser saw a carnivore the size of a small horse climbing in among them, and fell over backward in a scramble to escape. The maolot landed in the center of the truck bed. One massive paw slapped down on the laser and beat it from its mount, smashing stock and mechanism—and the maolot leaped over the farther side of the truck in the same instant, landing among the herd.

Through the herd he ran, slapping right and left at the necks of the wisents as he passed. Each slap sent a wisent bowling with a broken neck. So he raged on, as around him the other adults were also raging, killing as they went until they had beaten their way through and over

189

the mass of bodies, blindly struggling to escape.

Abruptly the maolots were on the other side of the herd and their job was done. The trucks were headed in all directions, the drivers now as panic-stricken as the wisents had been. The herd was a herd no longer. Instead it was innumerable terror-ridden animals scattering out from the point of their terror, ready to run until they dropped and not to be gathered together again, even with trucks, in under a matter of days.

The mist was dissipating. It cleared and the moonlight came clearly to illuminate the scene again, picking out a few—surprisingly few for all that wild panic—motionless dark shapes that were the bodies of slain wisent. The small number that lay dead would be written off without thought by the owner of this particular herd. Not so easy to write off, however, Jef understood suddenly through Mikey, would be the surviving beasts, whom no combination of drovers would soon be able to drive again in a northerly direction toward the newly cleared patch of forest. If the new patch of cleared land was to be populated with grazing wisents to prove the herd owners' need for it, new stock that had not lived through this night with the maolots must be gathered from much further south and a new drive begun. And by that time the satellite passing daily over this part of Everon would have recorded on its cameras a newly cleared area that had gone untenanted for several weeks.

The work of the older maolots was done. They turned away on a line of march that would intersect in a few hours with the route along which Mikey was carrying Jef.

Emotionally drained beyond anything in his life by the experience of riding in the mind of the mature maolot, physically worn out by riding Mikey and hollow with hunger, Jef slipped into a state that was part-faint, part-doze, lying along Mikey's back. He kept waking momentarily with the fear that he was slipping off. Finally Mikey got through to him.

I'll keep your arms and legs tight, Mikey told him. You won't fall.

Relieved, he let his mind relax, and actual sleep overtook him. He remembered how he had read about soldiers falling asleep on their feet while marching, but continuing to march. He had found it hard to believe, then. But now he accepted the fact that he could sleep while riding.

When he woke at last, it was to find Mikey descending a steep, sparsely wooded slope, apparently one wall of a small rocky hollow in what seemed to be mountainous terrain. The air was cold and thin and it was just about daybreak; bright enough to see, but with the sun not yet showing over the surrounding heights of rock. Below them a tiny stream ran through a hollow. They were approaching that stream and, in a moment, they came through a barrier of scraggly native trees and stepped into a small open space beside the stream.

A camp was waiting, sleeping bags laid out and a fire crackling. At the fire sat Jarji and Martin, Jarji facing Jef as he and Mikey arrived, and Martin with his back to them.

Jarji jumped to her feet, and Martin rose, turning about a fraction of a second later, as Mikey came to a halt and Jef slid off the maolot's back, trying to stand upright. His arms and legs were stiff and he had to struggle to stay on his feet.

"Jef—" began Jarji. She stopped and sat down again deliberately by the fire. "So there you are, Robini."

"There he is indeed, Jarji," said Martin, now facing Jef also. "Welcome, Mr. Robini. We've been most patiently waiting you."

Something popped in Jef.

"Damn you both to hell!" he exploded. "What's the matter with me? Am I the only one on Everon no one'll call by his first name?"

His knees gave way and he sat down, more or less cross-legged, on the ground where he had been standing.

A sudden, warm, good feeling was flooding all through him. He was aware of the other two coming hastily toward him, helping him up, helping him over to a seat by the fire; but he paid no attention to what they were saying, his mind was so full of a new discovery.

So this was what it felt like, he was thinking to himself. He had actually done it. After being formally addressed and verbally kicked about by these two from his first meetings with them. This time his resentment had not merely once again been buried in the non-feeling of a dreary indifference. Nor had it turned in him, curdling into the acid of that sad loneliness that had been his substitute for proper outrage all these years. He had actually gone off like a bomb. Without thinking.

Of course, he had not been really angry. Just irritated. But he had reacted all the same—snapped back instinctively, just as anyone might do. Now they were fussing over him in reaction—if two such unlikely characters as Jarji and Martin could be imagined fussing—trying to make him feel better. He could not quite make out what they were saying because he was so woozy with exhaustion, but their words were unimportant. It was their intent that mattered and that was now coming through clearly.

Actually, he felt fine. Weak, of course—but in all other ways he felt wonderful. The truth was, the way he was feeling was almost too good—there was a terrible sensation of power in knowing he was able to blow up at people like that. Now that he knew he might take anybody's head off for no reason at all, he would have to watch himself, be careful not to let the tendency get out of hand. He would not want to get into the habit of riding roughshod over others at the slightest excuse . . .

16

HE WOKE. He had never been so exhausted. Coming fully alert at last, Jef could not remember clearly past the moment in which he had been so ridiculously pleased with himself, on discovering he could lose his temper like anyone else. Beyond that there had been nothing but a dark valley of sodden sleep, interrupted only briefly by a few blurred periods in which he had woken for short, necessary moments and been helped out of his sleeping bag, then back into it again. But these had been only minutes at a stretch.

Meanwhile, time had moved—at least one day and one night had shuttered by and around him the world had patiently waited. Martin and Jarji had tended the camp and occasionally got him to swallow some soup or hot drink made from one of the Everon herbs. Mikey had lain by the fire as if on guard, paws crossed, neck erect and blind head turned toward Jef. He had been in that position whenever Jef had been awake enough to notice. In effect, around Jef the universe in general had seemed to pause, waiting for him to wake and rejoin it.

He had never been so exhausted. It was as if his bones had been dissolved and a vast emptiness had taken the place of his normal interior organs. He had been as weak as a baby sparrow. And yet . . . now that this was all behind him, he felt a great and peaceful sense of achievement. He was warm with it, almost as if he had gorged himself on a great meal of learning and was now busy digesting it, finding out what it actually was he had taken in.

He was aware of knowing more than his conscious mind could handle. He had been exposed to a great deal more of information than he could have identified or expressed to anyone. He could feel it there, bulging against his awareness; but so far he had only the most limited understanding of what it could mean.

Awake, now, he lay watching Mikey and the other two moving about the camp. The light-headedness from his recent weakness was undoubtedly to blame, he told himself, but he found he was deeply enjoying the simple activity of lying and watching the others. It was as if their ordinary movements about the camp were parts in some intricate ballet, commissioned solely for his pleasure.

Martin glanced over and saw him watching.

"Well now, Mr. Robini—Jef," he said, coming over and sitting down cross-legged, facing Jef in the sleeping bag, "here you are, alive again."

Jef gazed at him for a long moment.

"Yes," Jef said. His voice emerged from his throat a little rusty and effortful, but he found he could talk comfortably enough. "And speaking of being here, what are you and Jarji doing in this place?"

Jarji, hearing their voices, also came over. She stood looking down at them for a second; then, almost reluctantly, sat down herself.

"Back to normal, are you?" she said to Jef.

"Yes. Thanks," he told her.

She looked a little disconcerted.

"Nobody did anything special for you." But her tone was a good deal softer than her words might have indicated.

"I'm not surprised Mikey was able to find you," Jef said to both of them. "But how did you get here? And what are you doing together?"

"Well, now!" said Martin. "Is there some law against

our being in the same place at the same time?"

"Never mind," said Jarji to Jef. "We're together because I flew out of Beau's camp with him."

"True enough. No plan of mine, either," said Martin.
"I reached my flyer and found her already there, waiting
for me."

"But I thought you were in the bunkhouse—" Jef
stared at her.

Jarji snorted.

"Did you think I was just going to sit there with them
all around me, so that I couldn't do a thing?" she said.
"I told them I wanted to go to sleep early. Then, when
they weren't looking, I left a blanket rolled up under my
covers and slipped out. But Beau's got some woodswise
people among that group of his. One of them heard me
going and came after me. I had to take the first chance to
get clear—which was Martin's craft."

"That doesn't explain why you're both here, though,"
said Jef.

"Waiting for you, of course," said Jarji.

"Waiting for me?" Jef stared at her. "But how could
you know Mikey would bring me here . . ."

He ran down into silence.

"Ah, you've touched it, haven't you?" Martin said.
"Your Mikey knows we're friends of yours—on a world
where you've few of them, as I don't need to point out.
We're in the only pass to the high country in either direction for a few hundred kilometers. You had to come
this way; and when the maolot found us waiting here, he
brought you to us."

"How'd you know I'd be keeping on toward the high
country?"

"It's your stubborn nature, now," said Martin. "How
could we doubt that having started for that place called
the Valley of Thrones, on that map you told the Constable and myself about, you'd keep on in spite of all?"

Something about this answer woke a feeling of suspicion in Jef's mind, though he could not exactly identify what about it should so affect him. He tried to remember when he had told Martin and the Constable about the Valley of Thrones. Yes, it had been on the morning he had left for the upcountry. His hope then had been that the Constable might have a more correct map he could use to find the Valley; but Armage had evidently never heard of the place, and he had dismissed it as being any one of a thousand of such areas in the Everon wilds, which might have one name or several, depending on the number of humans who had passed by them.

If it was not the reference to the Valley of Thrones, then what had bothered him in what Martin had just said? Jef could not think what it might be. But something had.

"Why would Mikey bring me to you, even if he knew you were here?" He looked over at Mikey and felt a wave of reassurance, broadcast by the maolot—which was heartwarming, but hardly informative.

"You came in pretty chewed up," Jarji said almost sharply. "He may have thought you needed some of your own kind to keep you alive."

Jef switched his attention to her.

"Why are you still here?" he asked bluntly. "I'm all right now."

"With Beau and his people blocking my way back downcountry, where can I go but to the mountains?"

Looking at her, he suddenly had a strong feeling that there was at least a chance she had stayed because she was concerned about him; but of course there would be no hope of getting her to admit anything like that.

The memory of the nighttime drive and the counterattack of the maolots passed over his mind like the smoke of the campfire.

"On the way here I saw the wisent ranchers clearing forest and trying to move a herd into it," he told them. A gust of his rediscovered ability to anger shook him suddenly. "This whole planet's at war! The wisent ranchers on one side, Beau and the woodspeople on the other!"

"Don't go thinking Beau and his bunch speak for all us woods folk," said Jarji energetically. "And if it comes to that, even what Beau is, he was driven to."

"Do you know he's trying to import an illegal shipload of eland embryos?" Jef looked over at Martin. "You know about that. Tell her."

"Tell me nothing!" flared Jarji. "I'm no part of what Beau does. I just said he was driven to it in the first place. And he was! But what he's doing now's no part of me, or my family, or anybody else in the forest that I know. The trouble with you, Jef, is you've never been on a new world, never gone out to a new world, never probably even thought what it's like to go out to a new world. There's no going back to Earth from someplace like our Everon. Even if you could go back, you wouldn't. It's live or die with what you have—and that makes things different. It also makes it our business, not yours."

"No," said Jef, almost to his own surprise. "I'm hooked to Everon, now. Whether it's something more than my connection with Mikey I don't know. But I'll tell you this— I may be closer to what Everon really is than you or anyone else, even if I did just get off the ship a few days ago. Maybe I haven't lived here; but I'm willing to bet neither of you've ever seen what I saw, between the time I left Beau's camp and when I ended up here!"

On a surge of unexpected emotion he pulled himself out of the sleeping bag and stood up in his rumpled pants and shirt to tell them about the wisent drive and his long ride on Mikey.

" . . . But it's more than that, between me and Everon," he wound up. "On my first day here I stood on the Constable's porch and watched a shower that turned into a hailstorm; and, even then, I was feeling something. Maybe it was those eight years of growing up with Mikey, as I say. I don't know. But this world and I can talk to each other, in a way I can't even explain to you."

He paused, almost as surprised by his own words as they must be to hear them. Suddenly self-conscious, he wound up the lecture hurriedly.

"So," he said, "it's my business, too, what the wisent ranchers and the woodspeople and the officials down in Everon City are doing. I couldn't be outside it and leave it alone, if I wanted to."

He stopped, aware of having more or less run down rather than wound up with a strong, crashing statement. He half expected to find Jarji on top of him the minute he closed his mouth, ready and eager to cram his words back down his throat; but she did not, only stood frowning at him.

"That's a fine sensitivity you have there. Very fine," said Martin after a very short moment of silence. "Now maybe you'll tell us how it briefed you on all the economic and political struggles involved in this same matter with the woodspeople, the wisent ranchers and all those other fine gentlemen and ladies in government down in Everon City. Indeed, maybe this insight of yours is just the thing to cut through all that tangle of enmity and competition that's been keeping us baffled here, and produce an immediate solution, acceptable and fair to all!"

Jef opened his mouth, then closed it again. But Jarji turned on Martin.

"Why don't you tell him, then," she demanded, "instead of standing back and crowing over him because he doesn't know?"

"It's not something he could learn in a day—let alone in a few minutes," answered Martin.

"How do you know?" She swung back to face Jef. "I just told you it's not everybody! Most of the woodspeople can get along with everyone else. So can most of the wisent ranchers; even if they mostly haven't taken the trouble to think beyond their own side of things. But it's Beau and his group, it's the sell-out ranchers, the politi-

cians, and others like that who keep all this trouble
going, and make more when this starts to die down. Sure,
you'd have to live here ten years to learn all the ins and
outs and who's with who, and for what, just like *he*
says—"

She jerked a thumb at Martin.

"—But all you really need to know is that it's not the
real planters, not the ones who look to see forty generations of their descendents here. It's the sell outs that go
messing it all up for everyone else."

"Sell outs?" Jef said. The word was awkward on his
tongue.

"It means what it says. You don't know anything, do
you?" Jarji told him. "You think nobody ever went out to
plant a new world with anything but stars in their eyes
and a noble pioneering spirit, don't you? Of course you
do. That's what they all think, back on Earth; because
that's what all the ads and the articles say. Well, let me
tell you—no one ever pulled their life up by the roots and
went out to make it all over again in a howling wilderness
just out of some noble feeling. My folks came out here
because they couldn't breathe in Earth air, because they
couldn't—even with both of them working—have anything more than a third-rate living place. They came out
here because they saw there was no place decent for me
and my brothers and sisters to grow up in, back on
Earth. They came out and went through all the hell it
took to stay alive and build something here, just so they
could live for some purpose—and we, their kids, could
live for some purpose, too."

She stopped.

"I see," said Jef.

"No, you don't. You just think you do. Now, listen,"
said Jarji. "That's us—what we are, we Hillegases and
the rest of the real planters. But besides us there's other
people who came out, with other things they wanted.
Some of them, like the Constable and—well, maybe even

Beau; though, as I say, he had reason for what he did, to start with—came out here wanting to run things. They didn't have what it took to run things on Earth, but they figured to run things big, here. Others came to get rich, figuring to stay just to build up something, sell out and move on."

"Sell out? But you can't transfer planetary currency off-world and have it worth anything," said Jef, "except maybe for some of the strong Earth currencies, and interstellar credits—and private parties can't use interstellar credits. Only a bank or a government—"

"How thick is that head of yours?" said Jarji. "There's a few million ways to cash in, if you've really got something to cash: and the longer you hold something you've developed from the raw planet state, the more you've got to cash in. For every one like my folks, there's a thousand who haven't got the guts to be in the first wave of immigration; but they do have the wealth—in Earth and other world currencies—to lay back and wait until a planet is developed and safe. *Then* they buy in, in comfort, and the more they have to buy with, the longer they can wait to use it. Hell, didn't you know there're regular underground exchanges on Earth, where you can make illegal currency transfers, or get immediate quotes on any land or development you want, on any planet, anywhere? And with something like that going you think there aren't some who come in with the first wave, just planning to build up and sell out, then go on to the next new world they can find ready, and do it again? Do something like that three times over, Mister, and make it pay; and you can end up like a king on the last world you hit."

She paused to look at him narrowly.

"Of course," she said, "that takes guts—more guts than the late buyers have. But is it any wonder that we've got some people here who don't give a damn for anyone but themselves and their own profit, and are willing to tear everything apart for everyone else just to make their

200

property here as rich as they can, before comes time for them to sell out?"

"No," said Jef. She was right, of course.

"Certainly," said Martin, "that's it, in principle. But it's not by principle that situations like this have to be dealt with. It's by the effects of that principle—and those are none so simple."

Jef turned on him.

"You're still claiming to be a John Smith, are you?"

"That's what I am." Martin met his gaze dead-on.

"The Constable doesn't seem to think so. Beau seems to have an entirely different picture of you. And what they both think matches with that other set of identification papers I saw."

"In my luggage, that is, with never an apology or a feeling that you had no right to look," said Martin. Jef felt uncomfortable.

"You've got to admit you don't look or act like a John Smith."

"So you said once before," said Martin softly. "But what you mean is, I don't look or act as you imagined a John Smith. And both Jarji and I have just been pointing out how little your picture of things has to do with the facts."

"If you're one of the E. Corps top representatives, why don't you do something about what's going on, instead of hobnobbing with Armage and tangling yourself up with Beau, pretending in both cases to be something you're not?"

"Because," Martin said, "as I continue to tell you, matters are not that simple. Not just matters here on Everon. Matters on Earth. Matters wherever our race of humans are to be found."

"You've got the authority and the power—"

"That's just what I don't have," said Martin, "in fact."

Jef stared at him.

"Oh, to be sure, the powers are there for me and those like me, in theory. But have you any idea what would actually happen if I was injudicious enough to actually recommend quarantine for a world like this, with billions of credits tied up in it—back on Earth as well as here? In theory I've the power to right any wrong. But in fact I have to sail by the available winds in all I do. Did you think we were heroes, as the advertising legends say, we John Smiths? Just the opposite. We're trained villains, indeed we are, and measure our success by the depths of our villainies, performed in what we believe—but can never be sure—are good causes."

The emotion that had brought Jef up out of the sleeping bag to his feet, had begun to drain out of him. His knees felt weak enough to begin trembling.

"I've got to sit down," he said. He looked around. "Why don't we sit down by the fire?"

He led the way over to the fire and dropped down cross-legged next to it. It was good to be sitting, and the heat of the fire felt good to a body that had grown used to the cocoon of warmth provided by the sleeping bag.

Martin and Jarji joined him. He felt his left shoulder bumped from behind and discovered that Mikey had moved up and was now lying crosswise, right behind him. He leaned back against the backrest of the massively muscled side.

"I'm sorry," Jef said, looking across at Martin. "But I can't believe in your being what you say you are."

"You've a good deal of company" was all Martin offered by way of explanation.

But now Jarji was on the other side.

"That's right," she said to Jef. "You don't know anything about it, but that's all right. Just go ahead and make up your mind anyway."

"I'm willing to listen to him," said Jef doggedly. "He just hasn't told me anything."

"Have you asked him to?"

"Look," said Jef, "I may not be as fast with my tongue as either of you two—"

"Have you ever asked him?"

"All right," said Jef. He turned to Martin. "Tell me why you really are a John Smith."

Martin raised his eyebrows.

"I take it that's a question?"

"Of course," said Jef.

"In that spirit, then," said Martin, picking up a half-burned branch and using it to poke the fire, "I'll answer. I'm a John Smith because I'm doing a John Smith's job —in the only way that's available to me, or anyone, to do that job."

"Why can't you do it the way you're supposed to? Who's stopping you?"

"The human race is stopping me," said Martin. "You heard Jarji tell you about the human truths behind the people who plant a new world. Multiply that by the human truths behind all those on all the inhabited worlds —particularly behind those on the world called Earth— and you might begin to see for yourself why I can't do my job as you and the fictioneers of the popular press would see me doing it."

"All right," said Jef. "I can see you having troubles. I can't see you not being able at all to use your legal powers."

Martin sighed a little, looking at the fire.

"You grew up on Earth," he said. "What's it like there? I know, it's not easy to stand back and look at something when you're down inside it. But you've had a little time on Everon, now, and you claim to have been much enlarged by it. Tell me what you think of Earth from where you stand at the moment."

"Well," said Jef, "it's crowded, of course—particularly compared to a completely open, new world like this. It'd be bound to be."

He stopped. Neither Martin nor Jarji said anything.

"Of course," Jef said, "it's crowded. If you like, it's overcrowded—by definition. There're too many people, and not enough room. So there're too many restrictions. So competition is unbelievable; and there's very little left of what the wild Earth was to begin with—compared to a world like this one where everything's still natural. We live on concrete, and inside walls, back there. We have to. We breathe artificially cleaned air, because there's no breathable air that hasn't been artificially cleaned. The weather's got to be controlled to make sure the crops produce. People have to fit patterns, or there'd be chaos."

He found himself talking with a sense of relief that he had not believed was in him. He was saying things he had never said before, and it struck him suddenly that they were things he had wanted to say for many years.

"The people—" he said. "Maybe it's not their fault, but because of the way it is, if there's rough competition here, it's twice as rough there—only where it's in hot blood here, it's in cold, there. You step on other people back on Earth, because you know the machinery will chew up whoever's underneath, and that'll be you if you don't. Nobody talks about neighborliness back there— and means anything by it. There's no room for neighborliness, even if you wanted to practice it."

He looked at Jarji.

"You remember saying to me 'here we call it neighborliness—' or something like that, when I asked you why you were going along with me to Beau's camp? You know, I didn't really understand what you meant by the word. I've never known any neighborliness. I've never known any real kindness between strangers. To tell you the truth, now that I stop to think of it, I've never known any real kindness between individuals anywhere, except inside my own family. It's not that people were deliberately unkind, it's just that nobody had anything left

204

over, after the struggle to stay alive and make a living."

He stopped, to listen to the echo of his own words in his head.

"No, you're right," he said. "It's not very happy, back on Earth. Oh, maybe it's all right for the people who are on top of the heap—the political heads, the people in power wherever power is. No, I take that back. Not even for those people because even when they're at the top, they bargain and trade off with other people in power for what they want; and in the end they're caught up in the machinery like everyone else. Yes, by God!"

He turned sharply to Martin.

"It's the machinery—all the social and governmental machinery—that's the real villain back there!"

Martin nodded.

"It is, indeed," he said. "I don't know what the figure is now, but less than half a dozen years ago, over thirty percent of the job-holding population was working for one organ of government or another. Some twenty-odd percent were involved in the private power structure—in banking, the big cooperatives and corporations, twenty percent were in private occupation or illegals. It's a worldwide community of organizations and bureaucracies, our Earth, nowadays; and such have no human feelings or responses, for all they've got human parts to their mechanisms."

He poked at the fire. Jef waited for him to say more, but he did not. Jef opened his mouth to speak, but found himself without anything certain to say. He was still shocked at the emotional reaction in him that Martin's earlier question had evoked.

"What other way could it be?" he said at last.

"I don't know," said Martin. He threw the stick into the fire. "But some other way has to be found, or there's no justification for the human race to exist. Are we to be nothing more than a devouring plague upon the universe? All we can hope is that another way does turn up

—maybe on one of the new worlds. And there's the hope."

"The hope?" Jef echoed.

"Of course." Martin looked up from the fire at him. "I can't do the job I was trained and sent out to do. The E. Corps is a bureaucracy—in your words, it has to be—just one of the organizations. When you get right down to it, E. Corps doesn't really care what happens to Everon or any other world. All it cares about is that it, itself, goes on forever, getting more and more powerful, adding more and more staff, controlling more and more wealth and resources. Aside from that it has no desires—and no morals. Nor have the people in power within its mechanism—or else they'd not stay in power long. Others who agreed better with the soullessness of the organization would displace them, being an easier fit for their positions."

He paused. Jef could still think of nothing to say.

"So I can't crack down officially on illegal practices on Everon," said Martin. "I can't, because if you trace those illegal practices home to where they start, you find them rooted in the very organizations and the people in power in those organizations that sent me out here. My superiors aren't going to let me cut off their nose to spite their face—oh, not that they'd break the law themselves. But there's no end of ways of frustrating me within the regulations."

"Then—you might as well not be here," Jef said.

"Not at all, not at all!" said Martin with a thin grin. "I can still do anything I can get away with—illegally. And so I do. Under the cover of being what I am not, I work for what I believe in in ways that my cover specifically rejects and condemns."

Jef shook his head.

"And what do you believe in?" he asked at last.

"I believe," said Martin slowly, and he looked from Jef to Jarji and back again before going on, "I believe there's a way out. I believe that people deserve better than the mess they've got us into back on Earth, and if we can just keep them alive long enough, they'll find a way to be something more than selfish animals in clothes. So that's my real work. I do what I can to keep things going until that day."

"What are you doing now, then?" asked Jef. "And what's it all got to do with me—or Jarji?"

"A secret shared," said Martin with one of his thin grins, "is a secret no longer. You'll have to content yourself with the fact that I tell you I'm your friend."

"Still—" began Jef, and was interrupted by another shove from Mikey's broad head against his shoulder. "Mikey—not now!"

He turned, and felt a sudden powerful wave of feeling from the maolot, impacting in that same area of his perceptions that had already been sensitized by his long ride and the wisent drive.

"What is it?" asked Jarji sharply.

"I think he wants me to leave again—" said Jef, still watching Mikey. "No, Mikey. Not now. Tomorrow, maybe."

Mikey's closed eyes stared directly at Jef's face. The wave of feeling emanating from him intensified.

"Tomorrow!" said Jef, out loud to him. "I've just come to after the last trip. I need more rest; and food—"

He broke off and looked around. It was late afternoon and the blue of the sky was dulling to gray in the east.

"Mikey, I've got to eat and rest."

He was not at all sure how he was managing to interpret levels of specific meaning into the flow of emotion he was getting from Mikey, but he got the very clear impression from Mikey that besides the urgency of their leaving there were reasons he should not, in any case, eat anything.

"Why not?"

207

No explanation was forthcoming, only a renewed, overwhelming pressure to leave, and to leave without eating.

"He wants me to go right away," said Jef, turning helplessly to Jarji and Martin. They looked back at him in silence for a long moment, and then Jarji spoke.

"Well," she said. "What are you going to do?"

Jef opened his mouth, took a deep breath and shook his head, wearily.

"I don't know—yes, I do," he said, getting slowly to his feet as Mikey also rose. "I can't let him down. For some reason it's more important than anything else to him. I don't know why—but I've got to go."

"Wait a minute," Jarji swung aside to the pile of equipment and supplies, a little way from the fire. "I'll get some supplies together for you."

"No supplies—I don't know why that, either," said Jef. "But he acts as if it's a matter of life or death. I'm sorry. Thanks anyway."

Stiffly, he began to climb on to the waiting Mikey's back. Jarji had halted and half-turned back to face him. Her face was hard.

"You sure your head's working right?" she asked.

"I'm sure," said Jef, now on Mikey's back. "I'm sorry, Jarji. I've just got to go along with him, no matter how crazy it seems. It's not just that I owe it to him, after all these years—it's just that after that ride I told you about, I know he's got reasons for what he wants. I don't know what they are, but I know now they've got to be good reasons."

He looked from her to Martin.

"Maybe you'll see me again before you expect," he said, and tried to grin.

"We'd better," said Jarji.

"We will, I think," said Martin. "I've a feeling you can trust this Mikey of yours."

As if these last words had tripped a trigger releasing

him, Mikey turned and moved off through the trees. He was following the course of the creek by the camp, upstream. They would be heading through the pass that led on to the mountains.

There was nothing for Jef to do but hold on. Gradually he recognized that, once again, Mikey was causing his arms and legs to hold on instinctively. There was no danger of falling off, then, and no duty on him but to ride. Where Mikey was getting the energy to carry him so, without food on his part either, there was no way of telling.

After a while the day waned into darkness. Clinging without will to Mikey's working back, Jef found himself falling into intermittent dozes that finally flowed together into full sleep.

17

HE WOKE AT LAST to find Mikey standing still. As Jef blinked in the dim light around them, Mikey sat down and Jef slid off the maolot's back. He landed with a jolt, tried to stand up, and grunted with the sudden pain of movement.

His body felt like wood and each muscle twanged with agony on being stressed. He hobbled to a large boulder and sat down.

They were in a small, rocky depression holding a dark blue lake that was hardly more than an acre or two in area. Above the walls of the depression, mountain peaks stood up in all directions. The air was cold and thin; and it was just about daybreak, bright enough to see, but with the sun not up yet. Only a scattering of coniferlike Everon trees interrupted the rubbled slopes around the lake. As he watched, a small breeze ruffled the blue, lake surface and a second later touched cool fingers to his face and hands.

Jef woke suddenly to a terrible thirst. He pushed himself up from the boulder, staggered for a dozen steps or so down to the water's edge and fell on his face there. He drank deeply, and the stone-cold water made each tooth in his head ache separately, but his body seemed to expand like a sponge with the inflowing of the moisture.

Having satisfied thirst, he sat up and looked around at Mikey, who was standing now just behind him.

"Where are we?" Jef asked. "What's this place?"

The response he got indicated a distance yet to go. Mikey stepped around him to the water's edge and drank in his turn, crouching like a cat, but sucking up the water, rather than lapping it.

"Why are we stopping, then?" Jef asked, when Mikey was done.

Mikey's blind eyes turned toward him. An impression of an inability emanated from him, which puzzled Jef until suddenly his understanding awoke.

"You mean you can't carry me any farther." He was abruptly overwhelmed with guilt. It had been hard enough on him, riding. Granted that Mikey was now incredibly strong—to turn himself into a riding animal carrying a hundred and eighty pounds Earth-weight for over twelve hours, on top of having done an even heavier carrying job just a few days earlier, was incredible.

But Mikey had read his reaction and was now disagreeing with it.

"I don't understand—" began Jef; and then he did. It was not that Mikey was becoming more comprehensible. It was rather as if Jef was developing a stronger insight. He was beginning, he found, to interpret Mikey's emanations with an almost occult skill. It was as if the fatigue and lightheadedness from lack of food that he was feeling had touched him with the abilities of a seer.

"You mean," he said, "that from here on it's not possible to carry me over the terrain we'll be facing. We both have to go on foot. That's fine. That's quite all right. It'll feel good to me to walk for a change. . . ."

He was hearing his own words as if they were being spoken by someone else a little way off. Now that he had let himself notice it, he was lightly shocked to realize how hungry and exhausted he was.

"I don't know how far I can hike, though," he said.

Reassurance from Mikey.

"If only I had something to eat."

Negative. Not only should Jef not eat, there was nothing to eat.

"Can I rest a little while, first?"

That was all right—for a while. Mikey would like to rest, too.

They sat while day came to the sky overhead and the lake and the rocky hollow before them took on its full three-dimensional depths and shadows. Finally Mikey got to his feet. Jef tried to follow; but he tottered, once he was upright, and only kept himself from falling by grabbing at Mikey's solid shoulder.

"No, no, I'm all right," he reassured the maolot. "Just stiff. I ought to be able to walk that out of me."

Mikey led off through a narrow gap in the rocks that closed the far end of the mountain cup. The gap led into a narrow track or trail on which it was not possible for the two of them to go side by side. The way they followed led across steep slopes, so that the rock on one side of them would fall sharply away and on the other, a near-vertical rock face would rise, so that they were half-climbing, half-walking most of the time. In addition to the angle of the slopes on which they traveled, their footing was often on small rock or gravel, which slid and rolled as weight was placed upon it, so that at almost any minute a failure of balance could have sent either of them into a steep slide or tumble down a long pitch, and possibly over a cliff to a certain death-fall.

Between the weakness brought on by his fatigue and the uncertain footing, each step Jef made had to be considered individually before he took it. The effort seemed enormous. At any moment he would have believed that he had only another dozen steps left in him. And yet he went on, and on. Mikey was now in the lead, his four legs giving him a greater certainty of traction on the untrustworthy footing. As they went, the sun rose but the day did not warm greatly. The air was thin, and while there was blue sky to be seen, clouds were plentiful enough so that the brief periods of warmth when the sun shone would be cut short within minutes as a new vapor mass blocked its rays. A light, chill breeze blew steadily from the northwest.

In spite of all this the exercise and the moments of sun warmth began finally to reach and soothe Jef's stiff muscles. The pain of traveling ceased to be active and important. It moved back into the general structure of things. He began to notice the country through which they traveled and see beyond the space of the immediate next footfall.

For the first time he began to be aware of a difference that had come over him. It was a contradictory difference —at one moment he seemed to feel himself intensely within his body, and at the same time part way outside it. Now that his pain and the weariness had ceased to be important—they were still there, but it was easy to ignore them now—he was physically aware of the impacts upon his senses, to a degree he had never felt before in his life

The sunlight through the thin air, intermittent as it was, touched him with a warmth as precious as beaten gold. The chill breeze itself was as memorable as the taste of a strongly tannic, but unforgettable, wine. Altogether, the daylight showed him a world about him that possessed something like an added dimension. The solid bodies he looked at now appeared even more solid; he seemed to see more in rock and tree and mountain pinnacle or peak, than the eye could ordinarily discover. They seemed to reach off at one more right angle, giving a tesseractlike effect.

The sounds, few as they were—the rattle of pebbles underfoot, the thin singing of the wind, the far-off cry of one of Everon's birdlike native flying creatures, the buzz of occasional insects—were not only richer than they had ever sounded to his ear, but laden with new meaning. It was meaning he could not yet interpret, but it was so much more than he had ever read before in any such sound, that the information of it felt as if it must bulk like the contents of a book, compared to the brief information printed on its spine and front cover.

So it was, also, with the color around him. To a casual

glance he was moving through a drab landscape of grey rock, in shades of dark to light. Only occasionally was there the blue or silver glint of water, the dark green of upland vegetation, or the grey to brown of the trunks of native Everon trees. A tiny insect with green wings, a birdlike shape as a spot of dusky red against the sky, the sky itself with its hard, high-altitude blue and the unvarying white puffs of the swiftly moving clouds—these were the full range of the dramatic colors around him. Yet he could not have responded more to all that he saw if he had walked in the heart of a rainbow.

Each color that he found sang to him: rich and incredibly beautiful in its own right. Incredibly alive, as well. He recognized, for the first time in his life, the fact that no color was perceived as an invariant. Each one changed constantly, with each minute shift of light upon it, each change taking place in a fraction of a second, so that it was as if each color he looked at had a living, breathing existence of its own, in which it evolved—not merely in itself—but in him, who was resolving it from second to second into terms of human sight and memory.

On a similar level his areas of exposed skin sent him living, pulsating richnesses of sensation in the areas of temperature, pressure, and texture. These, and the sound and color images, blended together into a symphony of physical experience, echoing off each other, so that in looking at the trunk of a tree he passed at a distance of ten meters, he could, without touching it, literally feel the texture of its outer skin, the waxy sharpness of its coniferlike needles. The pressure and coolness of the air on his lips brought him a taste that was, at the same time, physically nonexistent and incredibly real, like the silent but real melody that violin strings might send forth into another dimension as they waited in the ecstatic anticipation of being played by magnificently capable fingers. Even the weariness and discomfort of his body had a meaning and a quality beyond ordinary perception, so that even this seemed to carry the burden of a message beyond ordinary communications.

But in the same moments that this great wealth of awareness was flooding him continuously, he was conscious of standing a little apart from himself. It was a sensation, like that of the richness of sensory input, that he had never experienced in his life before—and which even now he had difficulty believing could be possible. For it was a contradiction in terms. He had the benefit of detachment without being detached.

The detachment was one that seemed to open to him a great increase in inner vision. It seemed that never before in his life had his mind had such an ability, space and freedom to really process what life had fed into it from the moment of his birth. Now it could do so. Now there was a timelessness to all things and a liberty to work with them. He had escaped from the narrow confines that were the logical front of his mind, where thoughts had to come as if through a narrow door, one at a time.

Now, as if on a great plain, he saw moving together, milling about, all the things he had ever learned or come to understand. He looked down on that plain from some height, but with a telescopic vision that could see clearly the smallest detail of what was below. All that he knew was spread out before him like a horde of moving and mingled individuals; and, slowly, as he looked down, he began to sort, combine, and resolve the unstructured multitude into a gathering of coherent meaning. Gradually the information took form, acquiring the shapes of knowledges he had never imagined could exist, and offering a hope of answers beyond present conception. It was a hope that opened the available universe from something infinitesimal to something literally without limit, infinite and eternal in promise as well as in dimension.

His life came together for him. Everon came together for him. In his imagination he could now easily envision the hailstorm he had watched from the Constable's porch. The cloudbursts that made the floods of which he had heard, that had washed away dams and bridges the humans on Everon had built. Now he found he had no trouble picturing the weather that had bred the storms that flattened crops, the eggs that had hatched into the insects that destroyed planted seeds and growing plants. In his mind's eye he found he could now see all of this— and he saw it in connection, integrated and related, while at the same time, physically, he drank in the sound, the sight, the touch of the mountain land through which he traveled, painfully and carefully, in the tracks of Mikey.

He was still lost in the wonder of what was happening to him and what he was doing with his awareness of that happening, when they came at last to a closed-end canyon, surrounded except at its entrance by vertical, unclimbable walls several hundred feet in height. A small stream sprang from beneath a large boulder against the rock face at the far end of the canyon; and at the sight of it, Jef woke to the thirst in him.

Its awakening laid such a strong claim upon him that he hardly reacted to the fact that at the canyon's far end, up against the solid wall of great rocks barring progress, there were half a dozen mature maolots, sitting or lying as if waiting for him and Mikey.

Jef stopped when he reached the stream, dropped flat at its edge and drank heavily. This water, like that in the lake, was icily cold; and it seemed to him, still caught up in the acuteness of his senses, to be the most beautiful drink he had ever tasted. Slaked, he sat up on his heels and looked around.

The maolots at the end of the canyon stayed, waiting. Whether Mikey helped or not, he did not know, but with a little effort he found he could focus in on each of them from some observation point only a few meters or centimeters away. He did so now—and once again he found that they would not let him see their eyes. Those eyes, when his observation closed with them, were either closed or averted from his point of view.

But Mikey was communicating with them.

Jef could sense that the others were answering Mikey, but he could not understand them, even to the limited extent that he understood Mikey. Each one, he realized now, was subtly different in its communication. There was an individualism to each of them that did not interfere with Mikey's understanding, but baffled his human mind. He was like someone who has learned from one person to speak a non-native language with what he thinks is comfort and ease; only to find himself baffled by individual differences in other speakers of that tongue, when he tried to talk with them.

Should they go on, now, Mikey was asking the others.

The answer, Jef gathered, was affirmative. He got to his feet and joined Mikey. Together they went up the canyon toward the maolots. As he got to the great, waiting creatures who still kept their eyes hooded or averted from his gaze, Mikey led the way to the right of a four-meter-high boulder directly behind the sentinels.

Following Mikey around the boulder, Jef discovered that the base of it stood away from the cliff behind it, and hid a triangular crack in the cliff, something like a natural tunnel leading through to daylight beyond. Along the floor of this tunnel ran the stream from which he had drunk earlier.

The opening was a good two meters high and no more than ten meters in length.

Mikey called Jef to follow. Jef, who had hesitated at the mouth of the tunnel, moved forward again. Entering into its shadow, he stepped into the flowing water and it closed icecold fingers around his ankles. Mikey was just ahead of him. He began to wade up the stream, feeling the current plucking lightly at the sodden, lower ends of his pants. Midway, the ceiling lowered and he had to duck his head. But a few steps farther it rose again and only a little distance farther he came out on to an open hillside, sloping down to a mass of weathered rock spires, which blocked his vision of what lay farther on and lower down.

Go on, he felt Mikey urging him.

He went ahead and Mikey came behind him. They started down the slope. Here, once more, there was loose rock underfoot, so that he had to concentrate on each step if he wanted to avoid turning an ankle or falling. Shortly he was in among the spires of weathered, grey-white rock. It was like being in a forest of stone. Here the loose rock was even deeper and more treacherous. Jef concentrated wholly on his footing, holding on to spires as he passed, feeling his way down. So occupied had he become that it was not until he paused to catch his breath, that he lifted his head and saw that a mist had moved in about him. He was surrounded by a soft, white dimness that made even the nearest of the rock spires into half-invisible, vaguely looming shapes, like enormously tall, fog-wreathed gravestones in some burial place.

Holding on to the spire beside which he had paused, he turned to speak to Mikey—but Mikey was not to be seen.

"Mikey!" he called.

His voice died in the mist without an answer.

Jef stood, holding to the cold rock of the spire. Mikey had been right behind him. There had been no sound, no indication that anything had happened to him. Jef opened his mouth to call once more, then closed it. Instead, he put all his strength into a non-physical reaching-out; and then stood, trying to feel for Mikey with the new sensitivity that had been growing in him since he landed on Everon.

After a moment he thought he did indeed feel Mikey—but at some distance off. He made another effort to bridge the gap between them by empathic rapport.

Faintly he sensed a response from Mikey, a feeling of sorrow and regret that he could not be with Jef at this time. It was not clear, but Jef got the impression that Mikey was telling him to go forward alone.

With that understanding, a new calmness filled him. He became certain that his going on alone from this point was inevitable, had been inevitable from the moment of his landing. Everything he had done from that moment, from the first sight of Everon that had arrested him at the head of the landing stairs, had directed him to this place and time in which he would have to go forward alone to whatever had been waiting for him from the beginning.

The realization brought a feeling of peace to him. He breathed deeply of the damp air, taking it into his lower lungs. He let go of the rock he was holding and went on down the slope.

As he went, the mist thickened; and he was not surprised that it did. The mist was as much a creature of this moment as the hailstorm had been that he had watched from the Constable's porch, and that other mist that had obscured the moonlight just before the maolots' attack on the wisent drive. Very soon he could see no more than the next spire closest to him. Then he could see nothing at all but whiteness. He continued to grope his way forward, feeling the slope still angling downward under his feet, until finally he began to realize that either he had come out from among the spires, or he was in some open area where they now stood back a distance from him. He had not touched one for minutes, and still the slope led down.

But even as he realized this, the slope began to lessen. It became more gradual by degrees as if it was leveling out into a plain. The loose rock underfoot grew less, until now, more often than not, his bootsoles fell upon bare rock. At last a time came when he was walking on unrubbled surface that seemed perfectly level.

A burst of feeling from Mikey stopped him. He was there—wherever he was supposed to have come to.

He stood. For a moment there was nothing, only the mist around him. Then it started to lift and thin. It rolled back from him like sky-high curtains being drawn back, gradually revealing a vast amphitheater of rock surrounding him. He stood in a wide, circular depression in the mountains. The floor of that depression was flat, clean of loose rock and open. All around the sloping sides surrounding that central floor, however, rose the rock spires, but here they were broken off short, like a rubble of massive, flat-topped columns broken and shaped by the frosts of unbelievable winters.

As far as his eye could see, the rocks had tenants. One to each rock, the great adult maolots lay—as the last of the mist cleared—under an ice-blue sky, looking down at him. And he did not need to ask the name of this place to which he had come at last.

18

THE VALLEY OF THRONES.

In no way could it have been accidental that a young maolot cub had been found abandoned here, in this place where, he could now feel, as he felt his own breathing, nothing had been abandoned or mislaid for thousands of Everon years. This was no area of accident or chance. As the mist rolled back and he felt the pressure of the hundreds or perhaps thousands of mature maolot empathies, he knew this beyond any need for further proof.

There was no way to tell how many of the great beasts surrounded him. He could, either with Mikey's help or on his own, move in his mind's eye to a close-in point of view with any one of them, but he had no means to count them one by one or take an overview that would show all of them to him at once. But in fact it did not matter how many were physically present; for any not present could look at him through the point of view of any of those that were actually there. Still each one turned a massive head away, or closed eyes when he looked closely. But this, too, did not matter. In effect the Valley of Thrones held the presence of all the adult maolots of Everon—and this piece of knowledge, too, rode to him on the wave of the assembled empathies he felt as certainly as if it had been a physical pressure against him.

They were all here; and they were here because of him—to judge him.

He had never felt so tiny, so insignificant, in all the years of his life. He did not physically shrink from the watching multitude; but inside him his courage faltered;

and he looked around helplessly and almost desperately for Mikey.

There was a movement among the bases of the columns to his left, and Mikey came from among them, his eyes still as closed as those of any of his elders, though he had now grown so that size alone no longer distinguished him from the others. He crossed the open floor of the natural amphitheater to Jef.

"Mikey—" said Jef gratefully, when the maolot stopped in front of him. He reached out to touch Mikey's neck, but his hand dropped. The name of Mikey sat awkwardly now on this old friend of his, who had grown out of the diminutive address and role of playfellow-pet. Mikey was an equal, and more, now. He reached Jef and turned to sit down beside him, facing the surrounding watchers.

Jef felt Mikey being questioned on some matter by those who lay on the columns. He responded, rejecting whatever had been asked, and stayed where he was.

"What do they want, Mikey?" Jef asked.

Mikey indicated that he should be patient and wait. There were things yet to happen.

"What?" asked Jef.

Mikey directed his attention to the columns at the very edge of the open space a little to his left. Looking, he caught sight of figures emerging from between the rock uprights and beginning to cross the space toward him. Some of the figures seemed to be aware of what they were doing. Others moved as if dazed or under some silent order that gave them no choice. They were both human and animal; but with one exception all of the animal ones were Earth variforms.

In the lead were Martin and Jarji. They were two of those whose eyes were clear and sensible, and who appeared to know what they were doing here.

"Are you all right?" Jef asked as they got close.

"Of course," said Jarji.

"How did you get here?"

"Martin flew us in," said Jarji. The two reached Jef and halted. "In that craft he flew away from Beau's."

"Yes," said Martin. "I knew you'd end up here."

Jef looked past Jarji at him and their eyes held together.

"Of course you did," said Jef, and was surprised at the calmness of his voice. "You're Will, aren't you?"

"Yes."

They continued to look at each other for a very long moment. Jef had not seen William in over fifteen years; but now, staring at him, he could still wonder at the change in appearance of the brother he had known. The height was essentially the same, the thickness of bone was similar. In everything else, Jef looked without success for what he remembered.

"How long have you known?" asked William at last, a little hoarsely. All the rhythm of Martin's speech had dropped from his voice.

"Just since I woke up in your camp at the pass," Jef said. "Something about you bothered me from the first— I found myself liking you more than there was reason to. But I didn't know until the camp."

"What did I do at the camp?"

"It wasn't just what you did," Jef said. "Something's happened to me here on Everon, and I can see deeper into everything than I ever thought I could, or anyone could. Right now, I feel strange—sort of detached from everything, but with my mind very clear. Part of it seems to come from the fact that Mikey hasn't let me eat or rest."

"But the camp?" said Martin. "What happened at the camp to make you sure about me?"

"It was when you called me Jef that I knew for certain," Jef said. "I remember hearing about that once—or reading it, or something—that the voice and the walk are the two hardest things for any actor to disguise. You

223

must have known that, because you made a point all along of calling me 'Mr. Robini.' But I suppose you thought it'd be more likely to wake my suspicions if you kept on doing that after I'd blown up about you and Jarji calling me Jef. Only, you just couldn't manage to call me Jef without sounding like Will."

His brother nodded slowly.

"I thought it must have been something like that," he said. His eyes were dark. "Jef, you know it's my doing? I'm the one who got you into all this?"

"It's all right," said Jef. "It's what I would have wanted."

"All right!" said Jarji. "I think you both owe me at least some idea of what you're talking about!"

They turned to her.

"I started something when I sent Mikey to Earth— started it deliberately," William said. "I began something then that had to end here, with Jef, now. I didn't plan on you and other people being here, too. I couldn't see that kind of result from eight years beforehand."

"Then," said Jarji, "you came here the same time as Jef to make sure he got to this Valley of Thrones."

"Yes," said William. He looked back at Jef. "Jef . . ."

"I tell you, it's all right," Jef said. "But how could you have been sure I'd get a grant to come here, in the first place?"

"Oh, that," said William. "That just took a little wire-pulling. Anybody with my job could do that, in five minutes."

"Who else knows?"

"Only five other people, with the other four back on Earth at E. Corps HQ. Even that many was a risk. None of this was official."

"You've lost me again," said Jarji.

"I'm a test case," Jef told her. "He took Mikey back to Earth to grow up with me, as an experiment."

"We couldn't talk to the maolots directly—" William

nodded at the inhabitants of the rock columns. "It was an experiment on both sides. They gave me one of their children; I gave my younger brother, to see if we couldn't raise our own interpreters."

He looked at Jef.

"But it's worked, hasn't it?"

"Yes and no," said Jef. "But if you couldn't talk to them, how could you make the deal with them to take Mikey back to Earth?"

"I don't know," said William. "I don't really know how I did it. All I know is that, in the early years on Everon—even before the first wave of colonists was allowed in, I began to see that the maolots seemed to be showing more intelligence than animals should have had. I tried to observe some closely. They led me into the woods—you might as well say, they captured me—and brought me here. I was here, where we are now, for three days and nights with nothing to eat or drink. I think you're right, Jef. Something about being light-headed from exhaustion and deprivation makes communication with them easier. On the fourth day I started to go out of my head, and that's when they brought me Mikey. He looked like a fat, overgrown kitten that couldn't keep his balance even on four legs, he was so new. And then, somehow the other maolots and I got together on what I should do with him. It seems they'd noticed a difference in me, just as I'd noticed something more in them; and so they made this try to bridge the gap between us. They thought at first they could break the barriers just by wearing me down with hunger and thirst; but that didn't work. We're too different, we and they, to talk directly. But there's no doubt what they are. They're the first human-equivalent intelligent aliens we've met out among the stars. It's wonderful. They're our opposite numbers here, in the Everon life-chain."

"Not exactly," said Jef.

William stared at him.

225

"Why do you say 'not exactly'? What do you mean?"

"I mean that's not quite right," said Jef. "In a way, I think, the truth's even more wonderful than what you say. You see, they don't really talk at all in the sense we do—they *feel*, for and with each other, but what that *feeling* is to them, compared to what we're capable of, is like our speech compared to the grunts or howls of a chimp. Believe me. I've just touched the edge of that sort of feeling, once or twice since I've been on Everon. Even at that, I can't really feel with them, but I can come close to feeling with Mikey . . ."

He stopped.

"I'm sorry. There're no words in our way of talking that even come close to describing it. You'll just have to take my word for it."

"But if we can't communicate at all, then everything we've tried is no good!" William said. His face suddenly looked gaunt and old. "If the whole business has only got you to where you can barely communicate with Mikey, then the experiment's failed. We were dreaming of developing methods for talking to whoever, or whatever, is at the top of the ecological chains on the other new worlds. But if all we've managed to come up with is a special case—"

"It's better than that," said Jef. "It's just that it's too big a thing for me to see more than the edges of it. There're all sort of good possibilities, if things go right here. A lot of bad ones if they don't."

"What do you mean?" Jarji demanded.

He looked at her. He found himself shrugging helplessly.

"I don't know," he said. "I don't really understand what I get from them—or even from Mikey—the way you understand someone who speaks to you in words. There's never that concrete certainty that something's been said. I just sort of absorb a feeling—"

Exasperation and frustration came close to waking his

226

recently rediscovered ability to anger for a second.

"You know what a feeling's like!" he said. "There's no shape or size to it, no hard and fast terms to it. It's like that."

"But go on," said Jarji. "You were saying you absorb a feeling—"

"Yes." He tried to explain it to them. "I soak up the feeling, the emotion or whatever they're putting out to me; and then, inside me, in my own mind, little by little, I make sense of it. You know what it feels like to have something on your mind you can't quite grasp; and have it there, and have it there until suddenly it begins to make sense. What I get from them, and Mikey, is like that."

"What do you get from all this, then?" William swung his hand about to indicate not only the three of them, but the other humans and the variform animals that had come to cluster close around them.

"We've all been brought here so they can come to some kind of decision about us all—not just about me and Mikey. Something more than . . . We're a part of . . ."

Jef ran out of words and abandoned them. He looked around beyond the immediate circle of Will, Jarji and himself. All together, the group surrounding him made a small, tight gathering. A bull wisent, his heavy head lowered, his hair-shaded eyes clouded and dulled, stood only a step or two away from Jef. Almost as close were Armage and Beau, but on opposite sides of him, so that there was space between them. The two big men looked at each other with less of the stunned expression than was shown by the wisent and many of the others, but still without full understanding of where they were—although as he watched, with his new sensitivity Jef could feel them slowly coming back to full consciousness.

Beyond were a number of other variform animals; and men and women, some of whom he identified as having been at the dinner Armage had given for William. Among them was Yvis Suchi; and with her was the one Everon-native figure in the group.

It was her jimi, still associated with her at the end of the leash terminating in the collar about his neck. But now their situations were curiously reversed. Yvis's eyes were as unseeing as those of a sleepwalker. She held to her end of the leash as unthinkingly as if it had been glued to the palm of her hand. The jimi, on his part, grasped his own end of the leash at a body's width below its connection with his collar, and with that hold he was obviously leading Yvis about, instead of the other way around. Even as Jef watched, Yvis turned like a somnambulist to wander outwards from the group; and the jimi, without releasing his grip on the leash, moved to her side, took her arm gently and turned her back into the gathering. He held to her for a moment after he had turned her back, stroking her arm gently, and looking up into her unseeing eyes. There was no intelligence, but an obvious affection in his actions. Satisfied at last that she would stay where she was, he let her go and stepped back to continue patiently waiting with her at leash-end.

The rest of the humans there also seemed more or less dazed. So, too, did the variform Earth animals—the eland, the dog, cat, pig, chicken and duck Jef saw scattered among the humans. The variform animals seemed much more heavily affected than the humans—with one or two exceptions like Yvis Suchi. The humans showed signs of coming out of their dazes. Both Armage and Beau were beginning to show definite signals of returning awareness. They were now staring somewhat stupidly but angrily at one another, like individuals who had just roused from sleep to find an intruder in their bedrooms.

Something was about to happen. That which the maolots had brought them all here together for was waiting to happen; and on what happened would turn . . .

The implications of what he had just seen of the jimi

228

and Yvis Suchi suddenly crashed in upon Jef's conscious mind like a tidal wave.

"My God!" he said out loud. "We're on trial—that's what everything's been aimed at from the first—from the moment they first gave you Mikey, Will!"

"Trial?"

It was the heavy voice of Armage and the man himself, apparently almost back to his full senses, was turning toward them.

"That's what I said," Jef answered him, as well as Will and Jarji, who were watching him closely, now. "I should have realized it before now. They saw the difference between humans and themselves from the moment the first teams landed here. It's a difference that doesn't allow them and us to live together—here on Everon or anyplace else—"

"Anyplace else?" Will broke in.

"Yes." Jef looked at him, and from him to Jarji. "Anywhere."

"What are you talking about?" Beau broke in. "Are you saying these maolots think they can push us right off Everon?"

"Off of any world," Jef answered, still looking at Will and Jarji.

"You're insane!" burst out Armage. "I don't care what they are, they've got no technology. They couldn't stand up to what we can bring in here—"

"Who's going to bring it?" Jef was hardly conscious of the fact that he was answering the Constable and Beau. He was seeing more deeply into what confronted them every moment and the words into which he resolved what he saw were only the briefest notations of something his conscious mind was just beginning to grasp.

"Bring it in? We'll bring it in. Just a minute—"

He moved toward Jef.

"Stay back, please," said Jef almost absently. He had no time to concentrate on other humans now, when vast shapes were finally taking meaningful shape in his head. "Let me think."

Armage had stopped at Jef's words, but now he moved forward again, and Beau also rolled closer.

Will moved between Jef and both of them.

"You'll stay back," he said. All the lilt of Martin's speech was back in his voice. "Indeed, you'll stay back!"

For a moment more the two big men hesitated. Then, as if they had been practicing such teamwork for years, they moved forward again, spreading out a little, one on each side of Will.

"It's all right, Will," said Jef.

He hardly recognized himself in this moment, but he was suddenly sure of what he could do. He stepped past Will and lifted his hands slightly, one toward each of the two men.

"Stop," he said.

He reached out. His fingers did not touch either of them; but the feeling that had been growing inside him all this time seemed to coil momentarily within the very center of his body, and then suddenly extend itself through his fingertips like a living act of will, invisible but solid, and both men stopped as if their muscles had refused them.

"Wait there," he said, dropping his hands. "Let me think."

He realized then that he had not meant "think." What he had meant was this process of feeling and resolving in which he was now engaged and of which thinking was only a small part. He reached inward into himself again, and went on, more for himself than the others, resolving what he felt and knew into the verbal form with which he was most familiar.

"We don't fit," he said. "That's the trouble. We refuse to fit. Worse, we destroy . . ." He hesitated. "In self-defense they've got to integrate with or destroy us . . . here on Everon and on every world where we live."

"Earth?" said Will. He was watching Jef closely.

"Earth, too," Jef said absently.

"How?" burst out Armage. The other humans, awakening, were now beginning to drift closer to the five of them. "Will you tell me? How could they do anything to us?"

"Because this world is all theirs," said Jef, "and any other world they want to touch."

"What did you mean when you started to talk about who'd bring things in to fight them?" Jarji asked.

"Ships bringing any sort of weapons from Earth would never get here," Jef said musingly. "They can reach their own, anywhere. Of course! Why didn't I realize? They had to be able to reach Mikey, all the years he was with me on Earth. If they hadn't, he'd never have been able to fit in back here again. He'd have been—insane, I suppose you'd call it. They used Mikey and me, both, to get a look at Earth and the human race there."

He turned to Will.

"Will," he said, "there's nothing we can use to fight them—but they can use everything we have against us."

Beau grunted.

"A maolot can pilot a spaceship?"

"Not necessarily a maolot. Look—" Jef pointed to the Jimi with Yvis Suchi. "Those paws can do anything our hands can do."

"There aren't any jimis on Earth—or anything else that's Everon," said Beau.

Jef glanced his way for a second. "I thought I heard some talk of getting permission to export jimis as pets to Earthside," he said. "But it doesn't matter. There're the strains of all the variforms from which your Earth-derived animals were bred. They can reach those, because they can reach the ones here."

"Reach the ones here? What are you talking about?" demanded Armage.

Jef nodded at the wisent almost within reach of them.

"Look at him, and the other variforms with us here. They all walked out to us on their own. No one led them. They've been touched by Everon now, and Everon controls them when it wants to, just like it controls its own native creatures. Look again—"

He pointed toward the columns, sweeping his arm along. Between the bases of the columns flanking the open space, here and there a dot of color could be seen—the blue of a clock-bird, the grey and white of a galusha, the green of a leaf stalker—showing where those creatures also waited below the patiently waiting maolots.

"I don't believe it," muttered Armage.

"No," grunted Beau savagely. "But then you never did know anything about Everon."

They were staring at each other.

"Even if that was true," said Armage, "a few laboratory experimental animals can't take over Earth. There're hardly any animals left on Earth, compared to the number of humans."

"There're rats. As many rats as people, or more, even now," said Jef. "There're insects. There're water-life and insects. Finally, there're plants. If Everon flora can change itself so that it poisons variform elands, Earth plants can turn poisonous, too. The weather can turn against us. Humans can't live on Earth if they sterilize the world we live on."

"All right," Beau rumbled, deep in his chest, "what do they want from us here, then?"

"That's right!" said Armage suddenly. "Maybe we could split this world up. Make a deal. Give them a lot of the wild area as a reservation—"

"Beau was right," said Will, looking at him. "You're a fool."

"Fool! I've worked too hard to lose everything to maolots!"

"Do you think that matters?" Jef said. But he said it

232

without heat or emphasis, almost sadly. "It's bigger than that. We're not here to bargain. We're here to see if we can show some reason—"

He broke off.

"Reason, Jef?" Jarji prompted him. "Go on."

He heard her as if from a very long distance away. His mind was suddenly spinning, helplessly adrift like an oarless rowboat on an angry sea far from land.

"No," he said.

"No what?" he heard her ask.

"I can't! No. Mikey—" He reached out with the feeling in him, helplessly, to the maolot. "Mikey—"

He could not help, Mikey told him, also as if from a long distance away, although Mikey in the body was almost within arm's reach.

"Jef, what is it?" he heard faintly from Jarji.

"It's me," he answered her dimly. "That's what it's all about. That's what they've been waiting for. The whole business of planting Mikey with me so that we could grow up with each other. They want me to be the one to justify . . ."

He swayed. He was conscious of Will's hands catching him, holding him up.

"Justify what?" Jarji was asking.

"Everything!" It was a cry torn from the innermost parts of him. "They want me to tell them why they should try to live with us. They want me to give the answer. They want me to tell them why they should let the human race live!"

"Then you've got to try to," said Will.

"Try?" Jef turned blindly to him. He felt as if he was being torn apart and scattered to the farthest reaches of the universe. "Me? But I'm the last one in the universe to do that. I've got no use for the rest of the human race. I've been apart, lonely, and had no use for anyone outside our family from as far back as I can remember! I think we deserve to be wiped out—wiped out and forgotten!"

19

THERE WAS SILENCE in the Valley of Thrones.

It was as if all those present were holding their breath, as if the history of that place had come down all its centuries, only to pause in this moment of waiting.

"No," said the voice of Will. "I don't believe it."

The silence was shattered beyond repair. Jef turned to him.

"No," said Will, again. "You don't feel like that. I know you."

"Will," said Jef and his voice hurt his throat. "I do. It's been years since you saw me. The only part of the human race I had any use for was our father and mother. There would have been you, too, but you were gone so long, essentially you got dropped out. When they died, there was no one left."

Will did not move. He stayed, looking into Jef's face. His voice held on exactly the same level.

"Think, now," he said. "You say you really don't see any reason why the human race should live? No part of it? None of it? No one?"

"I don't . . . ." said Jef, and hesitated.

It was not that he doubted what he felt, and had felt since his parents' death. It was that Will's steady questioning raised an unreasonable fear in him that somehow he had overlooked something, forgotten something. He looked around him and saw Jarji.

She stood, watching him with a detached thoughtfulness, as if what concerned her had nothing to do with the question awaiting an answer from him. He looked at her, remembering her from that first meeting, sitting cross-legged across the fire from him, the crossbow laid out before her on the ground.

With that memory, suddenly, something else came back. Again he remembered standing at the top of the spaceship's landing ladder at Everon City spaceport, tasting his bitterness against the colonists he had traveled with. He felt it all just as he had then; but now for the first time he realized that all the time, underneath his bitterness, had still been his early dream that the people out here on the new worlds would be his sort, as he remembered Will being, and his parents being.

Now that he faced the truth, he recognized that that particular dream had survived even seeing the guests at Armage's dinner party, his encounter with Chavel and his early disappointment in a Martin who was Will in disguise; and it had taken life again when he had first met Jarji. For all her thorniness, she had been exactly the sort of human he had looked to find on Everon.

He faced facts now, accordingly. Will had always known him better than he knew himself. He had never really buried his hope of finding people he could belong to. His belief in his self-sufficiency and his own self isolation had been only a con game played on himself.

He reached out his hand to Jarji and she took it. The touch of her fingers sent an almost chemical heat flooding through his body.

"All right," he said to Will. "Have it your way. I guess I don't hate anyone that much, after all."

"Hate!" said Armage. "It's them—those maolots out there who hate us!"

"No," said Jef.

"No? What do you mean—no! Of course they hate us. It's the way they're built!"

"No," Jef told him. "Not the way *they're* built. Just the way we are. Look."

Jef pointed with his free hand to the jimi, now gently

235

pressed against the side of Yvis Suchi, the side of its head resting against the woman's elbow, as if it would send the warmth of its own small body into the numb one of the human.

"Some of them even love," said Jef. "The trouble is, love isn't enough. Not for them, or for us either, in this matter."

"I'm talking about the damn maolots!" said Armage.

"Maolots!" anger boiled up in Jef. "What's the matter with all of you, here? Can't you get it through your heads it's not the maolots you've got to deal with—it's Everon? All the life here, of any kind, from the maolots down to the damn viruses in the dirt!"

Armage stared at him. So, too, did Beau and those others who were conscious enough to understand his words.

"Can't you see what's under your noses? Look at that jimi!" said Jef. "It loves Yvis Suchi, but it brought her here, just the same. It hadn't any choice. Can't you understand? Everything on Everon is part of one creature— one total ecologic creature. The maolots are just the top link of the chain—the head-part. They can hear us and answer us. But it's the whole creature that needs to know whether it can live with us safely, or whether it has to destroy us to protect itself. Every insect, every amoeba, is in on that decision. Each of them is one of the real masters of Everon."

They stared at him. He saw that, even now, they did not really comprehend what he was telling them. Only Jarji and Will showed understanding—Jarji with a pressing of her fingers that signalled clearly her agreement with what he had just said; and Will, by nodding.

"Yes," Will said, almost to himself. "Yes."

"Anyone who lives here—who really lives here—" said Jarji, unexpectedly, "knows how everything's hooked together. Anyone who lives in the woods has seen prey walk right into the mouth of a galusha or a maolot, more than once. Even if you hadn't, you could feel how it is. The animals fit with the plants, and they both fit with air and the earth. It's all one thing, together. Jef's right!"

Beau's face was dark and twisted. In the area of his own new sensitivity, Jef could feel the struggle that the big woodsman was having with himself. But Beau said nothing.

"All right," said Armage. "What of it? Tell them what they want to hear and get us out of here. We can decide what to do about them later. Tell them they can live with us. Tell them we'll arrange to live with them. Tell them anything!"

"It's not that simple—" began Jef.

"Why the hell not?" shouted Armage. "How can they tell whether it's the truth or not?"

The anger Jef had felt a moment before licked up toward a total loss of patience, flared at the edges of explosion.

"It's not words they're waiting for," he said. "Don't you understand? It's something they'll be able to feel in us if we have it—and if we can't show it there for them to feel, then we're done for. They can seed the clouds with spores and raise anything up to a hurricane against us in the next ten hours, if they want. They can change the climate and freeze us out, or kill our crops where they stand in the field. They've never made any serious effort against us until now. But if they decide to, we're done for. They can turn every animal, bird and insect against us—even the variforms—to hunt and kill us. And that's what'll happen. Understand—the maolots won't do it; *Everon* will do it. It won't be a thought-out plan. It'll be a reflex, an instinctive striking back against their fear of us. The only hope is that I can somehow give them a feeling about us that'll disarm that reflex, make it unnecessary. Don't you understand?"

He stared at Armage, trying to read some flicker of comprehension in him. But Armage pinched his lips and looked away, back out at the rock columns and the waiting figures upon them.

"Jef," said Will, "you are going to try, then?"

Jef turned to him.

"I'll try. I don't know how."

Will nodded.

"What can I do to help?" he asked.

"Nothing," said Jef. "I don't even know if what they want is really in us—in me."

"It's in you," Jarji said. Her positiveness was like a powerful hand, holding him up. "Things wouldn't have gone this far, with them giving you Mikey to grow up with and their bringing you and all of us here, if it wasn't in you. The only question isn't whether it's there, but whether you can make them see it."

Jef nodded, steadying.

She was right. She had to be right. Things could not have gone this far, if there had been nothing in him. Had humanity lacked utterly what Everon wished to find, he and everyone else would have betrayed themselves for what they were, long ago; and in his case, he would have demonstrated his lack to Mikey, back on Earth. That would have been the end then—not only for himself but for Mikey. The Everon life-chain was all one animal, but the bond between its members was one of utility, not affection.

It was a matter of survival, not of affection. What had he said, himself, just a few minutes ago? It was something so basic. . .

The feel of it came to him then, clearly, for the first time. It came riding on a mental image of the Everon life-mass warily looking at the Earth life-mass, saying—"Can we combine? Can we interlock in an ecological sense? Can we be one animal?"

What Everon-life needed to know was whether what made up Earth-life followed the same rules as what made Everon-life. The same rules and patterns had to apply—

Everon had to know that Earth worked as it did, or that it could be made to work the same way. But all Everon had seen so far was a self-destructive, insane version of the rules it knew, a version in which one species had turned on the rest of its own ecological chain and was cannibalizing it to its private benefit.

What Everon wanted was proof that this was only a temporary sickness, not an in-born fault of the makeup of Earth-life as a whole. Nothing less than that would stop Everon, with the maolots as their head, from reaching out to destroy the structure that was the Earth-born ecological chain.

There would be no vindictiveness to such a destruction if it came to that, Jef thought. Many of the lower forms of Earth-life might even survive, incorporated into the Everon chain. But the sick part, the human part, would be removed from all worlds where it existed.

But humans were not all sick. Some were not. And the race as a whole had not been, once.

Once. . .

His mind slipped back in time, across the dusty ages to the very youth of man and woman, to the late Paleolithic when humans—no longer just man-apes, but true humans—were still a sound and wholesome part of the ecological chain on Earth. The animal paintings from the Magdalenian culture in the caves at Lascaux, in the Dordogne, France—running deer painted into life, with magic and a fellow-feeling—deer, horses, bulls. . .

From then, on down the millenia to the slaughter of the American buffalo. . .

A possible proof exploded in him suddenly. Still holding Jarji's hand, he made two swift steps to the bull wisent and threw his free arm around its head, lifting the shaggy skull so that he could look into its dulled and dusky eyes.

"Wisent . . ." he said to it, a low, angry voice. "Wisent, I know you. I knew you eight thousand years ago. I know you now. I know *you*, wisent. . ."

The dulled eyes stared into his. Deep within them there was something that might be a stirring, an awakening.

"Wisent," he said. "Listen to me, wisent. . ."

Something deep in himself had taken him over and was carrying him irresistibly away. His mind-image of what had been, and what was, of the very bones of man and animal together, was no longer half-formed. It was coalescing, taking solid shape; and as it did, the wisent was rousing from the influence of the Everon planetary mind that had dampened the natural fires of its spirit down to docility and driven it here. Jef let go of Jarji to grasp the woolly fur of the heavy head in both hands, and hold it eye to eye with him.

"Wisent," he almost whispered, "we're the same thing. We're the same blood and bone, part of the same life. Wisent, listen to me—"

The dullness was beginning to go from the eyes. The horizontal, slitted pupil stared back, dark brown and innocent, but at the outer circumference, the rim that was the conjunctiva was beginning to flush red with the beast's wakening of emotion. Jef felt the first faint onset of normal awareness in the wisent, the kindling of a reflexive panic, of a fear that was fury and a fury that was fear, breaking the surface of animal consciousness.

"Wisent," he was telling it, "I love you, wisent, but there has to be more than that. And there is—we're the same thing, you and I. We were always the same thing. We could never be anything else because we both belong to something that holds us both. You're Its wisent-shape and I am Its man-shape, but to It there's no difference between us. Do you hear me, wisent?"

The wisent was waking. Between his hands Jef could feel a growing tenseness, a rousing to a readiness to fight or flee. The uncomplex mind he faced was lifting swiftly from the cloudy waters of near unconsciousness to the light and clarity of decision and action. Jef ran his right hand down the neck and felt the great shoulder muscles quivering. The short, sharp horns began to lower. In a moment the wisent would be fully awake and he would attack out of instinctive fear.

But in the structure of Everon-life, such an attack did not need to happen. There were greater laws that reached out to dominate such fears and abort such reactions. If—but only if—such a law was with him, a maolot did not need to physically hold still a leaf stalker. The leaf stalker would wait by itself in those critical moments when the greater need of the whole, multi-species creature took precedence over the individual need and will; just as a jimi would lead an Yvis Suchi to the Valley of Thrones. If there was an equal response still in Earth bones and soul, then with what Jef had learned from Mikcy and Everon, he should be able to hold this wisent quiet, and abort the natural fear growing now in the animal.

"Wisent . . ." he whispered in its ear. "Wisent. . ."

It heard him and it did not understand. The eyelids lifted, showing a whitish brown. The elliptical iris widened, and the ring of the conjunctiva around it all reddened and swelled. Panic beat like a tom-tom in its deep chest. The two-thousand-pound body seemed to swell and loom over Jef.

He half-closed his own eyes. He sent his own mind out beyond the present moment, beyond the small known history of his two-legged race and reached back and back to where each other life form on the face of his native globe owned that world as much as he and such as he. Back . . . back to the time when they were all together, man and bull and all else that had lived and died on the continents of the late Paleolithic.

"We are the same. . ." he kept saying. "We are the same. . ."

For a long moment he rode the upsurge of fury-fear in

the awakened wisent's mind like a chip on the surface of a whirlpool—under its control, not it under his. Then, convincing himself, he began for the first time to feel the real power and presence of the great supra-species laws, the laws of a physics of life, beginning to emerge from the gloom of instinct to wake memories he had not known he had.

"*Brother bear. . .*" he heard himself murmuring. "*Brother bear, forgive me. I kill you so that my people may live. Brother bear, great bear, wise bear—wiser and greater than I am —bear, forgive me for killing you, so I can live. Brother wisent, forgive me. Wisent, great wisent, you are stronger and braver than I am, but I must hold you down, I must control you, so my people will live. Brother wisent, still . . . be still . . . stand quiet, brother wisent, so my people may live. . .*"

. . . And from beyond history, from beyond all the things known by the conscious mind, and from before the idea of time itself, came the operation of those great laws binding all life on Earth together, like massive girders reinforcing the little, individual structure of his own will . . . and the wisent calmed. Its panic and its fear descended, dwindled, sank back into a resignation, a willingness on the part of the wisent. The enormous, hunched shoulder muscles untensed, stretching out, going lax.

The red faded from the exterior circle of the eye, the iris shrank and the brownish-white disappeared as the eyelids drooped again.

The wisent stood still, passive and waiting, locked together with Jef by the invisible bonds of life that had existed before the earliest ancestor of either one of them had been conceived. Laws that were the counterpart of the laws of life on Everon.

Slowly Jef opened his hands. They had been clenched so hard in the hair on each side of the heavy beast-head that he could barely manage to unfold his fingers. About him was an aching silence that held all the people and beasts close about him, all of the watchers on the hill-sides, all of the amphitheater.

He felt Jarji close beside him. Instinctively he reached out and put an arm around her, holding her to him. Still the silence persisted.

Then, without warning, one of the maolots lying on a rock column directly before them lifted her head. The powerful jaws opened, and the ear-shaking roar of the species reverberated through the Valley of Thrones. Before it had even begun to re-echo, the roars burst forth everywhere. Not the droning hunting calls, but the full and absolute roar that could be heard, as Jef had heard it earlier, for kilometers.

Now the maolots on the columns were all roaring; and the sound, penned in by the rock walls and thrown back and forth by them, was stunning. Riding his empathic link with Mikey, Jef's vision swept over the columns before him, swept in close—and everywhere he looked from close up into the opened eyes of the maolots. Eyes of sapphire color, topaz, garnet eyes—each one different, each one deep with a knowledge and a wisdom he now realized would have defeated him utterly if he had seen it before he had learned to handle the great laws himself, for the power of those laws were there, visible in the eyes of the grown maolots, and if he had faced them before, he would never have had the courage to try to find such ancient and awesome power in himself.

He looked at Mikey with his own proper vision and saw Mikey's eyes, at last, were also open, and also wise. Joy flooded him. He hugged Jarji close to him in delight. Will put his arms about them both. All around them, the colonists, even the colonists, were staring at one another in stunned excitement; not understanding but absorbing, through the ancient marrow of their bones, the excitement of the feeling that, somehow, things had come out right.

Jef shouted to Jarji and Will, but they both shook their

heads. Nothing could be heard in such a din. He shouted again for the pleasure of hearing his own words, if only inside his head—he could tell Jarji and Will later, when there would be time for all the talking that might ever need to be done.

"Now we're ready!" was what he had shouted at them. *"Now, we're ready, at last!"*

—And Mikey pressed lovingly and hard against the three of them.

WAR
IN
2080

BY DAVID LANGFORD
(ILLUSTRATED)

THE SHAPE OF WARS TO COME

Since the beginning of recorded history war has been a
blight upon our species. And looking at current military
technology it seems likely that our warmaking proclivities
will flourish in the twenty-first century.

British physicist and science writer, David Langford,
spells out the progressive sophistication of armaments
from the slingshot to the neutron bomb, military hard-
ware and software of future wars in space. He examines
such 'science-fiction' concepts as planet-busters, death-
rays, ecological wars, climate control and even bionic
people able to become part of the weapons and machines.
And he considers the possibility of colonisation and of
encounters with aliens of a higher technological order,
elsewhere in the Universe.

WAR IN 2080 presents a grim and frightening picture of
a future world – which none of us can afford to ignore.

WAR   0 7221 5393 7   £1.50

WARLORDS

BY BOB LANGLEY

BRITAIN'S FUTURE?

Britain is on the verge of total collapse. North Sea oil has suddenly run dry. Rationing and unemployment spread like wildfire. And four elections in two months have plunged the nation into a terrifying chaos.

Across the Atlantic America decides it is time to step in and assist their one-time ally. BY FERMENTING NO LESS THAN A FULL-SCALE BLOODY REVOLUTION GUARANTEED TO BRING THE DYING NATION TO HER KNEES AND TO CHANGE THE COURSE OF WORLD HISTORY WITH ONE DEVASTATING, FINAL COUP DE GRÂCE . . .

Fast and furious, WARLORDS is a terrifying and disturbing vision of Britain at the mercy of the powerlords in the not-so-distant future!

ADVENTURE THRILLER   0 7221 5409 7   £1.25

THE GRAIL WAR

BY RICHARD MONACO

THE SOARING MEDIEVAL FANTASY

'A tall knight whirled an axe stroke at Parsival, who leaned
slightly away, and the blow chugged into a tree and stuck.
He didn't bother to return the compliment, just blocking and
ducking, keeping his nervous horse moving through the
frustrated, struggling mass of fighters . . . Another charged
him and then the horse jammed between two trees . . .
Another backed away from the thrust by Gawain and was
unseated by a heavy limb . . . Smoke cut the battle into
ghostly fragments . . . a man riding headless . . . a horse
dancing on another . . . a bodiless arm swinging, clutching a
branch . . . two knights wrestling in the blood-dewed brambles
. . . men climbing over one another, the ones underneath
creating a bridgeway over the prickly tangles, screaming . . .'

- THE GRAIL WAR

A magnificent, stirring and beautifully moving Arthurian tale
in the classic fantasy tradition of LORD OF THE RINGS.

FANTASY   0 7221 6165 4   £1.75

TERROR FROM BEYOND THE STARS

THE QUEEN OF THE LEGION

Jack Williamson

From the innermost core of the Nebula they swarm
forth in their nightmarish hordes . . . Beware the
shadowflashers: terrible parasites who will ruthlessly
enslave your mind and body. They have already
captured AKKA, the great secret weapon. They have
killed the Keeper of the Peace . . . and they will stop at
nothing. Who now can stand between the human
race and ultimate destruction . . . ?

Jil Gyrel, courageous daughter of a lost Legion pilot,
has inherited her father's prescience and his uncanny
navigational gifts. She is the first to sense the inhuman
danger . . . but can the strength of this valiant girl
alone save the future of Mankind?

QUEEN OF THE LEGION is the fourth novel in the
classic LEGION OF SPACE series – a thrilling tale of a
battle against the most monstrous evil ever to emerge
from the treacherous regions of outer space.

OLD TIME HAS ENDED BUT EARTH IS STILL AT WAR

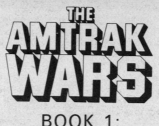

BOOK 1:

Cloud Warrior

PATRICK TILLEY

Ten centuries ago the Old Time ended
when Earth's cities melted in the War o
a Thousand Suns. Now the lethal high
technology of the Amtrak Federation's
underground stronghold is unleashed
on Earth's other survivors – the surface-
dwelling Mutes. But the primitive
Mutes possess ancient powers far
greater than any machine . . .

FICTION   0 7221 8516 2   £1.95

A SELECTION OF BESTSELLERS FROM SPHERE

FICTION

CHASE THE MOON	Catherine Nicolson	£1.95 ☐
BROTHERLY LOVE	William Blankenship	£1.95 ☐
FOLLOWER	Stephen Gallagher	£1.95 ☐
SOLITAIRE	Graham Masterton	£1.95 ☐
THE QUEEN'S MESSENGER	Robert L. Duncan	£1.95 ☐

FILM AND TV TIE-INS

THEY CALL ME BOOBER FRAGGLE	Michaela Muntean	£1.50 ☐
RED AND THE PUMPKINS	Jocelyn Stevenson	£1.50 ☐
THE RADISH DAY JUBILEE	Sheilah Bruce	£1.50 ☐
MINDER	Anthony Masters	£1.50 ☐
SCARFACE	Paul Monette	£1.75 ☐
THE KILLING OF KAREN SILKWOOD	Richard Rashke	£1.95 ☐

NON-FICTION

THE 101 BEST AND ONLY LIMERICKS OF SPIKE MILLIGAN		£1.25 ☐
THE MANUAL OF NUDE PHOTOGRAPHY	Jon Gray, text by Michael Busselle	£5.95 ☐
THE ESSENTIAL GUIDE TO LONDON	David Benedictus	£2.95 ☐
TWINS	Peter Watson	£1.75 ☐
SHADOWS ON THE GRASS	Simon Raven	£1.95 ☐

All Sphere books are available at your local bookshop or newsagent, or can be ordered direct from the publisher. Just tick the titles you want and fill in the form below.

Name _____

Address _____

_____

_____

Write to Sphere Books, Cash Sales Department, P.O. Box 11, Falmouth, Cornwall TR10 9EN

Please enclose a cheque or postal order to the value of the cover price plus:

UK: 45p for the first book, 20p for the second book and 14p for each additional book ordered to a maximum charge of £1.63.

OVERSEAS: 75p for the first book and 21p per copy for each additional book.

BFPO & EIRE: 45p for the first book, 20p for the second book plus 14p per copy for the next 7 books, thereafter 8p per book.

Sphere Books reserve the right to show new retail prices on covers which may differ from those previously advertised in the text or elsewhere, and to increase postal rates in accordance with the PO.